KILLING LOVE

An Inspirational Thriller

BOB LAURIE

Dedicated to:

To those whose lives are
navigated by God
and
anchored by Family.

PROLOGUE

Ten-year-old Sal Lovato was watching television with his babysitter Patty when the phone rang. It was followed by Patty shouting, "Oh, my God!"

Sal spent time at a hospital with people he'd never seen before. Then, he was taken to a police station where he sat at a desk across from a balding man who looked up and smiled now and then. Sal asked him and every stranger that shuffled him around where his parents were, but they all turned away, mumbling something about being sorry but not explaining anything. Sal was scared. He knew something was wrong when he was taken on a long ride to a building with bars on the windows and security guards at the doors. Inside was a large room with aisles of cots lined up wall to wall. The beds' occupants were all different ages and races, and the only thing separating the girls from the boys was a short wall you could see over. Sal hated it there. He considered it a prison of bullies and rejects that society didn't know what to do with. He was relieved when he saw his Aunt Carol two days later. He'd never forget the first words she said to him after getting into her car:

"Salvatore, your mom and dad died in a car accident. You're going to their wake tomorrow."

Sal knew she was telling the truth because of the way he was shuffled around for days among strangers who wouldn't answer his questions or look at him when he asked. His mom's only family were two sisters: Aunt Carol, the older one, and Aunt Connie. Sal didn't like either one of them. He recalled his mom saying they were both selfish people, and even though he was young, he understood why she said that. His Dad's father, and only relative who Sal called gramps, had died a year earlier.

Sal was taken to Aunt Carol's apartment, where Aunt Connie was waiting. They tried to be nice by offering cookies and milk, but Sal knew neither of them wanted him there.

They did nothing to shield him from their conversation about what to do with him. His Aunt Connie insisted her sister Carol take care of Sal because she was the more stable one, and that taking care of a kid would bog her down.

Sal sat alone at the wake, praying to God his mom and dad would just wake up and that everything would return to the way it was. Every so often, Aunt Carol would call him over to say hello to someone he didn't know. He was glad when it was over. Although he wasn't expecting what was to come.

Two days later, Aunt Carol sat Sal down and told him she couldn't care for him because Uncle Jeff got a job in Belgium, and they planned on traveling while they were there. Then she said: *"I've talked to the foster home people, and they'll find you a good home for a while. It may be a year before we return, and maybe you can come back and live with us. Uncle Jeff and I will be dropping you off tomorrow."*

The Nortons seemed nice when they picked Sal up at the foster home director's office. Mrs. Norton put him in the car's back seat, and nothing was said until they parked in their driveway. That's when Mr. Norton first warned him, "If you do as you're told, it will be better for you. Disobedience brings consequences." They hurried him into the house, and Mrs. Norton took him to the bathroom. "Strip your clothes here, get in the shower, and wait for Nat... I mean Mr. Norton."

Sal didn't understand Mr. Norton touching him, but when he was asked to reciprocate, Sal resisted, and Mr. Norton slapped him. Then he dragged Sal naked into a closet. "You'll have to learn to comply."

The days were long, and at times Sal didn't know if it was night or day. He spent a lot of time in the closet.

One day the lady from the foster home office where Sal was picked up, came to the Norton's home. Mrs. Norton rushed into the closet with clothes and told Sal to put them on. "Tell the lady you're being taken care of, and you're happy here. If you don't, it will be dreadful for you. Do you understand?

Sal nodded. *What could be more dreadful?*

The lady felt Sal's arms a couple of times and asked if he was being fed. Mr. Norton said, "Of course, we're feeding him. He eats like a horse."

The lady asked Sal, "Is that true, Salvatore?"

He shrugged.

The next day the lady returned with a doctor, and that was the last time Sal would ever see the Nortons.

Sal stayed with two other families until he ran away four years later at fifteen. Even though they seemed friendly and tried to make Sal feel at home. He never felt part of their family and refused to trust anyone after living at the Norton's house.

Sal found the docks of Venice Beach and took a job taking care of rich people's boats. It was there that he would find his new life.

PART ONE

THE
REDEMPTION

CHAPTER 1

The full moon shimmered on the bay, as rats scurried in the shadows of the large concrete pier that went by the name of Moss Landing. The restaurant built on the pier closed at ten P.M. The boats rubbing against the docks made an eerie, creaking sound. Sal Lovato sat in the darkness of his vehicle with the engine off and the windows open. His target was due at eleven P.M., and expected Sal to have two kilos of heroin to trade for fifty thousand in cash, but all Sal had for him tonight was a bullet to his head.

Sal's boss, Anthony Rinaldi, had told him to make the hit. Sal hadn't questioned the order, but he thought it was strange that a soldier of Carmine Simone's family was his target. If Anthony asked Sal to make a hit on a rival family, he knew the order came from Anthony's boss and uncle, Big Zac.

Sal never thought Anthony was the sharpest tool in the shed but being the nephew to Big Zac gave him clout. Anthony never did anything without Big Zac's approval, and that's why Sal didn't question orders coming from Anthony.

Typically, the drug transactions were brief. They didn't leave their cars and passed the packages through the opened windows, but tonight Sal needed the element of surprise. It was a few minutes to eleven when a car entered the pier. Sal got out of his vehicle, closed the door softly, and hurried behind a trash container a few yards away. He used the remote to flash the headlights and signal his location. As the car crept forward with only the parking lights on, he screwed the silencer into the pistol. The target stopped next to the vehicle, within inches of the driver's window.

Sal moved quickly and quietly from behind the dumpster and took aim. Two shots through the passenger window hit their mark. He looked around to be sure the noise didn't bring attention. The night was still dark and quiet, other than the sound of the car motor running and the boats rubbing against the docks. Sal reached into the dead man's car, took the satchel of money, and turned off the engine.

Sal mumbled, "Son of a bitch" when he realized the vehicles were too close together for him to get into his car. He went to the passenger side, dropped the bag in the back seat, and hopped over the console, which wasn't easy for a man of his size. He paused to look around before driving away. *Something about this hit didn't feel right.*

Sal and Susie arrived at Anthony Rinaldi's Labor Day party together. They met at his Memorial Day bash three months earlier, but Sal wasn't working as he was today. The moment Sal saw Susie, he couldn't take his eyes off her. He thought she was beautiful with long black hair and a tall, tan voluptuous body. She played hard to get at first, but Sal was able to crack her façade, and they've been dating ever since. Susie was spoiled and expected men to buy her nice things. Sal didn't deny her the comforts she expected within reason. Sal was tall, dark, and handsome and usually got the women he pursued, but there was a special connection with Susie — a bond he hadn't felt with the others. Sal also liked having her on his arm because they turned heads when entering a room together.

Today's Labor Day party was sunny and hot, with the temperature rising above ninety. Sal noticed more people with cell phones than there were three months ago. Almost overnight, they became smaller. The people at the party who had one enjoyed showing them off. Sal traded his large, clunky one for a model that looked more like a *Star Trek* communicator. He didn't care about the exorbitant cost because Anthony wanted him to have it, and paid so that Sal was always available. In 1992, the only people with cell phones were the elite and those who were respected for having one. Sal enjoyed the social status it brought him, but it wasn't long before Susie started pleading with him to buy her a cell. Sometimes Sal tried to stand up to her demands, but she was hard to resist when they were in bed. When he finally broke down and bought it for her, it was like he had given her a diamond ring. She kissed and hugged Sal for an hour before making the first call to her friend Maria, followed by many others listed in her phone directory. It had been a month since he bought the cell for her, and he sometimes regretted it. Especially when she called about unimportant nonsense.

Sal told Susie, before leaving her by the pool with Maria, that he was working and not to call unless it was an emergency.

Susie kissed him, "When will you come and spend some time with me?"

"I'll be busy today. Anthony has us on security alert. Not sure what's up, but I won't have much free time. You and Maria enjoy yourselves. I'll see you when I can."

Sal kept in contact with security via two-way radios. Anthony had given explicit instructions to make sure all guests entering the party had invitations, and the gates remained shut. Sal suspected it had something to do with Carmine Simone's soldier he whacked a week ago. Anthony had been on edge ever since. He usually told Sal why he wanted to heighten security, and the lack of discussion made Sal uneasy. Sal had a job to do, whatever the reason, so he focused on keeping in contact with his men and ensuring they stayed alert.

Sal sat in front of four monitors and a two-way radio, set in a room that overlooked the party outside. Susie's number appeared on his cell; it was the second time she'd called in an hour. He flipped it open, "Susie, I told you not to bother me. I'm working."

"I know; consider this a business call, babe. Two guys are harassing Maria and me. Can you please tell them to leave?"

Sal studied the screen. The guys standing in front of Susie looked young, and he couldn't make out their faces.

"Those two kids? How old are they that you can't get rid of them? You're slipping, Susie."

"I don't feel like dealing with them. Make them go away, Sal."

"Put the bigger one on the line."

Sal watched as the man reluctantly took the phone, "Hello."

"Who am I speaking with?"

"Vito. Who's this?"

"You know Mr. Rinaldi, Vito?"

"He's, my uncle."

"This is Sal, head of security. I believe the lady told you to leave, so be a good nephew and get lost before I tell your uncle you left here in an ambulance."

Before the young man returned Susie's phone, Sal heard him mutter, "What a bitch."

Then he heard Susie taunt, "I told you I could get rid of you with a phone call. Do you believe me now, asshole?" Susie and Maria giggled after the exchange. Sometimes — like now — Susie liked to abuse her power as his girlfriend. This wasn't the first time she had asked Sal to chase off the wolves. Even over the phone, he could tell she got a thrill from running guys off with a single request. Susie's beauty and body was a magnet to men, especially the young ones. She knew it, and she did nothing to make herself less seductive. Though her little games could irritate him now and then, Sal liked the way she dressed and never considered asking her to change. The men hitting on her didn't bother him as long as it didn't go anywhere. As one of Anthony's top men, Sal believed it was good to be envied and wanted a trophy woman on his arm. Besides, they made a great-looking couple.

"They're gone, honey, thanks. When am I going to see you?"

"I'll be making my rounds, and then I'll stop by."

"Tommy stopped by to see Maria twice."

"Tommy is supposed to be working. I've got to go." He closed his cell and called Tommy on the radio. "Come in, Tommy."

A voice garbled by static answered. "This is Tommy."

"Bathroom breaks don't include social visits with your girlfriend; Capiche?"

Anthony entered the room with his Hawaiian shirt open, exposing a forest of gray chest hair, "Have you seen anything?"

Sal spun his chair to face him. "I don't know what you mean by 'anything.' Why don't you tell me what it is I'm supposed to be looking for?"

Anthony locked the door and picked up the remote to turn on the television, but nothing happened.

Sal took it from him and whacked it with his hand. "Bad battery connection. What do you want to hear?"

"Anything, and turn up the volume."

Sal knew Anthony was about to tell him something serious. If the room were bugged, the background noise would make it impossible for whoever might be listening to hear their discussion. They sat on the leather couch across from the monitors. Sal leaned in when Anthony spoke in a voice loud enough for only him to hear. "The guy you whacked last week at Moss Landing worked for Carmine Simone."

"Yeah, I already knew that."

Anthony put his finger to his lips. "Keep it low; let me finish. I called my friend at the coroner's office to update me on the investigation. He told me the guy was an undercover detective."

"Shit, Anthony, you mean I iced a cop? Wait, all this extra security means you think they know it was our hit." Sal laughed, "Are you bullshitting me? If it were true, they would've raided us already."

Anthony nodded. "Exactly, because they don't know... yet. According to my friend, I was the first to know, but the police will be told soon... I doubt they'll be able to connect us to the hit. They'll be looking at Carmine first. Carmine found out about his dead soldier a couple of days ago. Can you imagine how that asshole will react when he finds out he had a mole working for him? He also didn't know who ordered the hit."

"You mean Carmine didn't have a sit-down with Big Zac on this?"

Anthony shook his head.

Sal's jaw tightened, and he felt his nostrils flare before he exploded. "I can't believe you kept this from me! I'm a target for Carmine Simone's crew and maybe even the police, and you didn't think you should tell me?"

"Keep it down, Sal, and listen. I didn't want you overreacting before the party because you would have taken unnecessary precautions. I told you to heighten security, and you did. Anything more would put my guests on edge. Don't worry. I doubt the police know anything, and Carmine would want to be sure who whacked him. When he finds out his soldier was undercover, he'll sit tight until the cops make a move. I haven't heard anything in the news about the dead detective. He may have contacted his superiors at a specific time, and they're not concerned until he misses the call-in."

Sal bit his lower lip, narrowing his eyes. "What's Big Zac saying about this?"

"Nothing. He doesn't know we iced the guy."

"How could he not know? He's the one who gave the order."

Anthony's head shook back and forth ever so slightly.

"You're saying he didn't give the order?" Sal said.

"I told Uncle Zac the guy was skimming, but he didn't care as long as he got his cut. It was coming out of my share, and he wouldn't do anything about it, so I did."

"You paid me five grand for the hit. Where'd you get the money?"

Anthony dropped back on the couch. "My personal funds. Don't worry. I repaid myself from the briefcase you took before I gave it to Big Zac."

"Where did Big Zac think the money came from?"

"I told him we hit a truck with televisions and got a buyer for the whole lot."

"Holy shit! You know Big Zac's going to find out. What the hell did you get me involved in? It wasn't bad enough having Carmine Simone and the police after me. Now you went and put me on the boss's hit list."

"Nobody's on a hit list. Relax. We're in a holding pattern, waiting to find out who knows what. Big Zac doesn't know what happened. Carmine isn't gonna do anything once he finds out his man was a mole, and the police most likely just found out as I did. They don't know anything yet."

Sal stood up and no longer tried to keep his voice low. "You make it sound like you have it all figured out, but you don't know shit, and no matter what you say, it's still my ass. Just so we're clear, Anthony, if I go down, so do you."

"Hey, take it easy, and sit. We're gonna work this out. Everything's cool."

The flicker of light coming from one of the security monitors caught Sal's attention. Each screen followed in sequence, displaying cars with strobe lights filling the driveway. "You son of a bitch, Anthony. You think we have nothing to worry about? C'mere and look at this."

Anthony jumped, barely glancing at the monitors. "We gotta get out of here." He flung the door open and ran. Sal ran after him, unsure of their destination. The guests hanging out in the kitchen moved out of the way as they barreled through. Anthony stopped to retrieve the key to the basement from under a decorative jar on the counter. Someone asked, "Is everything okay?"

"Yeah!" Anthony yelled before taking the dimly lit steps down into the dark basement.

Sal missed a step in his hurry and slid down the staircase the rest of the way on his butt. "Damn it, Anthony, where're the lights?"

The blue sky and puffy clouds brightened the basement when Anthony opened the slanted cellar doors at the top of old brick steps. "Hurry up!" Anthony shouted.

Sal was slow getting up from the fall. He made it outside just in time to see Anthony jump on a motorcycle and start the engine, taking off quickly down a dirt path toward the woods. Sal stood in bewilderment for only a moment before anger took over. "You son of a bitch, Anthony. I'm gonna kill you."

The house and surrounding grounds swarmed with police carrying automatic guns and tactical gear.

Sal ran to the woods, not looking back until a bullet whizzed past his ear, making him drop to his knees with his hands over his head. "Don't shoot!" he called. Within moments, three men in swat gear were standing over him. One pressed a rifle barrel against his cheek while the second bent his arms in unnatural ways to cuff his hands. The third recited the Miranda rights.

The back of the van they put Sal in smelled of urine, bringing back memories of Sal's childhood after his parents died. The Norton's foster home locked Sal in a room not much bigger than a closet, where he relieved himself in a bucket. He hated the odor he was made to live with then, and now the smell triggered memories he wished he could forget. Sal kicked the partition, separating him from the two cops in the front of the van. "Hey, it stinks in here."

He heard one of them yell back and laugh, "Hold your breath."

Freaking wise ass.... I can't believe Anthony did this to me. I was loyal. What the hell good did it get me? No matter what happens, he's going down with me.

CHAPTER 2

Sal was in a blue room with a large mirror and a single door. He sat in one of two chairs that shared a steel table in which he was shackled. He knew he had been watched for hours and wanted to scream profanities at the mirror, but he also didn't want whoever was on the other side to see the isolation getting to him. He occasionally sneered and gave the mirror the finger, and when he couldn't take the seclusion anymore, he yelled, "You're a bunch of clowns. You got nothing. Where's my attorney? I called him hours ago. You can't hold me here forever."

This wasn't Sal's first experience being held by law enforcement. He had been arrested twice before — the first time, at seventeen, for possessing a switchblade and smoking marijuana. He learned a lot from that arrest. Two cops using the stairwell connected to the mall parking garage just happened to be there and caught Sal and his friends smoking a joint. Lesson learned: Never do anything illegal in a public place without a lookout. The second time he was twenty-four and charged with assault for breaking the arm of a deadbeat who owed Anthony money. The freeloader also happened to be the brother of a detective sergeant in the Venice Beach police department. Lesson learned: Know your target's background.

Sal rehashed today's events over and over as he sat alone in the room.

I really screwed up this time. I broke my own cardinal rule, by not investigating the hit. Anthony gave the order and I trusted him. The guy was a cop, for Christ's sake. Alright, no one could have known, but Anthony never told me the order didn't come from Big Zac. Then Anthony leaves me to take the rap. He better hope I don't ever see him again.

Two men entered the room, one with spats, tan pleated pants, and a brown button-down shirt. His beer belly put him over fifty. The other, in a T-shirt and jeans, was barely thirty. Both had badges dangling from their necks. The older man had no facial expression and stood by the door while the other sat in the chair across from Sal. He didn't say anything while reviewing the file. When he finished reading, he gave a smug grin. Sal wanted to jump across the table and make him eat every sheet of paper he found so amusing.

He pointed to his partner. "He's Detective McGregor, and I'm Detective Burns." He took out his recorder, pressed a button, and placed it on the table, "Our conversation will be recorded. Please tell me your name?"

Sal shook his head and snickered in disbelief, "You just read my file, asshole."

Detective Burns expression and tone changed from amused to disdainful, "Tell me your name for the record, wise guy."

"I'm not telling you anything. Where's my lawyer?"

Burns irritating smirk was back. "Your attorney is on the way, but we wanted you to know something before he gets here so that you have a meaningful discussion."

Sal sat back. "I'm listening."

Burns removed a picture from the file and slid it across the table toward Sal. "Detective Franco was with the force for eight years. He had a wife and two girls, ages six and eight. We believe you're the one who killed him, but we don't want you. We want your bosses."

"Oh, I see. You want to make a deal?"

Detective Burns sighed, "You're a smart guy. Now tell me your full name for the record."

Sal clasped his hands together and examined the 'detective's face. "Okay, I'll play. Salvatore Lovato."

"Where do you live, Mr. Lovato?"

"2300 South Venice Boulevard."

"Do you work for Zachary Barrelli and Anthony Rinaldi?"

Sal slammed the table. "We're done. You want to make a deal? Put it out there or get out of my face."

Detective Burns closed the file and picked up his recorder. "Have it your way, Mr. Lovato. You want a drink of water or a cigarette before we leave?"

"No. I want to know what I'm doing here. What are the charges?"

"We're holding you for suspicion of Detective Franco's murder."

Sal laughed. "You have no proof. Let me go, or charge me. I have nothing else to say."

Detective Burns took out a pack of cigarettes and offered one to Sal. "Relax, Mr. Lovato.

You're not supposed to smoke here, but we'll make an exception while you wait for your attorney to get here."

The two detectives were leaving the room when Sal called, "Smoke's no good without a match."

"Oh, right, let me help you." Detective McGregor flicked his lighter and lit the cigarette between Sal's lips.

McGregor removed a thin black book from his shirt pocket. "Do you know what this is, Mr. Lovato?"

"Should I?"

"No, but you will. This is Detective Franco's log book, and it's going to put you behind bars. Maybe even get you a death sentence."

As Sal watched the detective flip through the book, he took a drag and slowly let out the smoke. "You've got nothing, or you would've charged me. What game are you playing?"

The detective opened to a page and read: "December eighth, 1990, Carmine and Chez meeting Anthony and his soldier at Santa Cruz harbor, ten P.M. shipment details to follow." He flipped to another page. "August twenty-third, 1991; meeting Barrelli's soldier at Moss Landing eleven P.M. to pick up two keys of smack."

Detective Burns jumped in. "Any of this sound familiar, Mr. Lovato?"

Sal took another drag and tossed the cigarette butt to the floor. "No. It means nothing to me."

Detective Burns put on a latex glove, picked up the lit cigarette, and extinguished it on the edge of the table. Then he took the crushed filter and put it in a plastic bag. "It's nineteen-ninety-two, Mr. Lovato. Have you heard about DNA? It's better than fingerprints. Amazing what they are doing in forensics today. They can tell me if you left your DNA at a crime scene." He held up the clear bag. "If you were at Moss Landing and anywhere around Detective Franco's car, we'll know."

Sal banged the table. "What's this, a setup?"

Detective Burns took out his recorder and looked for Sal's approval to continue recording. "The people in charge want to make a deal, Mr. Lovato. As for me personally, I'd rather see you fry."

Sal tried to read the detectives. They might be full of crap, but he decided he wanted to hear what they had to say. "Okay. But get to the point, and I'm not answering stupid questions."

Detective McGregor leaned on the table. "Were you ordered to kill detective Franco?"

Sal laughed. "I told you no stupid questions. Those questions will have to wait until my attorney is here."

"Okay, let's simplify it. Are you loyal to Anthony Rinaldi?"

That name was festering like a ringworm under Sal's skin. "Loyal?" He laughed. "Bring him here. I'll show you my loyalty when I rip his head off."

"Looks like he threw you to the wolves."

Sal wanted Anthony dead, but he knew what they were trying to do. "Give me an offer, or shut the hell up. I'm not your friend. Capiche?"

Detective McGregor was the older, calmer one. So, it made sense he should tell him the offer. They both knew Sal didn't like, or trust, his partner Burns.

McGregor crossed his arms. "I assume you've heard of the witness protection program — new life, no problems?"

"Yeah, I heard of it, but forget it. I am not spending my life as a shoe salesman, janitor, or plumber. I'd rather take the chair."

McGregor laughed. "A plumber just robbed me for a hundred and thirty dollars an hour to put in a new bathroom sink. Think about it? You'd be a legitimate crook."

Sal connected with McGregor's eyes. "Do I decide where I live and what I do?"

He nodded. "Don't ask for stupid, and they'll consider it, but I'm not the one to approve your request. Tell me you want to move forward, and the state attorney general's office will negotiate the deal. The U.S. marshal will make sure you live up to your end."

Sal gazed at the plastic bag with the cigarette butt.

Not many options. They may use that DNA crap to nail me if I don't accept. Let's see what I can negotiate. How about a nightclub with five hundred thousand for a start? If they want Big Zac and Anthony badly enough, they'll pay.

Sal nodded. "I'll discuss it with my attorney when he gets here. Is there anything else?"

"Yeah. Be prepared to tell all. Every gun and drug deal, every assassination. Anything less, and you'll spend the rest of your life in prison. Lie to us, and you'll fry."

McGregor kicked his chair back while his partner flung open the door. Their message was clear: Take it or leave it; live or die.

Sal didn't need to wait for his lawyer. He knew what he was going to do. All that mattered now was what he'd accept, as opposed to what they'd offer. He told them he'd give the idea of entering witness protection some serious thought.

Sal recalled what McGregor had said.

Whatever I wanted, "to a point;" I'll wait and see, but this deal could be sweet, real sweet.

Sal was taken to a cell before attorney Paul Tommaso arrived. "Hi Sal, sorry it took so long. I had a meeting with Big Zac and Anthony. I assume I'll be representing you."

Sal squinted. "Assume."

"I'll be honest with you, Sal. Anthony is concerned you are mad at him for leaving you behind at the house. I want to ensure we are still on the same team."

He looked at Paul with a sneer. "I'm an idiot… I forgot you work for them. You tell Anthony I'm more than pissed; he's going down, and so's his uncle Zac. I'd never trust Anthony again, and I'm sure that puts me on Big 'Zac's hit list…. So the hell with the both of them. You can leave now. I'll find my own attorney."

Paul turned to the door and waited for the guard to open it. "I'll tell them what you said, but you should reconsider what you're doing. It won't end well for you."

"Is that a threat, Paul?"

Paul looked at Sal. "You've been around long enough to know a threat if you hear one. I'll let the prosecutor know you need a public defender. Take care, Sal."

Sal felt weak in his knees and sat on the bed.

The witness protection program is my only hope of getting out of this alive. There's no one to turn to for help; all I have is Susie. I hope I can convince her to come with me. We've had a good thing going for a few months. We can continue somewhere new.

CHAPTER 3

The public defender recommended Attorney Matt Drake, after Sal told him he didn't want a free attorney who works for the same state trying to prosecute him. Sal liked Drake, as he referred to him. Drake listened and seemed to understand the gravity of Sal's situation. Although, Sal didn't like it when Drake told him he was not being let out on bond because of the cost of security in such a high-profile case. Drake explained the unique situation and why he thought Sal shouldn't fight them over it. "Listen, Sal, this deal won't go down unless you agree to stay in jail, and try not to be upset... they want you in solitary confinement. It'll only be until the trial is over. I told the judge I'd talk to you first, to ensure you're on board with the trial requirements. They're offering you a good deal because they want to bring Big Zac and Anthony down. Ride it out, Sal, maybe the police want to see you suffer a little, or they just don't trust you. None of that matters when the alternative is twenty-five to life."

Sal looked at him and snarled. "You mean I'll be in solitary? I can't believe this shit. Do I have a choice?"

"Not if you want to be a free man."

Sal dropped his chin and then raised his head with a smile. "I haven't seen Susie outside a plastic partition since being here. Tell them I want... what do they call sex visits?"

"Conjugal."

"Yeah. Tell whoever I want conjugal visits once a week."

Drake shook his head. "I'm not sure I can make that happen; you're not married, but I can tell them you're complying with the terms of the trial, and maybe they'll reciprocate by granting your request. If I can make this happen, you must promise to be good, or they'll take away any visiting privileges."

Sal nodded. "Go make the deal, Drake."

It took two months for the prosecution to confirm the facts of Sal's testimony before arresting and indicting Zachary Barrelli and Anthony Rinaldi for racketeering and murder. It took another two months before the trial started. Sal refused to be intimidated in the courtroom. Each time he took the stand, he held his shoulders back and chin up as he passed the defense's table. Big Zac and Anthony didn't say anything, but their eyes told him they wanted him dead.

The high-profile trial at the Los Angeles courthouse had more security than Sal had ever seen. The courtroom's majestic high ceiling and polished brass hardware accented the deep rich wood of the surrounding wainscot that conveyed the importance of the trials presiding there. When Sal became bored with the never-ending legal mumbo-jumbo, he'd imagine other high-profile cases of famous actors or corrupt politicians sitting in the same seat he occupied.

The media fought to have the trial televised, and Sal's attorney Drake was happy Judge Gladys Lacy didn't give in. Each day the correction officers escorted Sal in and out of the courtroom from a wood panel door behind the judge's bench that was invisible when closed. No cameras were allowed, and everyone needed a pass to enter the courtroom.

Susie came to see Sal every day before the start of the trial to wish him luck and tell him she was praying for him. Sal didn't understand her daily visits and contemplated her intentions.

She still hasn't given me an answer about coming with me into the witness protection program. Why would she care at all?

He chuckled.

Didn't expect her to say she was praying for me. When did she find religion? She must want something. What's her motive?

The judge stopped the conjugal visits when the trial started. Besides the sex and conversation, one of the things he missed was asking Susie to wear a sheer nightgown under her coat because he knew guards searching her would drool. Sal laughed when he shut the door. "Eat your heart out, boys."

When Susie left, Sal returned to his cell, angry about having to wait another week to see her. She was all he had between unbearable solitude and happiness. He missed lying together after sex and talking about anything but the pending trial. They had some good times in their short relationship and would laugh while reminiscing. Sal hated it when the visits ended because, in the isolation of his cell, his thoughts returned to the closet he resided in at the Norton's. He'd spent the better part of his life trying to erase them from his mind. But alone in his cell with nothing but his thoughts to keep him company, it was impossible not to relive the nightmare.

CHAPTER 4

After Sal's incarceration, Saturday night usually meant Susie watched television with a couple of glasses of pinot grigio before going to sleep. Sal didn't want her going to clubs by herself, and even though he made no commitments to her, she agreed. Susie fell in love with Sal during their conjugal visit talks. She always thought he was funny, handsome, strong, and classy, but he was compassionate and understanding during her visits. A part of him he'd never shown her before. The package was hard to resist. She wouldn't tell him about her feelings, fearing that he might leave her. Susie knew Sal well enough to know he would reject any talk of commitment. When Sal told Susie about the witness protection program, her first thought was *yes, of course,* but what she said was, "I'll think about it." She didn't forget how to play men by never accepting an offer right away. Either say "No", or nothing at all. Most men never give up on the first try and liked the chase.

I was playing with Sal by not giving him an answer, but circumstances have changed. How do I tell him?

Tonight, Susie allowed herself one drink to celebrate the exciting news that she's having a baby, then she'd switch to decaffeinated green tea or something healthy. She turned off the television, found a magazine, and took her glass of wine to the couch. She was tired of watching, listening, and reading about the *"Mob Boss Trial,"* as the media called it, but the public loved gangster stories. The networks, radio stations, and newspapers fed them daily doses.

The phone startled her, and she looked at the clock.

It's late; I doubt it's Sal. Who would be calling now?

"Hello."

"Hi Susie, it's Maria. It's been a while. What've you been doing? You don't call, I don't hear from you anymore.... What's going on? The last time I saw you was Labor Day weekend at Anthony's house when Sal was arrested. Have you been listening to the news? Anthony and Big Zac are screwed. I wonder who the rat is. Does Sal know?"

Susie's stomach jumped. "Um... No, Sal's just trying to cope with being in jail. The police keep stalling things, and it's starting to piss him off."

"Are they letting him out on bail?"

"I don't know. Sal tells me very little, and his attorney told me not to talk to anyone about the case."

"I'm your friend Susie, that doesn't include me."

Susie sighed. "Maria, can we change the subject, I received some good news today. This conversation is starting to depress me."

"Sure, I understand. What's the news? Wait, don't tell me. Let's meet at 'Le Park' for a few drinks and catch up."

Susie didn't know how to say no.

She's, my friend. I don't want her to hate me, and maybe I can take suspicion off Sal. I wish I had never picked up the phone.

"Sure, give me an hour to get ready."

Susie entered the dimly lit, crowded club vibrating with people dancing together to the flashing lights below the translucent floor.

She weaved her way through the crowd, searching for Maria. A tug on Susie's arm pulled her to the bar. Maria smiled, then turned and said something to the guy sitting next to her. He looked at Susie and jumped off the stool, motioning for her to sit. When she did, he left. "Who was that?" Susie shouted to Maria over the music.

"Some guy was trying to pick me up, and I told him he could buy me a drink and hang here until you arrived."

Susie gazed at the crowd. "How'd you get these seats in the first place?"

"Good timing, I guess. So, what's the news? Wait, let's get you a drink first. Pinot grigio, right?"

Susie nodded with a big smile. "I can only have one."

Maria frowned. "What do you mean one? You just got here. The night's young."

Susie jumped up, excited about sharing the news. "I'm having a baby!"

"Oh, um, that's great. How far along are you?"

Susie was surprised she didn't get a hug or a kiss to show Maria's happiness for her. "I don't know. I took a home test, and it showed positive. I have an appointment with my gynecologist this Monday."

Maria held out her glass. "Congratulations."

Susie tapped Maria's drink, and then took a tiny sip of her own. "Thanks."

"You know those home tests can give false readings."

She nodded. "I know, but I ran to the store and bought another brand, and it said positive, too."

Maria gulped her wine until the glass was empty and held it out for the barmaid to refill. "Does Sal know yet?"

Susie shook her head. "No, and I'm not sure how to tell him."

"Why?"

Before Susie could answer, a good-looking young man with dark hair squeezed in between them and shouted above the club noise, "I don't mean to intrude, but can I get a drink for you ladies?"

Susie thought he seemed pleasant enough and was going to say 'No', politely, but Maria spoke first, "Can't you see we're having a discussion here? Find yourself another piece of meat to harass."

He was still smiling as he walked away, apparently unaffected by Maria's rudeness. Susie watched as he pushed through the crowd to a woman a few seats down the bar and started talking to her.

"You were rough on him, don't you think?" Susie said to Maria.

"What's wrong with you, girl? You know you got to cut them off early, or they'll never let you alone."

Susie swirled the wine in her glass. "It's been a while, and Sal doesn't like me going to clubs without him…. Listen, can we get out of here? I can't drink anymore, and it's too loud here to talk."

Maria hopped off her stool and guzzled her remaining drink. "Sure, let's go."

The night air was humid and cool, with a strong breeze indicating that a storm was coming. The sky lit up with lightning in the distance. Maria took out her keys. "Ride with me, and I'll take you back to your car later."

"Okay, where're we going?"

"The Beach Diner. You know, the one by the marina. I can get a couple of beers, and you can drink whatever."

The storm grew closer, with frequent rumbles of thunder after they entered the diner's parking lot. They used the car's visor mirrors to freshen up their faces. They realized they were overdressed for the casual restaurant when most of the diners inside turned to stare at them. Maria didn't wait to be seated, pulling Susie by the hand to a private booth in the corner.

Susie told Maria how much she had always wanted a baby and never told anyone. Susie was excited and happy, but she felt Maria was barely paying attention.

While looking at her watch, Maria said, "So, do you want the baby to be a girl or a boy?"

"I hope it's a girl so I can dress her up like a princess! What's the matter, Maria? You seem distracted and keep looking at your watch. Do you need to leave?"

Maria slapped the table with her nostrils flared. "You're right. This charade has gone on long enough. Tell me the truth. Is Sal the rat?"

Susie's neck and shoulders tightened. *Oh my God, she knows.* "No. Why'd you ask me that?"

"Bullshit. Why are you lying to me? Do you think Big Zac and Anthony don't have friends all over, including in the can? We all know Sal's the rat, and you're his lying bitch. How could Sal do this to Anthony, who took care of and trusted him?"

A cold chill ran down Susie's back. She couldn't speak, and she couldn't look at Maria. All she could do was try to keep the water glass steady while bringing it to her lips. Her mind raced.

Oh my God. What do I say? How do I deny this?

Susie swallowed hard and said, "I don't know what you're talking about."

Before Maria could respond, they were interrupted by the waitress. "Can I get you something?"

Maria said, "Nothing, I was just leaving."

Susie grabbed her bag, ready to follow, but Maria stopped her and sighed. "Anthony has been my friend longer than you, and I'm not going to associate myself with the girlfriend of a rat. You can walk back to your car." She snarled and jabbed a finger toward Susie's face. "You're a marked woman. I hope you and Sal are incredibly happy together in hell."

Susie watched Maria storm out of the restaurant. So did the waitress, who said, "That was a little rough. Can I get you something to drink?"

Susie wanted to run outside for air; she felt like she was suffocating but had no strength in her legs. She sank back down into the booth and said, her voice shaky, "Decaffeinated coffee."

As Susie sipped from her cup, watching patrons walk in and out of the diner, she kept replaying Maria's words: *"You're a marked woman!"* As much as Susie hoped it was nothing but an empty threat, she knew

Big Zac and Anthony weren't low-level gangsters. They were the real deal. Sal had always called Anthony a captain, which reminded Susie of men wearing white hats with anchor emblems, but in Sal's world, being a captain meant you were more like a prince to the king.

She finished the last of her coffee, dropped money on the table, and left. It started to rain, but Susie began walking to her car anyway. She wondered if Maria had planned to desert her before calling her a rat's girlfriend and a liar.

It was a chilly February night, and the cold wetness enveloped her quickly. Susie wanted to get back to the car and home as soon as possible, so she took off her heels to walk faster. The darkness hid the littered glass that punctured the heel of her foot. She slumped onto the curb and sobbed under a street light, watching the wound bleed. There was no one to help her and no one to call anymore. Maria was the only real friend she thought she had. And now there was no one she could trust except for her sister in Colorado, and she couldn't do Susie any good right now. Susie was alone and scared. She took off her pantyhose and used them to wrap around her foot. She started walking again, this time at a slow jog, keeping her eyes trained on the ground to avoid further injuries. There was a half-mile to go in the cold, wet darkness.

Why didn't I call a car service? All I want is to crawl into my bed and cry... the evening started out so well.

She heard the music before she saw the lights at the club where she'd met Maria. She fumbled through her purse for the keys and pushed the button to unlock the doors. She thought it was odd when it beeped twice, indicating the car was not locked, or a door was ajar, but it didn't stop her from jumping in to start the car to get the heat going. She opened the glove compartment for tissues or anything she could use to mop the rainwater dripping down her face. She found a small pile of fast-food napkins and pulled them out. Looking into the rearview mirror, she wiped her face. The street light illuminated the eyes of a man sitting in the backseat. Susie gasped.

The man said, "We have a message for Sal. No matter where he goes, we'll find him." The man grasped her hair from behind and pinned her head against the headrest. Something moved across the left side of her face. It didn't hurt much until the man released her and jumped out of the car. Susie watched him run, then felt a warm liquid dripping on her hand. She pulled down the visor mirror. A wide, deep gash ran below her left eye to her chin. She pressed the napkins against her face and drove to Venice Beach Hospital. "Why God? I'm so tired. Why is this happening? I just want to go home, but now I have to go to the hospital. Please don't let there be a scar. Dear God. Not my face."

CHAPTER 5

Sal called Susie on weekdays after court was adjourned and on Saturday mornings around eleven because Susie liked her sleep and took the phone off the hook. On Sunday, he'd call at nine when phones were always available because the rest of the cell block was at religious services. It wasn't easy for Sal to schedule phone time from solitary, so he tried to ensure his efforts were well-spent.

Susie was always up, waiting for his Sunday morning call, and then would go to noon mass afterward. She said Sal needed her prayers. After multiple attempts to call her this Sunday morning, Sal slammed down the receiver.

Where the hell is she? Why isn't she answering? It's already nine-thirty!

He called numerous times throughout the day. His last attempt was half an hour before lockdown and the prisoners waiting for the phone were getting impatient. He tossed the receiver to the next guy who was mumbling, "Hurry up," and stormed back to his cell.

I'll talk to her tomorrow, and she'd better have a good explanation.

Sal remained in solitary confinement after the trial started and hated every moment. He told Drake that if he didn't do something, he would go out of his mind. It took over a week, but Drake was able to get him longer exercise time that was closely supervised, with only a few other inmates in the yard with him. Susie was the only contact he had with the outside world other than his attorney, and she hadn't answered or returned his calls for two days.

After his most recent attempt to contact her, he returned to his cell with an emptiness he hadn't experienced since his parents died.

Did Susie abandon me? I can't believe she'd leave me without discussing it. Tommy's girlfriend Maria may know where Susie is, but what will I tell Tommy when he asks questions…? Damn it, I can't take the chance! Where the hell is she?

An hour before they were due to take Sal to court, his attorney came to Sal's cell with a guard behind him. "You have a visitor, but you should sit before seeing her," Drake said.

"Her? Susie?"

"Yes, it's Susie, she begged to see you, and you're going to be upset when you see her. It wasn't easy getting this chaperoned visit right before the trial, so please stay calm. You'll have to talk through the bars. Do you understand? Any screw-ups and the visit's over."

Sal had never considered marrying Susie. Sure, they made a great-looking couple, but love was not something Sal was capable of and wanted no part of. He learned at nine years old love gave no guarantees and it could be taken away in a minute.

Sal was standing with his face pressed against the bars, stretching his eyes to see down the corridor. She walked through the security door at the end of the hall. Her long, heavenly body sauntered toward him.

She'd better have a good excuse for ignoring my calls. Wait… why's her face bandaged?

The corrections officer escorting Susie held his billystick out, keeping her at arm's length from the bars. The bandage partially covered her left eye, and there was noticeable swelling.

"Hi, Sal," she said, and winced when she tried to smile.

It took a moment for him to realize what had happened. "Those sons of bitches. They did this to you?" He reached toward her, and the officer yanked her back, ensuring she was out of reach. Drake pushed Sal's hand away. "I told you; no contact, and you need to stay calm, or this meeting is over."

Sal squeezed the bars until his knuckles hurt. "When did they do this?"

Susie's eyes welled. "Saturday night. Maria set me up. They're pissed, Sal… more than pissed. The guy who did this said they'd find you no matter where you go."

"Who was it?"

"I don't know. I only saw his eyes before he cut me and ran off."

Sal sighed, and then loosened his grip on the bars. "I'm sorry, baby. I never meant for you to get hurt."

"Eighty-six stitches. The doctor says I'll have a scar for the rest of my life."

"Don't worry, baby. We'll get you plastic surgery when I get out of here."

Drake interrupted. "You won't be able to have any contact once you're in the witness protection program. You'll violate the agreement if you get in touch with anyone other than your preapproved family members."

"So, tell them she's family. I never heard about any approved list… did I?"

"They went over it with you. I was there. Remember? You said you have no family."

He winked at Susie. "I forgot. She's a second cousin on my mother's side."

Susie took a small step forward, pressing against the officer's baton. "I have something to tell you, Sal. Please don't be upset. I swear I didn't mean to forget my pill." She didn't need to say the words, but she did it anyway. "I'm pregnant."

The first person to speak after a long and awkward pause was Drake. "That changes things. She'd be family through a blood tie. Assuming you both want the child."

Sal looked at her belly. It showed no signs of a bump.

She's going to throw this on me now. Does she think we're going to get married now? I'm not dealing with this… she needs to get rid of it!

"Susie, I warned you about forgetting to take the pill, and I also told you I couldn't help you if you got pregnant. Listen. I'll get you on the approved list and help get your face fixed, but a baby doesn't fit into the plan. You can see that, can't you?"

She pulled her shoulders back and stood erect. "As always, it's all about you, isn't it, Sal?" She turned to the guard. "Get me the hell out of here!"

"Hey, Susie, wait, let's discuss it."

She didn't turn back.

Sal wondered if Susie would ever see him again. Without her, he was totally alone, and that made his stomach tighten. Only one other time in his life, being completely alone, scared him, and that was at the Norton's. They took him from his home, friends, and everything he knew. There was not one person who could help him escape the nightmare he lived. The aloneness he felt today isn't unlike how he felt then. Sal's heart pounded in his chest, thinking about losing Susie.

I'll call her after she simmers down. She's a compassionate person. I've seen it. She even started going to church to pray for me. She won't just write me off… She can't.

CHAPTER 6

A month before the trial ended, Agent Talbot of the U.S. Marshals' office gave Sal his new identity. "Considering your previous history, you're going to be head of security at Kings Plaza Mall, in Brooklyn, New York, under the name Harold Murphy."

Sal laughed. "Yeah, right. You're screwing with me?"

"No, I'm not. The witness protection team puts a lot of thought into where you'd best fit in as a productive member of society. A deterrent for shoplifters seems perfect, wouldn't you say? A nice cushy nine-to-five job with benefits. It's perfect. No one would ever suspect a mall cop."

Sal wanted to wipe the smirk off the agent's face but refused to give him the satisfaction of seeing Sal angry. Instead, he leaned back in his chair. "I'm supposed to have a say in where I'm going, and you're a moron if you think I'm going to be a fat mall cop named Harold Murphy. Tell the prosecutor the deal is off. I'll tell the court I lied, and you'll have nothing."

"And we'll tie you to Detective Franco's murder. One way or another, there will be justice."

Sal laughed. "I'd rather be in jail than a rent-a-cop. We need a meeting soon to discuss where I'm going, or I swear I'm turning."

Agent Talbot opened the door to leave. "I'll let the team know. Someone will be in to take you back to your cell."

Before Talbot could go, Sal rattled his shackles. "It's lunchtime, and they have chili dogs today. How long are you keeping me here? Tell them they have twenty-four hours to get me to a meeting to discuss my future. After that, I'm giving Big Zac and Anthony a free pass to business as usual."

They'll get me to the meeting, or this trial will be a waste of time. The thought of being a mall cop makes me want to puke! What the hell were they thinking?

Sal knew what he wanted; it was supposed to be discussed, but they never asked. They had an agreement, but instead, they blindsided him with a ridiculous offer.

Since they're starting low, I'll start high: five hundred grand in addition to the cost of a liquor license and building. The nightclub won't be located in the boondocks, either. At least they got the city right. Brooklyn, New York, home to one of my favorite movies: Saturday Night Fever.

Sal was happy they acted quickly and scheduled a meeting for the following day at nine A.M., two hours before he was scheduled to be in the next court session. They took him to the warden's office, where the prosecutor, judge, and warden, waited for him to enter. His escorts uncuffed him and waited outside. The warden offered Sal coffee and a bagel, which he enthusiastically accepted. Bagels with lox and cream cheese weren't something you get in jail. A step up from dry toast, burnt eggs, and the brown water they try to pass off as coffee.

As they waited for Sal to take a seat at the conference table, he amused himself looking at their phony smiles.

Guess I got their attention.

The judge spoke first. "I hear you're thinking of reneging on our deal. Is this true?"

He didn't stop chewing to answer. "Yeah."

"You're not happy with the identity we chose for your new life. Is that true also?"

Sal swallowed his food. "Shit, yeah. I was supposed to have a say in my new identity, and you reneged first. So, the deal's off."

Mr. Gibbins, the prosecutor, was about to respond when Judge Lacey intercepted. "Sit down, Mr. Gibbins. I want to hear about the deal, especially because I don't seem to have all the facts." She turned her attention to Sal for a response.

He looked around the table at their blank expressions. "I can't believe you weren't informed, your honor. I'd think they'd tell you everything concerning the case you're presiding over."

The judge spoke sternly. "I'm not here to play games with you, Mr. Lovato. If you have something to offer, you should say it quickly."

Sal pointed to the prosecutor. "He said I would have a say in my occupation and where I go. That didn't happen."

Her stare was cold. "What do you want?"

He longed to hear those words and responded the moment he heard them. "I want a nightclub in Brooklyn with a liquor license and half a mil."

Mr. Gibbins jumped up. "You're out of your mind, Lovato. We made you an offer. Take it or leave it."

The judge stood and asked Sal to excuse her and her colleague. She pointed to the warden. "Stay with him until we get back."

Sal took another bite of his bagel with a grin. Few things excited him more than the feeling of being in control.

They returned after thirty minutes. When they did, the only person who didn't look angry was the judge.

She sat in the seat next to him. "If we agree to your request, you'll agree to no protection. You get made; it's because you were stupid. And just so we're clear, I consider your demands outrageous and reckless. How long do you think it will be before someone recognizes you at a nightclub? It's a small world, Mr. Lovato. The Justice Department offered you protection, and you refused it. You'll sign a piece of paper saying just that."

It was hard for Sal to hold back the chuckle. "So, it's a deal? Night club and half a mil?"

Judge Lacey told Sal she needed twenty-four hours. "We need to conduct some research to see what's feasible, but I'm reasonably confident we have a deal. For the record, the only people who will know about our pending agreement besides the Justice Department director and U.S. Marshal deputy director are in this room. So, I need to know right now, Mr. Lovato, will you maintain your confession with no further threats if we agree?"

Sal wanted to jump up and yell *TOUCHDOWN!* Instead, he looked around the room with a smile, not answering, just long enough to be sure everyone was annoyed, and then he said, "I'd want to hear the details and discuss it with my attorney, but yeah, it sounds like we could have a deal. Let's, meet again in twenty-four hours. Bring the documents with you for my attorney and me to review."

Judge Lacey stood and gathered her papers. "We'll send your attorney the agreement when it's done. I'll keep you off the stand until the papers are signed, but be warned, Mr. Lovato, any other attempts to derail this trial will be met with swift justice for your conviction. Do you understand what I'm saying?"

Sal nodded. "I got it."

Big Zac Barrelli and Anthony Rinaldi were convicted of racketeering, money laundering, and seven counts of murder: one count for Detective Franco and six more for hits made by Sal and ordered by Anthony. One thing Sal knew after the trial ended was that he couldn't trust anyone. Not unlike what he told himself after leaving the Norton's. But Sal didn't like being alone.

I have a new life now, and I need someone I can trust… I need Susie. I'll agree to the baby. Maybe we can have separate apartments after it's born. I must convince her to come with me.

PART TWO

THE
REVENGE

CHAPTER 7

On April 7, 1992, Sal and Susie received new identities and were escorted by two U.S. marshals to their new home and life in Bay Ridge, Brooklyn, New York. During the flight, the older of the two chaperones reiterated Sal's witness protection agreement. "These are your identifications: Mr. Sid Love and Ms. Diane Rivers. All the paperwork is here — birth certificates, Social Security cards, driver's licenses, bank accounts, and phone numbers."

Sal said, "The bank accounts better equal a half a mil."

"It's there, except for the fifty grand in cash you wanted. That money will be given to you when we depart company. Never thought I'd see our justice system bend to every whim of a confessed killer. They must have wanted your bosses bad."

He laughed. "Why can't you give me the cash now? What do you think I'm going to do, pay the pilot to take us to South America?

The marshal shook his head. "Maybe you should pay attention rather than making snide remarks. There's a small pamphlet titled 'History.' It will tell you where you grew up, the schools you attended, and a lot more. I advise you both to memorize that information." He jangled some keys in front of Sal. "These are to the nightclub and the apartments above. That about covers it. Let me see... am I missing anything? Oh, yeah, you're on your own. If you screw up and blow your cover, don't call us. We won't lift a finger to help you."

Sal snatched the keys from the marshal's hand. "Yeah, I got it. Do you get enjoyment out of saying it umpteen times?"

He heard a yelp and turned to Susie — no, she was Diane now. "Why're you crying?" he asked.

Susie held her belly. "The baby has no family except for us. It'll never know my sister Katie and her kids."

Sal threw his hands up. "How many times, Susie? How many times do I have to tell you to forget your sister? We discussed this, and I told you we can't take chances. Get over it."

Susie's face turned red. "You're a cold-hearted asshole, Sal. I thought I saw a different part of you. Maybe I was wrong. How'd I let you talk me into this?"

Sal didn't remember either of their escort's names, and he didn't care, but the older one reminded him of reality. "You don't start calling each other by your new names, it won't be long before you're both dead."

"He's right, baby," Sal said. "We need to use our new names."

Susie - Diane - squeezed past Sal's - Sid's - legs and said sarcastically, "I need to use the ladies' room. Excuse me, Mr. Sid Love."

After returning, she stood in the aisle gazing out a window, disregarding the empty seat. Sid stood and pointed to the vacancy. "Why are you standing? Come sit down."

"I'm good where I am."

Sid sneered. "Why're you mad? You know I'm right about your sister. Besides, I agreed to keep the baby, didn't I?"

She rolled her eyes. "That's the best you got? I give up my life, and you think you're the hero. It's always about you, isn't it?" She turned to the agent. "When the hell are we landing? I need to get away from him."

Sid's blood turned hot when the two marshals snickered. "You jerks think this is funny? Do your middle-class bullshit job. Someday when you grow a pair and want to become men, come see me."

An announcement came over the PA.

"We're cleared for landing and making our final approach to LaGuardia Airport. The current temperature in New York is fifty-eight degrees. Please, bring your seats and tray-tables to an upright position, and fasten your seatbelts."

Sid looked at Susie — Diane. "We're here. You ready? It's kinda exciting, don't you think?"

Diane maintained her gaze out the window and only nodded in response.

They all exited the plane at ten A.M. Once Sid and Diane had their baggage, the younger escort said, "You're on your own." Then the two marshals turned and left.

Sid held up his middle finger, "Good luck to you, too." He flagged down a baggage attendant, and hailed a taxi. He opened the cab door and told Diane to get in, but she wasn't there. He snapped his head in different directions, shouting her name.

He turned to the cab driver, loading their baggage into the trunk. "You see the woman I was with?"

The driver pointed to the terminal. "I saw her walk into the coffee shop."

Sid focused on the glass doors, took out a twenty-dollar bill, and handed him the money. "Stay here, and you get to keep that on top of your fare and tip. I'll be back soon."

Sid entered the coffee shop calling out Diane's name. The customers sitting quietly with their magazines and coffee were yanked out of their literary world when Diane jumped from her seat and said, "My name is not Diane. It's Susie, and I'm done with you, Sal."

Sid felt a hot rush of blood to his head. He grabbed Diane under her armpit and dragged her toward the exit.

"I'm not going with you! Someone, please… help!"

A young man stepped in front of Sid. "Come on, let her go."

Sid released some anger when he chopped his hand into the guy's throat, making him fall to his knees and gasp for breath. "That's what you get for not minding your own business."

When they exited, Diane yelled louder. Sid squeezed her arm until she submitted to the pain. "It hurts. Stop, Sal."

"My name is Sid. Say it, *Diane*. My name is Sid."

She winced. "Okay, your name is Sid. Please stop. You're hurting me."

Sid looked around and whispered directly in her ear. "You're acting crazy. If we're recognized, game over. Capiche?"

Diane nodded. "Yes."

"Good, behave yourself, and let's see our new home."

The forty-five-minute cab ride from the airport to the nightclub was silent. Sid brought up the plastic surgeon they would seek out to fix her face. He thought it would make her happy, but instead, she turned away, ignoring him. He took a deep breath and whispered so the driver couldn't hear, "Fine. Don't talk to me, but it's too late to change your mind. This is not a game. If you become a liability, they'll never find you."

Her wide eyes connected with his cold stare, and she nodded. Sid knew she'd read his message loud and clear.

The taxi stopped in front of the address, and Sid found himself pleasantly surprised. He liked that it was a corner building, and the stone façade made it look like a castle. On the roof above the entrance was a large white horse and knight in armor holding a lance. Below the giant sculpture was the neon sign that read: Camelot Dance Club. Across the entrance doors was a yellow banner that said, "Closed. Keep out by order of police."

He pushed the key into the cylinder, but it didn't move. He wrestled with it until it snapped off. "I swear. If those bastards are screwing with me."

Diane stood beside him. "Are you sure it's the right key?"

"Doesn't matter anymore. It broke off in the lock."

Sid took a step back and kicked at the door multiple times, with no result. His face became heated, and he kicked harder until his foot hurt. "Son of a bitch."

He looked around the corner of the building. "Stay with the luggage, Diane."

The rear yard didn't offer an easy solution for access; a steel door and a window with security bars were the only openings. Sid pulled on the handle of the door, which had multiple locks. The steel rods protecting the window were old, and one of them was nearly rusted through on the bottom. He pulled at it, and to his surprise, it came free. He swung the bar back and forth until the top broke off. The opening was large enough for Sid to squeeze through, but he needed to break the window first. He smashed the glass with the rusted bar and removed the shard pieces from the opening.

Sid stuck his head inside and used his lighter to illuminate the interior. The sink below the window was filled with dirty dishes, and he saw something scurrying through the filth.

They could've at least cleaned the place.

The slime he touched as he pulled himself through the narrow opening made him gag. He squiggled back and forth, pushing and twisting his body until he fell to the mold-infested floor. He jumped to his feet, and a wave of nausea rushed through him. Though he targeted the sink, the roaches there made him turn away, and he covered the nearby stove with his puke.

He looked for something to wipe his mouth with and was happy to find a half-used roll of paper towels on a shelf across the room. He pulled a few sheets off and used one to mask his nose against the overpowering stench.

Sid went to the nearest door and searched the walls for a light switch. He found two and flipped them up and down with no result. Trying to keep his lighter burning to illuminate the room, he burned his finger and screamed. "Those bastards didn't turn on the electric?"

As his eyes adjusted to the dark, he was able to make his way past the swinging metal kitchen doors and into a larger room. The heavy drapery covering the windows revealed a glimmer of sunshine. He pushed the cloth to one side of each window, revealing a room with medieval décor.

Outside, he could see that Diane was talking with a police officer. *Why the hell are the cops here?*

Sid went to the entrance and released multiple locks, except for the slide bolt that needed a key, which none of his fit. He kicked the door and yelped when it didn't budge.

Sid banged on the window, and both Diane and the cop turned. "I can't get the lock open," Sid called. "I need a locksmith."

The officer yelled, "You need to come outside and give me your identification."

"I'm not crawling through the kitchen window again. If you want my ID, you better get a locksmith."

The officer said something to Diane and went to his patrol car. "What's he doing?" Sid shouted to Diane.

She cupped her hands to tell him, "He's calling his captain."

Sid threw up his hands. "Screw him. Diane, find the yellow pages and get a locksmith."

While he waited for help to arrive, Sid used the time to look around the club. He liked the venue and envisioned a dance club that people from all over would want to experience.

The police officer stood by while the locksmith opened the door. Once they got it open, the cop dragged Sid outside and patted him down. Fury ran through Sid's veins.

These idiots are going to make him look bad in front of his new neighbors.

He called to Diane, "Get these morons the deed."

It took time for her to go through the envelope the marshals had given them and find the document. When the cop released Sid, he turned to the sidewalk, where there was now a crowd watching the scene unfold. He said, loud enough for all to hear. "I own this place. Anyone looking for a job, bring me your résumé." He pointed to the officer and clapped. "Great job. You almost let an innocent man get away."

The group of spectators laughed. Sid studied them and knew this encounter had helped him gain some respect in his new neighborhood. It felt good. Respect was something he'd been missing.

When the crowd broke up, Sid had the locksmith stay to secure the building with new keys. While waiting for the locks to be fixed, he went to the apartment above the club. It was a shambles, and it smelt like something had died inside. Sid called a car service to take them to the nearest hotel. It would be weeks or months before they could live above the nightclub.

The first day of Sid and Diane's new life hadn't started well, and the first night was no better. Local hotels were booked because of a convention, so the best accommodation they could find was a Marriott near JFK Airport.

Sid went to the front desk and asked for a room with a king-size bed and a Jacuzzi.

The clerk looked at the monitor. "I'm sorry, Mr. Love, but the next available room will be at three. There's a lounge on the second floor if you'd like something to eat or drink while you wait."

Sid hadn't relaxed at a bar with a cold beer since before he was arrested, so the idea sounded appealing to him. He put his arm around Diane's waist. "Come on, babe, let's relax while we wait."

Diane pushed his hand away. "I may have agreed to my new identity, but I didn't agree to any relationship with you."

Sid sneered. "Fine, fine. I'm just trying to be nice. Have it your way." He stepped away from her and made his way to the bar. She didn't say anything but followed him.

The dimly lit room had a large circular bar at the center with bar tables on one side and a stage on the other. Sid chose a table and told Diane to order him a beer while he went to the restroom.

As Sid washed his hands and checked his hair in the mirror, a man entered and glanced at Sid before entering a stall. Sid felt his stomach flip.

Where have I seen this guy before? He looked at me. I'm sure he looked at me. Better watch what he does.

Sid threw multiple glances over his shoulder on his way back to the table. When he arrived, Diane was missing. The only thing at the table was a bottle of beer. He surveyed the room, but Diane was nowhere to be seen. He turned quickly back to the bathroom entrance. He hadn't seen the guy leave yet, so he kept an eye on the men's room while he flagged down a waitress. "You see a tall woman with dark hair and a scar on her face? She was sitting here?"

The waitress barely looked up from her notepad. "Nope."

"Then who served the beer to this table?"

She picked up her head and looked around the room. "That would be Barry. I don't see him. He must be in the kitchen."

"It's important. Can you get him, please?"

"Yeah, I'll get him."

Before Barry arrived, the man from the bathroom walked directly toward Sid. Instinctively, Sid reached for his piece — or, rather, he reached where he used to carry it. The only thing the witness protection program refused to supply was a gun. The man from the bathroom reached inside his jacket. Feeling panicked, Sid flashed a glance around, searching for a place to take cover if the guy started shooting.

The man took his wallet out and put money on a table. The woman sitting there got up, took the man's arm, and together they left.

Sid laughed as relief washed over him.

Now I know who he looks like, he thought. *That young detective who badgered me the day I was arrested. Yeah, that's it. Burns. Guy's name was Burns. My mind is working overtime; I need to chill out.*

A voice came from behind. "You wanted to see me?"

Startled, Sid turned abruptly with a clenched fist raised. The young man standing there held out the tray he was holding to block the punch.

So much for chilling out, Sid thought.

He put up his hands, palms out. "Sorry, man, didn't mean to scare you. You must be Barry. You see where the woman went, the one that ordered the beer?"

"She went to the ladies' room." Barry rolled his eyes and shook his head before turning away.

When Diane returned, Sid slammed the beer bottle down on the table. "You can't leave without telling me. I thought you got kidnapped or something."

She laughed. "Excuse me for having to go to the bathroom, and now you are going to pretend you care what happens to me?"

"Believe what you want, but you must tell me what you are doing and where you are going for your safety and mine."

"When did you become so paranoid?"

Sid pursed his lips, not sure what to say. "I'm not. Where's the server? This beer is warm."

CHAPTER 8

Sid had the best night's sleep since before he was arrested. The car rental next to the hotel was Sid's first stop after eating breakfast. He wanted a full-size Caddy or Lincoln. He always had a large luxury car and wasn't about to let his new life start with anything less. The lady behind the counter told him all the full-size vehicles were reserved and tried to give him a mid-size Ford Taurus.

Sid took out his billfold and put a twenty down in front of the woman. "Maybe a reservation for a full size got canceled."

"I'm sorry, sir, there are no cancelations."

He slapped down another twenty. "You sure? Why don't you check again?"

The woman giggled and stared at the money. "I'm sorry, sir, but we have policies."

He put two more bills down. "I'm sure you do but go ahead and check again. I'm sure there was a cancelation."

She looked around before taking the money. "Wait here, and I'll see what I can do."

Anthony Rinaldi sat in his cell after being transported to the state penitentiary, where he was sentenced twenty-five to life. Even in prison, Big Zac had the clout to ensure he and Anthony were in the same cell block. So, when Big Zac entered, he wasn't surprised.

"Here we are, Anthony… and you know what? I still don't understand why. That's the question that keeps coming back to me, Anthony. Why?"

Anthony slid over on the bed. "Please; sit?"

"I'm not staying. You told me your man Lovato was loyal, yet he turned on you. Why? He testified you ordered the hit. Why? I've given orders to start seeking out your rat Lovato. You are the point man for all communications and will report directly to me with the information received. Is that understood?"

"Of course. I'll work out the details."

"You're damn right you will. I want Lovato alive — those are your instructions. When my experienced interrogators question him, he'll give them the truth. The '*why*' questions will be answered."

Anthony watched Big Zac leave.

At least I have some control over this. Sal dying in an altercation would not seem unlikely. He can never be questioned. If he is, I'm a dead man. Sal must die.

Sid and Diane arrived at the police precinct in Bay Ridge at ten A.M. People were hustling around the entrance. Sid took Diane by the hand and navigated their way to the front desk. A hefty officer with rolled-up sleeves, an open collar, and significant sweat marks didn't look up when Sid asked for a firearm permit application.

"Have a seat. I'll be with you shortly."

The building and its inhabitants made Sid uncomfortable, even with his new clean record. "Will this take long? We're in a hurry."

This time, the officer looked at Sid. "I said, have a seat. When I'm done here, I'll help you."

Sid pointed Diane toward a bench, and they both sat down. He spoke loudly, "Typical bureaucrat. Can't do more than one thing at a time."

On the wall behind them were pictures pinned to a bulletin board. Under each photo was the word, **WANTED**. Most images were of young men and women wanted for robbery or auto theft. There were a couple for rape, and one for homicide, but the one that caught Sid's attention was Vito Rosa, who was wanted for illegal gun sales. In the picture, Vito wore a jacket and tie, and his hair was well-groomed, which told Sid that Vito wasn't some local hood. He asked Diane for a pen and found a piece of paper to write down the name.

A voice bellowed from the front desk. "I'm done with my one thing. What do you need?"

Sid ignored the officer's sarcasm. "A firearm permit application."

The officer retrieved the documents and slammed the metal cabinet shut. "Fill this out and mail the white copy to the address at the top of the form. Then return the yellow copy here. The state will be in contact to schedule you for fingerprints and a background check."

"Fingerprints... state..., how long is this going to take?"

The officer chuckled. "Twelve weeks for a standard permit, and conceal and carry could take months or even years."

The officer's amusement rubbed Sid the wrong way. "Our government has two speeds: slow and stop."

"Yeah, I know, and we only do one thing at a time. Have a good day, sir."

Sid kicked the door on his way out and muttered, "Bunch of clowns."

Inside the car, Diane asked, "Why are you so mad?"

Sid punched the steering wheel. "Because we need to protect ourselves. We could be dead in twelve weeks."

Sid was angry for allowing himself to be vulnerable. He was always prepared; it was his job, and he did it well up until now. As much as he tried to suppress his feeling of vulnerability, it brought back memories of the helplessness he once endured.

Diane scowled at Sid. "We could be dead in twelve weeks? What the hell are you saying?"

Sid turned the ignition. "Take it easy, I was exaggerating, and I don't like not having protection for twelve weeks." Sid smiled at Diane. "Forget I said anything. You don't need to worry; I'll take care of it."

Sid was surprised when Diane reached over and patted his leg. "You'll figure it out. You always do."

"It's nice to know you have faith in me."

I want to trust Diane, but her recent behavior puts her loyalty in question. Still, she's all I got; I'll give her time to adjust. My main concern now is to find a way to track down this Vito Rosa guy and get a gun.

Sid stopped at a convenience store. "I'm getting a cold drink; you want something."

"Water, thanks."

When Sid returned, he opened her bottle and handed it to her. It had been more than five months since Sid had been intimate with Diane. He gazed at her shapely legs and firm breasts. The visible bump in her belly also aroused him. He leaned in for a kiss, but she turned away, leaving just the scar for him to look at. He grimaced.

"You don't own me, Sid. You need to make up your mind about what kind of relationship we have."

Sid leaned back in his seat. "What do you mean? I said I will take care of you and the baby."

Diane shook her head. "You can't even look at me. How long will it be before you toss me aside for another woman?"

Sid bit down on his knuckle and grunted. "I told you I would pay to get your face fixed. What more do you want from me?"

She looked down, putting her hands over her belly. "I want to know that the baby and I will not be alone in this new life with no family, no friends, and always waiting for you to give us a handout."

"I never lied to you. You're here because I want you here."

She looked him in the eye. "The only reason I'm here is that you wanted someone you could trust and control."

He laughed. "Your pregnancy hormones must be kicking in. You're talking crazy."

"There's always someone else to blame," she said. "Never you."

Sid and Diane cruised the neighborhood for a real-estate office. Sid was hoping for an apartment vacancy within walking distance of the club. The hotel was too far and expensive for them to stay more than a few nights.

Driving past his soon-to-be renovated club, Sid took notice of his neighbors. The businesses across the intersection included a laundromat, a dollar store, and a pizzeria. The neon sign in the window next to the club read: "Psychic – Tarot - Palm Readings." Sid chuckled.

I want to support my fellow entrepreneurs, but I doubt I'll be going for a palm reading.

Sid found a real estate office a few blocks away. When he turned the corner to park, the bridge that spanned Brooklyn and Staten Island appeared before him like a great monument.

Diane's jaw dropped. "That's magnificent."

"*Saturday Night Fever* was filmed here. One of the best movies ever."

The search for an apartment took longer than Sid could ever imagine. The agent introduced herself as Tracy. The first apartment she showed them was in the basement below a two-story building.

It took Sid less than thirty seconds to spin Diane around and leave. They stood by the car, waiting for Tracy. When she returned, Sid ignored her apologies and smiled. "Do I look like a low life to you, Tracy? I wouldn't let a dog live there."

Tracy looked through the pages on her clipboard. "The only other availability is not far but not walking distance; and it's a bit pricy. It's two blocks from the Verrazano Bridge and on the sixth floor, oversee-ing the bridge and Shore Road Park. They're asking for eight hundred a week."

Sid whistled. "You mean a month, right?"

"No, it's per week with one-week security."

Diane cleared her throat. "I'd love to see what it looks like."

Sid opened the car door. "Great idea, let's go see it."

The view from the apartment was spectacular. Diane liked the ter-race breeze and the ocean air. Sid was fond of the Jacuzzi and was sur-prised by the stocked bar. "The place comes with the booze?"

Tracy chuckled. "Yes and no. Replace what you use, or you're billed for what you drank when you leave."

Sid opened the refrigerator and cabinet doors. "Fair enough, but I want to make an offer of six hundred a week."

Tracy shrugged. "I'll convey the message, but he usually gets his price."

Sid responded quickly. "If he did, it'd be rented. We need the place for two or three months while renovating my building. I'm sure the leaser would rather have the rent than not."

"I'll let him know."

Sid wasn't happy with the answer. "Call him now? I want to move in today."

Tracy took out her phone and dialed. She turned away and walked to the far end of the room. After a minute discussion, she said he would accept seven hundred and fifty.

Sid opened the pantry door, not caring what was inside. "Tell him six hundred and fifty, and I'll give him free drinks at my club for six months after it opens."

Tracy quickly finished the conversation and smiled. "Good call, Mr. Love. He said yes."

"Great, we'll go to the hotel and get our things. I'll bring the first week with security in cash to your office and pick up the keys in a few hours."

Diane enthusiastically talked about the apartment as they drove back toward the hotel. "The view of the bridge is amazing, and the place is so bright and cheery. I love the colors; it has everything we need — furniture, bed, and even the plates and silverware."

Sid hadn't seen Diane excited about anything since before his arrest. Her change in attitude cheered him and even aroused him a little. "How about some champagne tonight in the Jacuzzi to celebrate?"

She frowned at him. "You know I can't drink."

He glanced at her belly. "We'll get you the nonalcoholic stuff. We can still have some fun." He put his hand on her knee. "It's been a while."

Diane studied his face with her brow lowered and lips pursed. Then she nodded. "I guess we have to make this work. We only have each other."

Sid stopped at a red light, and she leaned over to kiss him. Her scar was not something he wanted to see up close. "Hey," he said, squeezing her knee. "Let's get an appointment tomorrow to see a plastic surgeon."

She turned to look out the window. "It bothers you, doesn't it?"

"Of course. Doesn't it bother you?"

She pulled her hair away from her face and gave Sid a good view of the scar. "Yes, of course. It's *my* face. But when *you* look at it, you're disgusted. Like now."

He accelerated when the light changed. "What are you saying? You don't want to get it fixed?"

Diane shook her head. "I'm saying you're a superficial, selfish jerk."

Sid swung the car into a parking space at the hotel. "I don't understand you. I'm trying to help. What do you want from me?"

"Nothing, Sid, forget it. Let's check out."

CHAPTER 9

Evan Locke looked at his watch and began putting away his fishing gear. He wanted time to set up the apartment before the new renters, Mr. Love and his girlfriend, moved in.

Everyone in the area nicknamed Evan "Ahab", because of his captain's cap and white beard. From April through October, whatever the weather, he could be found fishing on the pier under the bridge.

On his way back, Evan avoided the neighbors he'd usually stop and talk with, but couldn't dodge the mailman, who handed him his mail. "Catch anything?"

Evan smiled and walked to the elevator. "No luck today."

Leslie Richards from the fifth floor was alone in the elevator with a laundry basket. "Hello, Ahab; how are you?"

A tingle went through his body. "Hi, Leslie. Always a pleasure to see you. That's a nice dress. You fill it out beautifully."

She blushed and pushed the button for her floor again. "Thank you."

He reached into her basket and felt her undergarment sitting on top. "That's nice material. What is it silk?"

The elevator came to a stop and dinged when the doors opened. "I don't know," she said. "I have to go. Nice talking to you."

He watched her hurry down the hall before the doors closed. She was, and still is, one of his favorite performers to sublet his apartment. Then she bought her own condominium on the fifth floor two years ago. The video recordings of Leslie were included in his collection of favorite performers.

He entered his residence, put his fishing gear away and changed his clothes. Then he entered the room with the sign that read, COMMAND CENTRAL. Inside, six computer monitors sat on a large table against the wall. Above them were reel-to-reel voice recorders. When Evan flipped a switch, all the monitors lit up, with red and green lights glowing against the electronic equipment. He studied each monitor and made notes with a pencil and pad: Camera 1, ten degrees left; Camera 2, five degrees up; Camera 3, good; Camera 4, good; Camera 5, ten degrees down; Camera 6, good.

He tore off the sheet of paper, took off his shoes, put on latex gloves, and checked the corridor before locking up his apartment. Evan lived in apartment 6A for fifteen years and most residents knew him, but he sublet apartment 6C and kept his ownership a secret from the neighbors. He was always careful not to let anyone see him entering or leaving.

The cameras Evan kept in the air vents sometimes moved. The rattling of the ductwork jarred them, requiring him to come in and adjust the viewing angles, but it was still the best-concealed spot in each room.

Evan used a step stool from the pantry to access and remove the duct vent covers. He checked the microphones and tweaked the cameras in the kitchen, bedroom, bathroom, and living room, before replacing the registers and tracing his steps to ensure he left no evidence of his visit. Then before leaving he surveyed the corridor, confirmed it was clear, and locked up before returning to Command Central. The cameras were set up for optimal viewing. He checked to make sure the motion detectors were on, and a new video cassette tape was inserted.

Evan chuckled when everything was ready. "All we need now are the new performers."

Diane was hungry on the way back from finalizing the paperwork at the real-estate office. "Can we stop for something to eat? It's past two."

"What do you want?"

"Salad or fish, something good for the baby."

Sal sighed. "Okay, let's see what we can find."

He found a small restaurant on Fourth Avenue on the way to the Shore Road Condos. It had laidback, cozy Italian decor, and the food was fantastic. Diane got a tossed salad and grilled snapper, and Sid had calamari over linguini and sautéed broccoli rabe.

The owner stopped by their table to introduce himself when they were finished. "Hi, I'm Paul Denali. I hope you enjoyed your meals."

"Best food we've had in a while," Sid said, shaking Paul's hand. "You'll be seeing more of us. We're moving to an apartment on Shore Road, and I own the club on Eighty-second and Seventh Avenue."

Paul nodded. "Oh, sure, I know the Camelot. Hottest nightclub around here until the newspapers published a gruesome article a couple of years ago."

Sid felt his eyes widen. "Gruesome article?"

"The story said the kitchen was used to chop up and dispose of bodies. Supposedly mafia-related, but I doubt it. Not their style to use the same place… According to friends that I know."

Sid's knees went weak. "No one told me about that."

Paul put his hands up and chuckled. "Don't shoot the messenger. The newspaper article said they couldn't confirm the allegations because the owner went missing. I never read any more about it. Could be nothing more than a bad story. Hard to be sure."

Sid took Diane's hand. "I hope there's no truth to it. Thanks, Paul."

Sid waited until they were outside the restaurant. "Those bastards gave me a club with a bad rap! This story better not be true. I don't care what I signed or agreed to. They'll be hearing from me."

Diane smiled at Sid. "Let's forget that for now and enjoy the moment. We have an hour to kill. I picked up a tourist pamphlet at the hotel. Did you know Shore Road Park is a three-mile-long path that passes our building?"

"Sounds like a good place to kill time."

Diane blurted. "Doesn't it."

Sid and Diane walked half a mile of the three-mile path along the Hudson River that included a fishing pier, bike path, and both tennis and basketball courts. They leaned against the railing, looking at the boats and barges beneath the Verrazano Bridge.

Diane spun around and gazed at the children playing on the swings and monkey bars. "I like it here. It'd be a nice place to bring up the baby."

Sid nodded. "I like it, too, but the plan was to renovate and live above the club."

Diane gave a sarcastic snicker. "Yeah, in separate apartments."

Sid smiled and put his arm around her. "I can get used to this place. Maybe I'll rent those rooms above the club and see if we can buy a condo here."

She pointed to her belly. "Did you forget the baby?"

"I didn't forget. There're two bedrooms, so we can all live in the same apartment."

Diane tilted her head and peered at him through squinted eyes. "Why the sudden change of heart?"

"This place makes us both happy. When was the last time *that* happened? And like you said, we've only got each other. Of course, I haven't renovated the apartment yet, and it'll be a few months before it's done. My main concern is getting the club open. The shithole apartment upstairs can wait." He looked at his watch. "It's almost four. Let's get going."

It took Sid two trips to carry the luggage to the apartment while Diane took a couple of small bags and went ahead with the key. When she entered the apartment, she opened the blinds on the terrace door to reveal a fantastic sunset.

Sid dropped the last of their things in the bedroom and went behind the bar to make a drink. "You want soda or water?" he called to Diane, who was sitting on the terrace staring at the red and orange sky while listening to the Hudson River crash against the riprap. She sang Elton John's *"Don't Let the Sun Go Down on Me."*

Sid took his drink outside and placed a bottle of water on the table next to Diane. "You're happy."

She nodded and smiled up at him. "I am."

Sid sat back with his drink. "It's beautiful."

They stayed there, watching the sunset in silence until the sky deepened from red to purple and finally a twinkling black. Along with the night came a cool breeze that had Diane searching for the thermostat. Sid switched on the television and started filling the Jacuzzi. "You want to join me?" he asked, wrapping his arms around Diane.

She leaned back into his embrace as he caressed her body. "Yes."

Evan Locke sat inside Command Central, watching the new performers. He looked at the lease. "Sid Love and Diane Rivers. Not married but expecting." This was the first time he'd be taping a pregnant performer. Even with the bulge, Evan considered her body one of the best he'd seen. He zoomed in on her face and mumbled. "What happened to you?"

On camera, Sid was all over Diane, so much so that Evan couldn't see anything but the back of his head. Evan sighed and left to make a sandwich then returned ten minutes later to find the couple no longer embracing. He chuckled. "Finished already, lover boy?"

Evan put on the earphones and turned up the volume. It was hard to hear what they were saying above the sound of the bubbling water.

Sid said, "I'll fill out the firearms application tomorrow morning and drop it off. In the meantime, I'll see what I can find out on the street."

Diane closed her eyes and leaned back against the tub, using a jet to massage her foot. "You don't know anyone here."

"No. You're right, but what difference does it make? We wouldn't know anyone no matter where we went. So, what's wrong with here?"

She nodded. "Nothing. Just be careful."

Sid finished his drink and stood. "Starting tomorrow, I'll be at the club all day, and I'll get to know the neighborhood and a feel for who's running things."

Diane sat up and looked at him. "It's a small world, Sid. What if you're recognized?"

Sid kissed her head. "I doubt it, but it's a chance I'm willing to take."

Evan was fascinated by their conversation.

Guns and a secret past?

These two were quickly becoming the most exciting performers he'd ever recorded. Evan focused on watching Diane get out of the tub and dry off.

He grunted when Sid picked up the television remote, and Diane slipped into a robe. "Not much else is happening with the new mystery couple tonight. Don't worry; I'll find out who you are soon enough."

CHAPTER 10

Sid dropped off the state's copy of the application to the post office and the police copy to the precinct before going to the club. Immediately upon entering the building, he opened every door and window to try to air out some terrible smells. He bought spray cleaner and some clean towels to wipe down the corner booth by the window to use for his office until the electricity is turned on.

He spent the morning arguing on the phone with the electric company. Afterward, he put the cell phone on the table and walked outside to clear his mind.

The dollar store and laundromat were busy at eleven A.M. Sid watched as an older, white-haired man struggled with a security gate while opening the pizzeria and decided it was a perfect opportunity to introduce himself.

The man was about the same age as Sid, he thought, seeing him from a distance he thought he was older. The silver hair was deceptive.

"Hi, I'm Sid. Sid Love. The new owner of the Camelot."

After opening the pizzeria door, the man hoisted several large bread bags into his arms. He didn't acknowledge Sid's presence until Sid leaned down to pick up the rest of the bags. "Did you research the dark history of the property before you bought it?" the man asked.

Sid's mouth went dry as he recalled what the Italian restaurant owner had told him about the club.

Maybe it's not just a rumor.

"No," he replied.

The man went around the pizzeria, flipping switches. "I have something to show you, Sid. Would you mind taking that bread behind the counter? I'll be right back."

Sid moved the bags, but when he turned around, the man had disappeared into a back room.

Sid waited by the front door. When the man returned, he handed Sid an old newspaper with a headline that read: "Brooklyn Night Club Used as House of Horrors." The picture below the headline was of the Camelot.

Sid grabbed the paper and read about murder, dismemberment, and the club owner's suspected involvement. Sid finished reading the article and looked up at the man, who began kneading dough on the counter. "Is this true?"

The man didn't look up from his work as he replied, his voice cracking. "People were disappearing. One of them was my wife. The article was the only story that ever officially came out. Anything else has been rumors."

"Sorry to hear about your loss. What's your name?"

"Tony Rappa. My wife, Darlene, told the police what she heard and saw, and it had nothing to do with the Camelot. She told them about the fortune teller next store, and then she went missing."

"What'd she tell them?"

"To make a long story short, our pizza delivery man Henry was in some trouble and asked Darlene if he could borrow some money; he asked for more than Darlene wanted to give. Later that night, after we closed, Darlene was waiting for me in the car. She told me she saw Henry in the alley next to the Camelot with two people in robes from the psychic place. That was the last time anyone saw Henry."

Sid shrugged. "I assume your wife was able to identify the men."

Tony stopped kneading and stared at Sid. "Why do you say that?"

"She wouldn't have been a threat unless she could identify them. Did she tell you who they were?"

"No. Only that she saw them previously entering and leaving the building next to the Camelot." Tony went back to working with the dough. "Be careful of the neighbors you share the alley with," he added.

Sid glanced out the window. "You mean the palm-reading place?"

Tony ladled sauce on top of the stretched dough and started sprinkling cheese on top. "They're not who they appear to be."

"You mean they're mob-connected?"

Tony opened the oven. "No. I'm saying they make the mob look like choir boys."

"How's that?"

After sliding the pie into the oven, Tony said, "They're not just bad. They're evil."

Sid could relate to the difference between bad and evil. The Nortons were the evilest people he ever knew, unlike the mob who did bad things for business reasons. "Evil. Why do you say that?"

Tony let out a sarcastic chuckle. "Anyone who makes people suffer and then murders them is evil, wouldn't you agree?"

"Yes, but how do you know that's what they're doing?"

"When our delivery man Henry first went for a reading about three years ago, Darlene and I laughed. He was shy around women and wanted help meeting somebody. It seemed to work for him. He found a girlfriend about a month later. Soon after, Henry got paranoid about his girl cheating on him and told us he thought people were following him. He'd go away with his girlfriend for weekends and come back looking like somebody drained the life out of him. Darlene saw what was going on. She told him to break it off with the girl for his own good. He didn't listen. He just kept getting worse, and then one day, he up and quit. Didn't say why and we didn't see him again until he came around asking Darlene for money, months later. Then he went missing or got murdered. Nobody knows what happened. I suppose we'll never know for sure, but one thing I can tell you is he was a pretty normal guy. At least, before he went in for that psychic reading."

"That doesn't prove anything. Maybe the girl got him hooked on drugs or something."

"Believe what you want, but Darlene knew him well. She was a nosy neighbor type. Not like me. She liked to sit at the table by the window and watch what was happening outside. More than once, she told me that she saw people go into that storefront wearing robes and hoods. I didn't think anything of it at the time, but now it makes sense. They're an evil cult."

The aroma of fresh pizza woke up Sid's senses. He pointed to the oven. "I'll take a slice of that if it's ready. Listen, Tony, I'm just finding out about this history of the Camelot and these neighbors that you say are evil. I'm not turning back even if I could, and I'm not going to worry about the past. The Camelot will reopen, and it'll be better than before."

Tony pulled the pizza out of the oven and said, "You sound determined. I wish you luck, but I'd still advise you to stay clear of that place, or you just might go missing like your predecessor."

Sid laughed. "Don't worry, I can take care of myself. So, what do you know about the previous owner?"

Tony sliced the pie and handed Sid a piece. "Rick went to that fortune-teller almost every day. Darlene and I figured he was one of those people who believed in palm readings and such. Not my business; to each his own, right? But then he went missing a week or two after Henry. The story was never confirmed, but the rumor is the police found Rick's head washed up on the rocks under the bridge."

"That's quite a story, but I'm not convinced. The newspaper says the police found blood and a severed toe when they searched the club, but it doesn't say why they were searching or whose blood and toe it was."

Tony started working on another pie. "The article came out about a week after Rick went missing. I think it was his disappearance that got the police to search the club. The strange part is the press never followed up. Even the police stopped sniffing around. And then, Darlene disappeared after talking to the police. I'm telling you, Sid, I went down to the precinct every day. All they would tell me was, 'We're investigating, and we'll let you know if we find anything.' Tell me something, Sid. How can *three* people go missing without any clues? None. Zilch."

Between bites of pizza, Sid said, "It's not that hard to make people disappear."

Tony narrowed his eyes. "You sound like you're talking from experience."

Sid laughed. "Nah, I just like gangster movies and detective stories."

"Where're you from, Sid?"

The question made his stomach jump. He read through the history the witness protection provided but didn't recall where they said he was from and couldn't answer. Sid chewed and swallowed the last bite of his slice. "Hey! I just remembered I left the building open. Not that there's anything to steal, but I oughta be getting back. Oh, there *is* one thing you can help me with. Can you recommend a good contractor? I want to start renovations, but I don't know anyone in the area."

Tony dug in a drawer under the counter, pulled out a business card, and handed it to Sid. "My nephew Dan is good and will give you a fair rate. Tell him you're my neighbor."

"That's great. Thanks, Tony, this was a very enlightening conversation."

Sid crossed the street, looking at the lit neon palm reading sign in his neighbor's window. *I must pay them a visit and find out what they're all about. If they're evil people, they'll also be good liars as the Nortons were. But I've since learned how to see through bullshit. If Tony's right and they can't be trusted, I'll know.*

CHAPTER 11

Diane made spaghetti and meatballs for their first dinner in the new apartment. She had never cooked before, though she did remember helping her mom shape the balls from seasoned meat when she was a kid. The jarred sauce and spaghetti were easy, but she wanted to make the meatballs herself. With the baby on the way, it was time to get more domesticated, even if the word previously made her cringe. It hadn't been hard to stop partying when she got pregnant, but she'd found it challenging to stop pampering herself. Her beauty always paid for her luxuries through men that paid to have her on their arm. Sid was different. She stopped playing other men after she met Sid.

The doorbell chimed. Before answering, Diane gulped the last of her water and washed her hands. A middle-aged man with a white beard and a friendly smile greeted her at the door.

"Hi, I'm Evan, your neighbor. I wanted to introduce myself. Whatever you're cooking smells wonderful."

Diane rolled her eyes. "Smell is one thing. You haven't tasted it."

Evan reached into his shirt pocket. "Take my card. I'm a financial consultant. Phone number and email are there."

Diane peered at his card. "I've heard of email, but I don't know what it is."

"New technology can be confusing. Don't worry; the phone still works best."

"That's sweet of you, but I don't think I need a financial consultant. Please come in. I don't want the sauce on the stove to burn."

Evan clapped his hands and followed her. "We'll get along fine if you don't call sauce 'gravy.'"

Diane stirred the pot and lowered the burner. "My mom always called it sauce."

"You must be Italian, or a food connoisseur like myself."

"I'm Italian, but I'm hardly a food expert. Believe it or not, this is my first attempt at cooking."

Evan grabbed a wooden spoon by the stove and lifted the pot cover. "Mind if I give it a taste?"

She didn't like his forwardness but nodded.

"Very good," he said. "Did you use fresh tomatoes?" He put the spoon back by the stove.

Diane felt herself shudder a little.

Does he honestly think I'm going to use that spoon after he put it in his mouth?

"Yeah, fresh out of the jar."

Evan stayed close to her — too close, she thought — as she stirred the sauce.

I wish he'd leave.

"How'd you get the scar?" He said while attempting to push her hair back to see it better.

Diane took a step back to avoid his physical contact. "It's a long story. Can you please leave now — I need to finish cooking."

Diane could feel his eyes on her and became increasingly uncomfortable with his presence.

I hope Sid gets home soon. This guy is creeping me out.

Evan took a celery stalk from the cutting board and chomped on it with a smile. "Celery. It's good for the libido. Maybe your boyfriend should eat some."

Now he frightened her so that her legs became weak. "I didn't tell you I have a boyfriend."

"Well, you're obviously cooking for two. I just assumed since you don't have a wedding band."

Evan leaned against the counter, facing her. "Where're you from? Your accent tells me you're not from around here."

She grimaced. "You need to leave. I've asked you nicely; now, please go!"

Evan smiled and chomped down another bite of celery. "Hey, I'm just trying to be friendly, I'm sure we'll be seeing more of each other. I live just down the hall, apartment 6A, if you ever need anything or just some good conversation."

Diane followed him to the front door, the chopping knife and dish towel in hand.

I doubt I'll be visiting you, ever.

Before leaving, he looked her up and down. "You have my number and know where I live. Let's get together for a friendly drink sometime."

Diane flung the door open. "I'll ask my boyfriend and get back to you."

"Sure, let's all get to know each other."

When he was gone, Diane leaned against the door, took a breath, and blew it out slowly.

I feel like throwing up. He was gross and creepy. Sid will be pissed when I tell him I let him inside.

After returning from the pizzeria, Sid took a chair outside the club to sit in the sunshine. He left a message asking Dan, the contractor, to call back today. The people passing were local residents who smiled and said hello as they passed. Sid kept a close watch on the psychic-reading shop, but there wasn't any activity.

Maybe Tony's right, and it's a front.

He decided to take a walk over and peer inside. Behind the neon sign was a black curtain. He went to the door, which also had black drapery concealing the interior. Sid turned the handle.

Time to know the neighbors… It shouldn't take me long to figure out if it's a front.

A bell chimed when he entered. There was a long counter separating the storefront from the back room. The strange décor on the walls included large round wooden plaques with bronze metallic emblems at the center, animal skulls with horns, and painted silhouettes of what he thought looked like men with goat heads, all of which were hard to ignore.

A woman entered. "Can I help you?"

Sid clocked the woman at fifty-five or sixty years old. She wore a black shawl around her shoulders over a long black dress. Her hair hung nearly to her waist and had streaks of gray running through it. Sid thought she looked like fortune tellers he'd seen in horror movies.

"How's it going? My name's Sid Love. I'm the new owner of the club next door. I wanted to introduce myself and say hello. So, what's psychic reading exactly? I only know what I've seen in movies."

The woman showed no emotion, and her response was slow. "Knowing the future and connecting with the spiritual world can help resolve problems. That's what we do here: help people. Do you have troubles you'd like to resolve, Mr. Love?"

Sid took a closer look at one of the metal medallions on the wall. "No, but I wouldn't mind some information. I've seen a few shady characters, and it'll be a while before my gun permit gets approved. Do you know where I can get a pistol until I buy one legally?"

This time, she responded quickly. "Are you a police officer?"

Sid chuckled. "Lord, no."

"Wait here."

The woman walked into the back room through a black curtain. Sid ran his fingers along the strange figures carved into the metallic emblem:

men and women with animal heads were standing over corpses with daggers and swords, and some bodies were dismembered. Sid's neck tightened when he thought he recognized a face of a decapitated head.

This is spooky shit, but I think I found out what their real game is; guns.

A tall, well-groomed man entered the room. "Can I help you?"

Sid recognized him instantly from the wanted poster at the police station. "Are you Vito Rosa?"

"Do I know you?"

Sid took out the paper with his name and showed it to him. "I got your name from a wanted poster at the police station. I was hoping I'd run into you."

"Why is that?"

"As I told your friend back there, I'm looking for a gun to protect myself until I can buy one legally, and the poster says you're an illegal gun dealer."

"I'm not in that line of work anymore."

The comment irritated Sid. "The police don't post pictures of innocent people, so don't bullshit me."

"I may be able to help you, but what will you give me in return?"

Sid snickered. "You get me a gun, and I pay you. I'm sure this isn't the first time you are doing this."

"I don't need money. If you want my help, you'll need to offer something other than cash."

Sid recalled Tony's warning: *"Be careful. Your neighbors are not who they seem to be."* *This doesn't sound like your average gun deal. Let's see what their game is.*

"I pay cash. What the hell are you talking about?"

"Something of great personal value: A keepsake, jewelry, a body part, a relative."

Sid frowned.

Tony wasn't kidding when he said these people are evil. I'm not sure how to even respond to this asshole.

"Is this a joke? Body part? Relative? What the hell is wrong with you?"

"Those are our terms for the type of transaction you have in mind. If you'd prefer a simple psychic reading, we do accept cash for those. The cost is sixty dollars for the first reading and forty-five afterward. Madame Beth is available now, or you can schedule an appointment."

Sid laughed and turned to the door. "No, I don't want an appointment. And you're a nut."

He looked back twice, walking to the Camelot.

I can't believe that guy. What the hell are those people capable of? They're evil, to say the least, and they can't be trusted.

CHAPTER 12

Sid rushed Diane to get ready. "I have a ten o'clock appointment with the contractor and still need to drop you off at the dealer. Pick up the pace."

Diane poked her head out of the bathroom. "I'll be ready soon. I forgot about your appointment. I'm almost done. I'll meet you at the car in five minutes."

They arrived at the dealership as it was opening. Diane turned to Sid. "Can I have some cash?"

"How much?"

She pulled down the visor and popped up the mirror. "Two hundred."

Sid reached into his pocket. "That's a lot. What're you getting?"

"I saw a cute baby store, and I want to pick up some things for the baby's room. It's a mom-and-pop shop, and they might not take credit cards."

He handed her the money. "Don't go crazy. The baby's not even here yet."

Diane tilted her head. "Do you want to know the sex?"

"I haven't thought about it. Do you?"

"I'd like to decorate the baby's room in the right colors."

"Gender and color don't matter to me. Do what you feel is right. I've gotta go. Drive by the club later and show me the new wheels."

Diane slammed the door. "I'll do that."

Dan, the contractor, was sitting in his pickup when Sid arrived. Sid went up to the driver's window. "Hi, Dan. I hope you didn't wait too long."

Dan dropped his newspaper. "No. A few minutes. I'm always early." He got out of the truck and shook Sid's hand. "Tony told me the place was sold. I never thought that would happen, based on the rumors."

Sid laughed and pulled the keys from his pocket. "They made me an offer I couldn't refuse. Gimme a minute to open. It's dreary outside. We may need a flashlight. The best the electric company could tell me was they'd be here sometime today."

Dan shook his head with a grin. "I'll get my flashlight. Don't be surprised if they don't show up. I waited a whole day last week, and they never bothered to call to let me know they rescheduled." Dan looked at the building while Sid unlocked the doors. "Outside's in good shape. Are you keeping Sir Lancelot up there on the roof?"

Sid pulled the door open. "Isn't it grand? I'm keeping the name also. One of my favorite movies is *"El Cid"*, with Charleston Heston. Have you ever seen it?"

"Can't say I have. The only thing I remember about knights is a childhood fairy tale about a knight pulling a sword out of a rock when no one else could."

Sid chuckled. "King Arthur and the Excalibur sword. I know the story well. I did a lot of reading when I was younger. Sometimes it was all there was to do."

Dan flicked on his flashlight. "I was never big on reading. I usually wait until the movie comes out. Where's the utility box? Is there a basement?"

"I think so. There's a trap door behind the bar. I haven't opened it yet. I was waiting till we had lights. Who knows what's lurking down there."

Dan swung the light around the room. "We'll check it out. So, what do you want done?"

Sid outlined his vision while they roamed the building. Dan took notes and advised on costs. A car honking outside got Sid's attention. A new black Jeep Wrangler sat outside his front window. "I'll be back in a minute, Dan."

"No problem. I'll check out the basement."

Sid walked around the vehicle before giving Diane a kiss. "Jeep? Surprised you didn't get a convertible."

She shook her head. "I'm thinking about the baby now, and a convertible wouldn't be practical."

Sid smirked. "I'm finishing up with the contractor. Stay for lunch. The pizza across the street isn't bad."

She shook her head. "No, I still have errands. I'll stop by Denali's and pick up some dinner. What time can I expect you home?"

He shrugged. "Who knows. I'm waiting for the electric company. I'll call you later."

After Diane drove away, Sid went inside just as Dan came up from the basement. "Find everything?"

Dan handed Sid a large manila envelope. "Yes, you have an updated two-twenty-amp service, so any rewiring shouldn't be difficult."

Sid looked at the packet. "What's this?"

"I don't know. It's sealed. I was checking out the electric panel, and it dropped out of the ceiling." Dan chuckled. "If there's money inside, remember who found it."

The envelope was slim but heavy. Sid bounced it in his hand. "Doesn't feel like money. Maybe a magazine. Anything of value, you're in for twenty-five percent."

"Don't worry, there's nothing worthwhile in it. I've never been that lucky."

Sid tossed the envelope on the bar. "When can you get me a quote for the work?"

"Tomorrow, I'm still waiting on subcontractor and material prices."

The pizza lunch crowd was dispersing when Sid arrived and grabbed a booth.

Tony brought over a stromboli and sat across from Sid. "Thought you'd like this, hot out of the oven. He looked out the window. I see Dan is still here. When do you plan on opening?"

"Dan said he'd have a price for me tomorrow. Then we'll talk schedule. I was hoping around three months or sooner."

Tony smiled. "You should've seen this place before Dan performed his magic, and he got done within the sixty days he promised. Don't worry; he'll take care of you. You had any other run-ins with your neighbors?"

"No, and I don't want to."

Tony's eyes narrowed, and he tilted his head. "How could you not know the history of the Camelot before you bought it? I'm sure you could have found a better investment."

Sid paused to swallow his food. "Some questions are better left unanswered," He murmured.

Tony shook his head. "I don't mean to pry, but you're obviously a smart guy. How could you not know what you were buying?"

"Leave it alone, Tony. I swear to you, my reason for the investment was justified"

Tony gazed at Sid as if he were trying to read his thoughts. "So, you *did* know about the Camelot? Tell me what you found out, Sid. I'm still trying to gather any information I can about my wife's disappearance."

"The only thing I can tell you is the purchase wasn't solely my choice. I accepted an offer. Leave it at that."

"Whoever made the offer must have told you something about the history. I want to find out everything possible; wouldn't you if it was your wife who went missing?"

Sid dunked the last bite of the stromboli into the sauce. "I don't know what I'd do, but I'm telling you as a friend. Stop asking questions I can't answer. If I knew anything about your wife's disappearance, I'd tell you."

Tony nodded. "I'm sorry. I didn't mean to upset you. It just makes me crazy when I think about her being gone. She may have been nosy, but she didn't deserve whatever happened to her."

"I get it. And if I find out anything that can help, I promise I'll let you know."

Sid watched three electric company trucks pull up in front of the club. He stood and dropped a twenty-dollar bill on the table. "They're finally here. I gotta go. Maybe they can get the power on today. The stromboli was awesome. You can keep the change."

Sid was optimistic the power would be restored until one of the workers told him the lock on the meter could only be released with payment. "I'll call my supervisor to release the hold on the account. Do you know if the bill was paid?"

"I recently purchased the building, and I doubt the transaction would've gone through if there was a lien on the property for unpaid bills. Tell your supervisor I have a copy of the deed if he needs to see it."

It took less than an hour for the lights to come on, and when it did, it was as if the energy surged through Sid's body. He jumped up and shouted, "Yes-s-s! We're in business."

By three o'clock, when Dan and the power company techs left, Sid was alone in the building with the lights on for the first time. As he walked around, he realized just how much work it needed. "This place," he muttered, "is a shit hole!"

With nothing else to do, he went behind the bar and opened the cabinets and drawers. He found a book of matches, a box of swizzle sticks, and a rusted corkscrew. When he opened the refrigerator, the odor made him gag. He heard the motor running, and the light was on, but whatever was inside had started growing fungus long ago. He quickly closed the door.

I pity the person who has to clean that.

His eyes focused on the top shelf above the cash register. He saw the neck of a bottle hidden by a fallen poster. Standing on a chair to reach it, he found that the bottle was half-full, but it was the label that excited him; twenty-five-year-old bourbon. He jumped off the chair. "This has turned out to be a good day!" He looked around for a clean glass but soon realized wiping the top of the bottle with his sleeve was the only sanitary option.

The first swig burned on its way down, but the second felt like an old friend. As he lowered the bottle, his eye caught the yellow envelope Dan found, on the bar. He was about to reach for it when his cell rang. "Hello?"

"Hi, Sid. Would you have a problem with cartoon characters on the carpet in the baby's room?"

Sid laughed out loud. "What the hell are you talking about?"

"We haven't discussed what we're doing to decorate the baby's room. I'm at the store now, and I love this carpet. It's colorful, with baby Disney characters.

The slug of bourbon had Sid feeling good.

Why does she think I give a shit about the baby's room carpet? I guess I should sound like I care to make her happy… it's better than listening to her bitch.

"I wouldn't want the kid on any other rug. Hey, the lights are finally on down here at the club. I'll be leaving soon. Forget the takeout. Let's meet at Denali's at about four-thirty."

"Sounds good. I love you. Bye."

As he hung up the phone, he tried to recall ever hearing Diane say those words before. In fact, he couldn't remember the last time *anyone* told him they loved him, other than his mom and dad.

I'm happy Diane's with me, but I told her our relationship can't go there, and she knows I'm not going to reciprocate those words.

He took another drink.

So why say it?

Sid reached for the envelope. It was closed with a metal clasp, but the glue seal hadn't been used. He bent the hook open and poured the contents onto the bar.

The photos that splayed out before him were of people in black robes standing in a circle around naked, bloody bodies. Along with the images was a single sheet of paper that contained a handwritten note:

If you've found this envelope, I am most likely dead.

The people in these pictures are members of a cult called Renewed Bones. They reside undercover in the psychic-reading business next door. I met with Madame Beth, the psychic medium, who told me my ex-wife Karen planned to ruin me. She made me a believer by telling me personal things about my marriage and divorce she shouldn't have known. She said I would be bankrupt, and the Camelot will be closed within six months. I was horrified and asked what I could do. That's when she introduced me to a man named Trent, who offered to get rid of my ex-wife problem.

Then Trent said they don't work for money. "If you want to draw blood, you must give blood", he told me. I still can't believe I agreed to give them my pinky finger. They had to recite a secret ritual just before the finger was taken. I thought that was the end of my payment and my ex-wife, but I was wrong. They told me I had to be present during my ex-wife's sacrifice. I told Trent I no longer wanted to go through with it, and he told me backing out was not an option once I made the payment. A man I'd never seen before, and Trent, took me blindfolded, to a warehouse. The location couldn't have been more than a few miles from the Camelot.

Karen was unconscious, naked, and tied to a steel table. Five others besides me were dressed in black robes around the table. Trent stood at the center with a dagger and started a chant that the others followed. I couldn't believe what was happening and that, somehow, I had initiated it. I asked them to stop, but Trent raised the knife and plunged it into her. Afterward, they had their hands all over her body, like they were working with fin-ger-paints. Trent took my hand and put it over the hole in her chest that was still spurting blood. I tried to pull my hand away and wanted to flee, but he held me there before laying out a towel next to the body and pressing my hand down on it. My only thought was, "Oh my God, what did I do?"

Soon after, they wanted to use the Camelot for ceremonies and rituals. They said they would send my handprint with Karen's blood to the police if I didn't let them. I knew there was no way out, so I complied. After the first sacrifice was performed, I hid a camera, thinking I could blackmail them into letting me out of the cult. To this day, I don't know how they found out about the camera, but it became apparent I was being followed. I knew they wanted to kill me, so I hid the photos I had before they took the camera, hoping that if they did murder me, whoever found the pictures could bring them to justice. Please turn this note, and the enclosed photos, over to the authorities.

Rick Tully
Owner of the Camelot

Sid read the note three times and studied the pictures. They showed four different sacrifices: one of a woman and three others of men. All were lying naked on a table, surrounded by people in robes. He recognized Vito, the gun runner he'd met at the psychic shop, and mumbled. "What the hell am I supposed to do with this? I can't show this to anyone. The Camelot will become a national spectacle with tele-vision cameras and reporters, which would negate me from being the whistle-blower. Besides, this bum got in over his head with those crazy evil people. Sorry, Rick, but you're not my problem." Sid thought about tearing up the contents but didn't. Instead, he put them back in the envelope and slid the packet under a pile of papers on his desk.

It was three-thirty that afternoon when Sid stopped at Tony's for a soda. Tony was busy with a crowd of teenage customers recently let out of school. Sid stood three customers back, waiting to give his order. When Tony saw him, he raised one finger, then two. Sid shook his head and pointed to the soda machine.

As Sid leaned against the wall waiting for his drink, he noticed the décor for the first time. There were numerous photos of Tony and a woman, who must have been his missing wife. With shock, Sid studied her face and realized she could be the woman in the cult sacrifice photo. He shook his head and pushed the thought away.

It doesn't make a difference. I can't tell Tony or anyone about the envelope. I'm not even telling Diane. She'd freak out.

Sid watched Tony working behind the counter and felt the heaviness of guilt.

I like Tony. He reminds me a little of my dad in the way he uses his hands when he talks. He's a good guy, and I wish I could help him, but I can't. I'm sorry I had to lie to you, buddy, but there are other lives at stake. Damn it, why did Dan have to find those photos?

Tony handed Sid his soda. "Too busy now. Pay me tomorrow."

"Sure, thanks." Sid pointed to the wall. "That your wife, Tony?"

Tony paused, suddenly motionless, as if no one else was in the room. He nodded, and Sid thought he saw the glint of a tear in Tony's eye. "Yes."

"Beautiful woman. I'm sorry. I didn't mean to distract you."

Tony gave Sid a stiff smile and went back to work.

Sid took a gulp from the cup and walked back to the Camelot, never taking his eyes off the psychic crazies building.

After leaving the Norton's house, I promised myself that I'd only look out for myself, and that's how I've lived my life; so why is not telling Tony what I know making me feel like crap?"

CHAPTER 13

Evan did his personal chores before going to the library at three P.M., and luckily, the only microfilm reader was available. He found *New York Times* articles about recent hi-profile trials but wasn't sure where to start, so he went backward from the present. After two hours of poring through only a month's worth of articles, the library was closing. He realized his research would take a while. But he was in no rush. It was just a matter of time before he'd know their true identities. Then he'd have fun watching them squirm, knowing they'd been found out.

Sid arrived at Denali's restaurant twenty minutes early to meet Diane. There were no patrons yet, and even the service staff seemed absent. He sat at the small bar and waited.

Paul, the owner, entered the dining room and spotted him. "Hey. Nice to see you again."

"I told you I'd be back. Where is everyone?"

"We're between lunch and dinner crowds. My favorite time of day. It gives me time to prep and clean. Where's your lovely lady?"

"On her way. Can you get me a bourbon, neat, while I wait?"

Paul slipped behind the bar and put down a coaster. "You want it from the well, or top shelf?"

Sid laughed. "After the day I've been having, money is no object. Give me the best you've got."

When Paul placed his drink, he asked, "How are things going with the Camelot? You find out any more about the rumors?"

"Yeah, I guess I did. My neighbor across the street thinks his wife went missing because of something that happened at the club. The police didn't offer much help finding her, and they seem to have swept her disappearance under the rug."

Paul stopped wiping the bar and looked at Sid. "Maybe there was some truth to the story. But why would the police cover it up?"

"I don't know. I'm getting a lot of this in bits and pieces on what happened. It doesn't take much for rumors to get started. Maybe something terrible happened, and maybe it didn't, but it was over two years ago. My contractor will start renovations soon, and the bad history will soon be forgotten after the Camelot's opened again."

"You're probably right about that. People have short memories. So, when are you opening?"

Sid took a sip, smiled, and raised his glass. "Smooth. My goal is ninety days or sooner if possible. I'll start doing promotions when I confirm an opening date."

"Good luck with the renovations."

Paul brought a basket of bread and butter just after Diane arrived. "Can I get you a soda or non-alcoholic wine cooler?"

Sid shook his head and didn't wait for Diane to answer. "I'll take the real stuff, a bottle of merlot and the chicken parm."

Diane looked up from the menu. "Just water for me, and I'll have the tossed salad and salmon."

After Paul left, Sid studied Diane's face. "You look out of it," he said. "Did you have a rough day?"

"I'm tired. I did a lot of shopping. I'm looking forward to taking a bath and going to bed."

"I'm no doctor, but shouldn't you be taking it easy?"

Diane looked at Sid for a moment as if she wanted to say something, but then she pursed her lips and reached for her water glass.

"You're giving me a look," Sid said. "Did I do something to upset you?"

Before she could answer, Paul brought their food over and opened a bottle of wine. Diane shook her head. "Let's just eat," she said. "We'll talk later."

Sid thanked Paul and waited for him to leave. "No, let's talk now. If you have something on your mind, spit it out."

"Okay, you want to know? I'll tell you. Because you want nothing to do with the baby. It's all on me. All you care about is the club. The baby isn't going to have a father, and that makes me dislike you."

Sid looked over at the people being seated. "Keep your voice down. I'm giving you everything you asked for: a car, money, and a shared apartment. How can you say I don't care? What else do you want?"

"Love. I want you to love us."

The churning of his insides usually preceded an angry outburst. He wanted to yell that he was not capable of love, but he didn't. He's never told anyone, but he knew it was true. Instead, he asked, "Why're you bringing this up now?"

"Today, when I called you about the carpet, I said, 'I love you' and you didn't say anything. You just hung up. Weren't you even surprised to hear me say that? We can't be a family without love, and the only person you love is yourself."

Sid washed the food down with wine and looked at the people across the room. He responded in a low voice. "The deal was that I take care of you. Love, marriage, and family were never part of the package. If you didn't understand what you agreed to, that's your problem, not mine. We're stuck with each other, Diane, like it or not. So, why're we having this discussion?"

She shook her head without looking up from the table. "You're right. It's my problem. Let's eat and go home. I'm tired. Forget I said anything."

Evan Locke entered Command Central at five-thirty that afternoon and viewed the monitors; glad to see Sid and Diane weren't home. He knew he'd have to work quickly; he was determined to find out who Diane and Sid really were. Evan removed his shoes, put on latex gloves, and checked the corridor was clear as always before entering their apartment. Once inside, he immediately went to the bedroom and opened the dresser drawers. Evan paused when he found Diane's lingerie. He removed a pair of panties, smelled them, and tucked them into his pocket. He would've liked to browse some more, but he knew there was little time and couldn't afford to get sidetracked.

Inside a night table drawer, he found two envelopes. One was labeled *Sid Love,* and the other *Diane Rivers.* He took both packages and tucked them under his shirt. The sun was going down fast, leaving the room in shadows. Evan tripped over a suitcase and fell into a lamp, knocking it over and smashing the decorative glass globe. Knowing he didn't have time to clean it up, he rushed to the door but stepped on a piece of glass. Evan hobbled to the light switch and flipped it on. "Shit," he mumbled when he saw the trail of blood. Now he would have to make it look like a burglary gone wrong.

He spotted some jewelry on the dresser and took it. Then he opened a few drawers and scattered the contents onto the floor. He didn't want to leave a trail of blood back to his apartment, so he hurried into the bathroom to find something to stop the bleeding. There were no medical supplies he could find, so he cut a towel into strips with his pocketknife and tied it around his foot. Before leaving, he left the lights on and the door ajar. *That would do,* he thought.

Sid and Diane finished dinner and politely refused Paul's offer of cheesecake and coffee. Diane stood and pulled keys from her purse. "Thank you," she said. "The food was wonderful." She turned to Sid. "I'll see you at home."

He nodded. "I'll get the check. I'm right behind you."

Paul took the money. "I hope she's feeling better, Sid. She looks pale."

"The pregnancy hasn't affected her until lately. She's tired a lot, and her emotions are on overdrive."

Paul laughed. "I remember those days. It gets rough for a while, but when the baby's born, and you both hold that little miracle in your arms, any anxiety you endured will've been worth it."

Sid nodded and smiled. "Thanks, Paul. I'll have to wait and see" *But I doubt it.*

As Sid drove home, his thoughts kept jumping from Rick Tully's note to his guilt over hiding the information from Tony, and now Diane wanting a family, a real one. When he parked the car, his shoulders were tight, and his head was pounding. He took a deep breath before heading to the apartment.

Sid entered the elevator and greeted a blond woman. Sid could tell right away she was one of those people who couldn't be on an elevator with someone else and not talk. "Hi," she said. "I'm Leslie. Are you the new tenant on six? You're subletting from Ahab?"

Sid shrugged. "I got the apartment from the realtor, don't remember the landlord's name."

"Sorry, I don't mean to be nosy. I used to sublet your apartment before I bought my own on five. It's not waterfront, but it's mine with cheaper monthly payments. I was sad to leave the beautiful view of the bridge. I guess you haven't met Ahab, the owner, yet. He's a nice guy… in a weird kind of way."

"It's a very nice place we like it a lot," Sid said. The elevator stopped on the fifth floor.

Leslie smiled. "Nice meeting you. Maybe we'll run into each other again."

Sid took a breath before getting off on his floor and hoped Diane wouldn't spout any more crap he didn't want to hear.

Not tonight, Diane, please. I need a drink and maybe some Sinatra. Don't give me shit, please.

Sid took out his keys but noticed the door wasn't closed. As he pushed his way inside, he called, "Hey, Diane, you left the door open." The lights in the bedroom were on, but he headed to the bar and popped in a Sinatra CD before making a drink. The bedroom was quiet.

She couldn't possibly be asleep already; I was only five minutes behind.

He shouted. "Hey Diane, did you go to bed?"

Sid plopped down on the couch when the sparkle of shattered glass caught his eye. He stood and followed a red trail along the white carpet that ended at the broken lamp in the bedroom. "Hey, Diane, what the hell happened?"

The bedroom was empty, but Sid immediately saw that it had been trashed, the contents of the dressers thrown all over the floor. "Diane, where are you?" He knelt to take a closer look at the stain on the carpet and swiped a finger across it. "Blood." The realization weakened his knees first and then twisted his stomach.

Is it Diane's blood?

He yelled, "Diane!" before she walked in.

"What?"

"Where've you been?" he asked. "Are you hurt?"

She set a couple of shopping bags down on the coffee table. "I'm fine. I had to go to the drugstore to get my prenatal vitamins and other stuff. What's wrong with you?"

Sid turned off the music and pointed. "Take a look in the bedroom."

He followed behind her and watched as she took in the sight of garments on the floor. "My jewelry's gone!" she said. "It was right here on the dresser — my diamond necklace, my tennis bracelet, some earrings. We've been robbed!"

Sid nodded. "Certainly, looks that way. The robber must have broken the lamp and got cut on the glass, which explains the stained carpet. Let's look around and see what else is gone."

It didn't take long for Sid to realize their envelopes were missing. "Damn it. The asshole stole our identity information. I can't believe this."

Diane's eyes widened. "Oh my God, Sid."

Sid picked up a piece of broken glass. "There's nothing in there about our previous identities, but if they read those folders, it's gonna be obvious that we're not who we say we are. Did you take all your documents out of the envelope? License, passport?"

"Yeah, the only thing I left in the envelope was the history outlines of Sid Love and Diane Rivers. We were supposed to study them and get rid of the information. We've only briefly looked at them. That's why they were still here."

Sid tossed the shard of broken glass into the wastebasket. "That's good. I doubt the past information about our new identities will offer anything incriminating to reveal our past. I guess we'll have to call the police to get a report for the insurance. That tennis bracelet I gave you was worth a couple of grand. How much was your other jewelry worth?"

"They were gifts. I don't know."

Sid sneered. "Old boyfriends?" He didn't wait for a response. "Was any of it insured?"

Diane sighed. "It was in Venice Beach, but I canceled the policies before we moved."

"Then there is no reason to get the police involved. They'll start asking questions we'd rather not answer. Now more than ever, I need to get a gun. I guess we're shit out of luck with the jewelry. All right, let's see if we have supplies to clean this mess up."

Evan watched the monitors while removing the towel from his foot to see if he had stopped bleeding. When Diane entered, Evan listened intently to their conversation. He yelled out, "Bingo!" when she said the jewelry he had stolen was insured in Venice Beach. "You just narrowed my search, sweetheart. It won't be long now before I know your true identities."

Evan went through Diane's envelope. It described her family dying in a fire and living in Long Island, New York, with foster parents. It provided every detail, including addresses, parents' names, schools she attended, jobs she had, and even vaccinations she received. Sid's envelope supplied similar information, except his parents had been killed in a car accident, and he had lived in Rochester. Supposedly, they met at a club in Manhattan a year ago.

Even Chuckled. "Witness protection provided them with nitty-gritty details. I wonder what they'll do when they find out their secret is out of the bag. I'll play with them a little and leave a few anonymous notes. I bet Mr. Love will freak out. This should be fun."

When they began cleaning, Evan shut down Command Central to tend to his injury. His foot recoiled quickly when he went to stand. He hobbled to the bathroom and went through his first aid kit for the antiseptic and bandages.

I must be careful next time; I should've waited, but solving this mystery is the most exciting thing that's ever happened with my performers.

Diane was picking up the clothes in the bedroom when Sid walked in.

"You look white," he said. "Are you okay?"

She sat on the bed. "I need to lie down."

"I'll finish up here. Go to bed."

Sid put away the cleaning supplies, but sleep wasn't an option for Sid. His thoughts jumped from the burglary to the note and photos, giving him a headache. He went to the living room, put the music on softly so as not to wake Diane, made himself a drink, paced the room, and mumbled. "On top of everything else today, now I've got to worry about our identities. What if the burglar found something incriminating and is smart enough to figure out, we're in witness protection. The first thing he'd do is try to blackmail us. I'll have to wait and see what happens. If it happens, I'll deal with it then. Hopefully, the burglar was a stupid amateur that won't figure anything out. Either way, one thing I'm sure of is I need a gun ASAP. I'll have to deal with this Vito character, but I'll do it on my terms."

CHAPTER 14

Sid woke up after eight the following day and jumped out of bed. "Hey, Diane, can you get that coffee going while I shower?"

Diane didn't answer or move. Sid stumbled over to her side and shook her. "You hear me? I'm gonna take a shower. Can you *please* get me some caffeine?"

She grunted and turned on her back. "I'm not feeling well. Give me a few minutes."

Her pale complexion and lifeless expression concerned Sid. It reminded him of the first time he looked in a mirror after leaving the Norton's home. Not unlike Diane's appearance now. "That's okay, forget the coffee. I'll stop at the diner. Maybe you should see a doctor?"

She groaned, falling back on her pillow after attempting to sit up. "My appointment is tomorrow. I'll be okay. I just need some rest."

"Yes. It's obvious you do." He kissed her. "I should be done early; I just need to finalize with the contractor. I'll call you when I'm done and pick us up takeout at Denali's on the way home."

She took his hand and squeezed it. "You do care."

"Never said I didn't. Go back to sleep."

Sid opened the club doors at nine-thirty and flipped on the lights. He looked around. "This place looked better in the dark. I'll be happy when the demolition gets started."

His meeting with the contractor wasn't for an hour, so he kept an eye out for Vito Rosa.

If all goes as planned, I'll be scheduling renovations and have a gun by the end of the day.

He surveyed different windows looking for a good angle to keep an eye on who was entering and leaving the psychic's building, but there wasn't one from inside the Camelot. Sid took his coffee, roll, and the envelope he had buried yesterday off his desk and went outside to sit in his car, eat breakfast, and watch for Vito.

The dollar store and the laundromat were busy, but it didn't look like his psychic shop was open yet. Tony arrived at ten to open the pizzeria.

Sid picked up the pack of photos and looked through the contents. He peered at the photograph of the dead woman. It could be Tony's wife, but he wasn't sure.

It looks a little like her… wish I could help Tony, but I can't. This infor-mation gets out, the Camelot, and me as the new owner, will be all over the news, and I can't allow that to happen. I should burn this. Or wait… I have a better idea.

Sid was watching the neighbor's building when Vito walked past him unexpectedly from behind. Sid jumped out of the car. "Hey, I want to talk to you. Give me a minute."

Vito didn't turn but stopped walking.

Sid ran to catch up with him. When he turned, Sid was a foot away and realized his eyes were black?

You're a creepy dude.

"I'm ready to make a deal." Sid stuck out his arm and pointed to his watch. "It's a Rolex worth seventy-five hundred. Get me a thirty-eight pistol with six additional boxes of ammo, and it's yours."

Vito gazed at the watch. "It has a special meaning for you?"

Sid chuckled. "Yeah. The special meaning is that it's worth seventy-five hundred bucks."

Vito sidestepped to get past him. "The object must have meaning other than money."

Sid grabbed his shoulder to stop him. "What the hell's with you? All right, I'll get you something with meaning, and I'm sure it will satisfy your morbid obsession. Meet me at my club this afternoon at four and bring the gun with the additional bullets."

Vito nodded and walked away.

Sid watched him disappear inside the psychic shop. That was it. Sid was done playing this game.

I'll give him something with meaning when I crack his head open.

He returned to the club and wrote a note telling the contractor he had to run an errand but would be back soon. He pinned it to the door and locked up. Then he headed to the local copy shop to get some Xeroxes made.

He entered a storefront on Eighty-sixth Street. The clerk was moving boxes and had his back to Sid. "I'd like to get some color copies made."

"Sure," the clerk told him. "Color copies are thirty cents each."

Sid was about to hand him the envelope but pulled it back. "They're kinda personal. Can I make the copies myself?"

"I'm not allowed to let anyone behind the counter. Don't worry, I won't look. I stick the papers in the automatic feeder, and the machine does the rest."

Sid slid the contents out. "There's a note and four pictures. Keep the note on top."

The man snickered. "I promise I won't peek."

A few minutes later, he handed Sid the originals and copies, still holding them facedown. Sid paid and headed to the bank, where the witness protection program set up his and Diane's accounts. There, he set up a safety deposit box to hold the original photos and notes.

Evan Locke checked the monitors in Command Central. Diane was alone and sleeping. He wanted to stay and watch her get dressed before leaving for the library but didn't want to risk having to wait for the microfilm reader.

He got on the elevator with Ian McBride, the building maintenance man. "Hi, Evan. Where's your pole and gear?"

"I'm giving the fish a pardon today."

Ian handed Evan one of the flyers he was holding. "Glad I ran into you. Saves me a trip. The fire department is doing a fire and smoke detector test next week. They'll need access to your apartment. If you can't be home, I'll let them in. It only takes a few minutes to test the devices."

Evan studied the paper. "This must be new."

"A law was passed last year in New York. All apartment buildings over three stories or older than twenty-five years must have an updated fire alarm system and be tested once a year."

"When will it be? I'll try to make sure I'm home."

Ian pointed to the paper. "It's on the sheet. Wednesday, April twenty-first. They'll be testing floors one through three then, and four through six on the twenty-second. Like I said, you don't need to be home. I'll let them in and make sure they don't touch anything."

The elevator dinged at the lobby and Evan folded the paper. "Thanks Ian, but I should be home."

Evan walked through the lobby trying to recall where the fire devices were in the performer's apartment. He'd need to check the locations and make sure they're clear of his hidden wires and cameras.

I hope I won't have to remove any equipment, but for now, let's find out who Sid and Diane really are.

"Tony said you were going to take care of me," Sid said, tossing Dan's proposal across the table toward him. "This can't possibly be your best price."

"A hundred and twenty thousand is the best I could do. I included the restoration work, even though I could take a huge loss on that."

"I'm sure you've got some fluff in the quote. Come on, man, show some goodwill."

Dan sighed. "I'll take off five grand if we have a deal right now."

"That works, but there's one other thing we need to discuss. Your proposal says twelve weeks; I need it done in eight."

Dan shook his head. "I can guarantee my work will be done, but I can't do the same for the restorations. If I rush and ruin your medieval relics, you wouldn't be happy."

"Okay, we'll leave it twelve weeks, but would really like to get it done sooner. I lose money every day the clubs not open."

Dan nodded. "I'll do my best."

Sid put out his hand. "Deal. When can you start?"

"I'll put in for the building permits today. It could take two or three weeks before they're ready."

Sid grimaced. "What? That's unacceptable. You need to get started right away."

Dan shrugged. "Out of my control. But hey, listen, I'll see if I can talk to the right code official. Sometimes they'll expedite the demolition permit in a couple of days. Then we can get started while we wait for the building permits."

"Start on Monday, and I'll have a ten-grand deposit waiting for you."

Dan nodded. "We'll be here."

Sid and Dan had lunch at Tony's and then returned to the Camelot. Before Dan left, they walked around to discuss and finalize some of

Sid's ideas. After a while Sid looked at his watch. "Dan, I have another appointment I need to get ready for. I look forward to getting started."

When Dan left, Sid began making preparations to meet with Vito. He went to the kitchen and picked up a rusted knife. "Too messy. I need a bat. There must be something around here I can use." The wooden table by the door caught his eye. He turned it over and rocked one of its legs back and forth until it broke off. "That'll do," he muttered to himself.

In the main room, he pulled the drapes shut. His watch showed three-forty P.M. He ran out to the car, retrieved the photocopies, then returned and flipped a series of switches, leaving the room dim without being in total darkness. He checked to ensure the kitchen and alley exits were locked, and then opened the front entrance to ensure Vito would have no choice but to enter there. He used chairs to hold open the interior vestibule doors, and then stepped behind the door leaf with the table leg in his hand.

Everything was set to give Sid the element of surprise. He assumed Vito wouldn't be alone and hoped there wouldn't be more than one accomplice.

Vito and a larger man walked in a few minutes after four. Sid heard them but couldn't see them from his hiding spot. They stopped at the threshold. He recognized Vito's voice. "Hello, is anyone here?"

Sid had to wait for them to come into the club if he hoped to surprise them from behind. They took another couple of steps, but still not far enough.

Come on, asshole. Just a little bit further. What are you waiting for?

One of the men said, "I don't like this. Let's get out of here."

Sid wasn't about to let that happen. He pulled the framed occupancy sign off the wall and tossed it into the center of the room.

The taller man stepped inside to inspect the noise. As soon as his head was visible, Sid brought up the club and hit the man under the chin. He fell backward and landed hard on the floor. He tried to scramble to his feet, but Sid landed another blow to his head, rendering him unconscious.

Vito quickly pulled out a gun. "Stop! What are you doing?"

"This table leg has a lot of meaning for me, especially now. So, let's trade. You can have this, and I'll take that gun."

Vito raised the pistol and aimed at Sid's head. "Why would I do that?"

Sid ignored the threat and walked to his desk to retrieve the photocopies. "I'll show you why; just wait a second." He turned up the lights and thrust the papers at Vito.

Waving the papers away, Vito brought the gun closer to Sid's face. "What's this?"

"You can read the note from the previous owner of this establishment at your leisure, but I'm sure you'll find the pictures most interesting. Look here, Vito. Isn't that you? You're very photogenic."

Vito pressed the pistol against Sid's head. "You're making a big mistake."

Sid maintained his grin.

I can't show fear. He has to believe I mean business.

"Maybe I forgot to tell you. These are copies. The originals are in a safe place and will only be revealed if something should happen to me. So, why don't you hand me the gun, and we can all go on our merry way."

Vito's black eyes and cold stare made Sid uncomfortable.

I can't read this guy, I don't know what he's capable of, but he must believe I'm not afraid and I'm in control.

"Well, what's it going to be, tough guy? Either shoot me or hand it over."

Vito lowered the gun, hesitating momentarily before handing it to Sid.

Sid checked to see that it was loaded, then slid it behind his belt.

Sid went behind the bar, filled a dirty pot with water, and poured it over the unconscious man's head. The man groaned and rubbed his head as he struggled to get up. His eyes widened when Sid aimed the gun at him. "Don't be a hero; you and your boss can leave now. But first put the additional ammunition on the table."

The man looked at Vito, his face puzzled. Vito shook his head, and the two left without saying a word.

Sid snickered as they walked out. "You should've taken the Rolex, dummy."

It had been a while since Sid had roughed anyone up. He felt empowered by the engagement, not to mention the pistol he now owned. The weight of the cold steel in his hand felt like an old friend.

It was almost four-thirty when Sid called Diane. She picked up on the second ring. "Hello."

"It's me. How're you feeling?"

"I'm better, when are you coming home?"

"Sorry, I had some urgent business. I'm leaving now."

Sid shut off the lights in the club and locked up. Vito and two men he didn't recognize stood outside the psychic shop, watching him.

He yelled. "You guys got a problem?"

They didn't answer.

Sid watched them go into the building.

Who knows what the hell they'll do? Even with a gun, these people worry me. With the evidence I have on them, they're not going to do anything now, but just the same, I'll be looking over my shoulder. Evil people are sadistic. The Nortons made me suffer for their enjoyment. But these crazies don't just torture; they murder their victims when they're done. I will take no chances with them. If they attempt anything, I'll do whatever I must... even if that means torching their building with them in it.

CHAPTER 15

Evan arrived at the library, went to the *Los Angeles Times* archive, and began the search one year before; April 16, 1991. He stuck to the major headlines and didn't waste time with the small back page articles. He thought he got lucky when he read about a police undercover agent being murdered in late August.

Twenty minutes before the library closed, Evan found a headline: Reputed Mafia Bosses Indicted for Murder. The story went on to say an unidentified informant was helping the prosecutors indict Zachary Barrelli and Anthony Rinaldi for murder, racketeering, and drug trafficking. He rushed through the archive to find any follow-up to the story. None of what he found said anything about the snitch, but logic told him it had to be this Sid Love character. A photo with attorneys outside the courthouse caught his attention. Standing in the background was a man who Evan thought looked a lot like Sid Love. He hurried to the woman at the front desk. "I'd like to print a picture from the microfilm reader. Can that be done?"

The librarian continued her work checking in books. "Yes, but we're just about to close."

"I know, and I'm sorry. I've been searching through the archives all day and finally found what I was looking for. You'd be doing me a huge favor if you could print it out now."

She called to her assistant. "Carol, please help this gentleman while I start closing up." When Carol handed him the photos, he thanked her and stopped in front of the librarian. She had taken off her glasses and released her hair bun. *You're a looker under the facade.* He raised the papers. "Thanks, I owe you. Can I buy you dinner?"

She lifted her hand. "If you didn't notice, I'm married."

"I'm only asking to buy a pretty lady dinner. It doesn't have to go any further unless you want it to."

The librarian scowled. "Don't make me sorry I helped."

Evan was surprised by her response. "What's with you? I was trying to be nice."

Sid arrived with Denali's take-out at five-thirty. Diane was lying on the couch watching television and was slow to get up. "I'm starved. I'll get the utensils, and we can eat here."

Sid stopped her. "You're still white as a sheet. Did you rest today?"

Diane reached into the bag of food and took out a piece of bread, stuffing it in her mouth. "That tastes so good. Yes, I rested all day but didn't feel like eating. I'm finally hungry. I'll get what we need from the kitchen. Get yourself a drink from the bar and I'll have a ginger ale."

They watched television as they ate. Sid paused to watch Diane devour her food. "Hey, I know you're hungry, but you have eaten before, right?"

She smiled and licked her fingers. "I don't know why I'm famished. I had to force myself to have toast this morning and skipped lunch because you told me you'd be home early, remember?"

Sid reached behind his back and pulled out the pistol. "This is the reason I'm late."

Diane stared at it. "Those things always make me nervous, but I'm glad you finally got a gun. I know you were worried."

Sid set the revolver on the table. "Worried? This has nothing to do with worrying. It's about being prepared."

She buttered a piece of bread. "Whatever the reason, I'm happy you can now keep us safe."

"You wouldn't believe what I went through to get it. I had to teach my bizarre neighbors not to screw with me. I think they got the message."

Diane widened her eyes and swallowed. "Be careful. You don't want to get in trouble with the law."

"Trust me, they won't be calling the police."

She narrowed her eyes. "Is there something you are not telling me?"

With food in his mouth, he muttered. "You don't need to know everything."

Diane grasped his wrist. "I'm not just here for the ride. If you go down, what happens to us? To me and the baby? I need to know what you're doing. Are we clear on that?"

He pulled away. "No. You don't need to know everything. I'll tell you when I think it's important. When are you going to start trusting me? We're in this together. I'm not about to throw you to the wolves."

Diane sighed. "You're very capable, Sid, but you've never had to take care of anyone else before. Except maybe for Anthony and that's not the same." Diane cupped her belly with her hands. "I need to be sure we're as important to you as you are to yourself."

Sid's neck and shoulders tightened. "You make me sound like an arrogant, self-centered jerk. I'm not. I've already made my promises to you. If that's not good enough, you shouldn't be here." Sid got up, made a drink, and went outside to sit on the patio.

Diane followed a little while later. "I'm sorry. I just… I see you getting involved in things that scare me now because of the baby. I'm so worried something will happen to you, and we'll be all alone." She smiled and took his hand. "But I do trust you."

He smiled and looked at her pale complexion. "You seeing the doctor tomorrow?"

"Yes, I have a ten-thirty appointment."

"You want me to go with you? I don't have anything to do at the club until the renovation work starts Monday."

She giggled and threw her arms around him. "That would make me incredibly happy, thank you!"

Sid hugged her.

It used to be gifts and jewelry that made her react like this. Now it's accompanying her on a doctor's visit. Diane is not the same person; I guess it's the pregnancy. There's something sincere and humble about her new attitude.

Evan arrived home at five-forty-five P.M. and entered Command Central. Once the monitors came to life, he focused on Sid. "Distinct resemblance. He's lightened his hair and grown a mustache. We'll soon find out if you're the snitch, Mr. Love."

Evan turned up the volume when he saw Sid take out a gun but didn't hear how he obtained it.

If he's who I expect, he either bought it illegally or stole it.

He listened to Diane complain about Sid not taking care of her and wondered why she was with him, to begin with. *The article didn't say there was more than one informant. Like a pregnant girlfriend. It'll be interesting to see what they do when the cats get out of the bag.*

Sid woke up first and tapped Diane. "Are you getting up? It's nine o'clock?" She didn't budge. "Hey, you should start getting ready." She still didn't move. Sid sat up and shook her. "Diane, are you okay?"

Diane grinned and reached for his hand. "I'm alright, Sid. Go shower. I love you for caring."

Sid nodded.

Why did she have to say that?

"You should get up; it's getting late."

Sid walked Diane into the doctor's office and gazed at the room full of women. "I'm going to wait in the car. Are you going to be, okay?"

Diane sat. "I'll be fine. Get yourself breakfast. You haven't eaten."

He nodded. "That's exactly what I'm going to do. I need a cup of joe. Call me on the cell if you need me."

Sid found a diner on the corner and bought coffee and an egg sandwich, then picked up a copy of the *Daily News*. He ate in the car, reading and listening to Sinatra. His cell phone rang half an hour later. "Hello."

"Hi, Sid. Doctor Givens wants to talk to us together. Please come back to the office."

He dropped the paper on the passenger seat. "Is something wrong?"

"The doctor called it something. I don't remember the name. He hasn't given me the details, but he seems concerned and wants to make sure I have family support. I told him we live together and that you're the closest thing I have to family."

"I'll be right there."

I knew she didn't look good. I hope it's not serious.

He walked through the crowded waiting area to the receptionist behind the sliding-glass window. "The doctor asked to see me."

"Are you Mr. Rivers?"

He shook his head. "No, but I'm here for Diane Rivers."

The woman pressed a button to let him in. "Second door on your right."

Entering the doctor's office, Sid noticed Diane's eyes were wet and red. The doctor stood and shook Sid's hand. "I'm Dr. Givens. Thanks for joining us."

Sid sat next to Diane. "What's the matter? Why are you crying?"

The doctor jumped in before she could respond. "I was just explaining to Diane that she has a condition called pre-eclampsia. It's not uncommon for women in their thirties and third trimester. If it goes untreated, it can have serious consequences, and in rare cases, it can even be fatal to the mother and baby."

Sid frowned. "What is it with you, doctors? You're not happy unless you're scaring the crap out of people. Tell us the best-case scenario, not the worst."

Dr. Givens opened the file on his desk. "I'm not trying to frighten you, but you need to know this is very serious. Diane, your blood pressure is one-sixty over a hundred. It distresses the baby and causes a strain on your internal organs, which can lead to seizures and kidney failure."

The doctor wrote something on his pad and handed the sheet to Diane. "This is a prescription for blood pressure medication. Get it filled and start taking it right away. You'll also need plenty of bed rest and a special diet until the baby comes. I'll monitor your condition and the baby's development closely. Talk to the nurse on the way out about scheduling weekly visits. If possible, we'll try to take the baby early through a cesarean delivery. The sooner you deliver, the better it will be for both of you."

Diane nodded, wiping away her tears. Sid took her hand and slid forward. "Tell us the truth, doc. Chances are, she and the baby will be fine, right?"

The doctor stared at Sid for a moment, and then reclined in his chair. "Yes, the odds are good, but she needs to follow the treatment plan. The nurse will give you instructions on your way out." The doctor closed the file and stood. "If you have any questions or concerns, feel free to call me."

Sid stood and helped Diane up. She thanked the doctor, but Sid said nothing and waited for her by the door.

She should have gotten rid of the baby, like I said. I don't want to see anything happen to Diane. I care about her, but I don't need this shit in my life right now with everything else to think about.

Evan missed fishing on such a glorious morning, but in this case, it was like giving up going to the arcade to go to Disneyland instead. He watched the performers dress as he wrote his message and saw them leave as he finished.

I wonder where they're going. After I drop off my letter, I'll need to stay glued to the monitors. I can't miss their reactions after they've read my note.

Dear Mr. Love,

Do you remember the prosecutors who charged Zachary Barrelli and Anthony Rinaldi with murder, racketeering, and drug trafficking in the attached photo? More importantly, do you recognize the man in the background? That's you, Mr. Love. You were the snitch for the prosecution. I can keep this a secret, but you must do something for me first. At nine o'clock tonight, take your pistol to the trash can on the corner of Ninety-second Street and Third Avenue and drop it inside. If you do as I say, we can become friends. I especially want to know the beautiful Miss Rivers. You're not married, so I guess she's fair game. I'll keep your secret as long as we can all play nice together.

Evan took the paper from the printer and read it over with a grin. "This is going to be better than an all-night orgy." He put the note and the photo in an envelope and went to the lobby. It took him a few minutes to find the mailbox key. He hadn't used it since he started subletting the apartment. He inserted the envelope and snickered after he locked the box. *Game time.*

CHAPTER 16

At three P.M., Sid pulled into their condo's parking lot after filling Diane's prescription, only to find a red Ford Taurus in his assigned space. He hit the steering wheel. "Son of a bitch, who the hell would park in my spot?" He reached for the door handle to get out of the car.

Diane grabbed his arm and stopped him. "What're you going to do?"

He flipped open his pocketknife. "The cost of parking in my space is four flat tires."

"Wait! Maybe somebody had an emergency and needed the space. Don't do anything to bring bad karma."

Sid laughed. "Karma? Where the hell did you get that from?"

"Hurting innocent people can come back to you. Let it go."

He studied her face with tightly pressed lips.

I don't believe in karma, but maybe she's right, and there was an emergency. Just the same, I can't let it go without doing something.

"Do you have a pen and paper?"

Diane fumbled around in her purse. "I have a pen."

"Forget that. I've a better idea. Give me your lipstick."

She handed it to him. "What're you going to do?"

Sid stepped out. "Watch and see."

He went to the Taurus's front windshield and wrote in lipstick: I SHOULD HAVE GIVEN YOU FOUR FLATS. PARK HERE AGAIN, AND I WILL!

She was laughing when he returned to his car. "I should have known you couldn't let it go. But thank you for not getting violent about it. I'm sure they won't be taking your space again."

Diane retrieved the mail on the way to the apartment and dropped it on the coffee table before she plopped onto the sofa. "I'm going to sit here and rest a while. The doctor wants me to start taking the pills right away. They're in the bag, you brought in. Can you get them for me with a glass of water?"

Sid nodded.

I hope she doesn't think I'm going to wait on her until the baby's born. "Sure thing."

When Sid returned, Diane was going through the mail. "They're doing a fire test next week and need to get into our apartment. Hey Sid, what do you think this is?" She held up a manila envelope with *Mr. Love* handwritten on it.

She handed it to him. "Strange that there's no address or postage. I wonder what it is."

Sid used his pocketknife to open it and slid the contents out. He looked at the picture first and then the note. His stomach flipped, and his shoulders tightened, pulling at every tendon and nerve ending connected to his head. He squeezed his eyes shut, trying to stop his insides from shaking. He ran into the bathroom, and with his empty stomach, all he could do was convulse into dry heaves.

Diane ran in behind him. "My God, Sid, what's wrong? What was in the envelope?"

He handed her the note, which had crumpled a bit in his fist while he was heaving.

Diane examined it. "That looks like Big Zac in the photo."

She smoothed the paper on the counter and read the message. Her eyes widened, and her mouth fell open. "No, No, No! How can this be? What're we gonna do?"

"I don't know. I need a drink to calm down and figure out who sent this. How is it possible that we've been found out this quickly? Something's not right." He took the note and photo to the bar and filled a glass with bourbon.

Diane was even whiter than she'd been before. He took a large gulp of his drink. "You need to sit down," he told her. "Take your medication. Don't concern yourself. I'll take care of this."

Her eyes welled with tears. "I'm scared."

Sid sat next to Diane and took her hand.

This isn't good. I'm worried too, but I can't let her see it.

"Don't be afraid. There must be a clue in this note as to who sent it, and once I figure it out, I'll find the culprit and take care of this."

Sid was truly frightened for the first time since he was ten. His fear took him back to the sound of the door unlocking the room he was captive in. He never knew if they were there to hurt him or throw him some food. It was the uncertainty that scared the hell out of him. The same uncertainty he was feeling right now.

Big Zac and Anthony can't possibly know yet. I'll find out who wrote this, I have to.

Diane studied Sid. "You're worried; I don't think I've ever seen you look worried."

Sid held up the papers. "They haven't contacted anyone yet, or they wouldn't have sent this. Can you please sit, Diane? You don't look good."

She nodded. "Okay. But one thing I don't understand. The note says they want your gun. You just got it. How could anyone know about it?"

Sid took another sip of his drink. He studied the message, then clapped his hands.

Vito, of course, no one else knows about the gun.

He kissed Diane. "That's the clue! I know who sent this. Don't wait up. I'll be late."

"Wait. What are you going to do?"

He smiled. "I'm going to get rid of the problem."

Tears rolled down her cheek. "Please be careful. I need you to come back."

"Don't worry. Now that I know who sent it. Everything will be fine."

"Please hurry back. I'll be going out of my head until you do. I love you, Sid."

He kissed her again. "I know you do. Don't wait up for me."

There it is again. It's becoming more frequent. She needs to stop saying "I love you." One day maybe I'll explain why I can't reciprocate, and she'll stop saying it.

Evan had stayed home half the day, waiting for Diane and Sid to arrive. He was so excited he felt like a child waiting to open gifts. When Sid and Diane finally entered their apartment, Evan turned up the volume in Command Central and leaned forward in anticipation to watch Sid open the envelope. The response was even better than Evan had expected.

Evan was entertained and amused until the audio went silent. He adjusted the controls, until the sound returned moments later. He heard the last part of what Sid said. "I know who sent this. Don't wait up. I'll be late." For a moment, Evan felt his blood cool.

That's impossible. There was no way Sid could know it was me. He must have thought the note came from someone else. But who?

Evan dashed to the stairs to try to beat Sid to the parking lot. After Sid drove away, Evan followed far enough behind not to be noticed.

Sid drove to the club, parked in front of Tony's Pizzeria, and went inside. Tony was serving the early dinner crowd. Sid waved to him and took a table by the front window where he could see who was entering and leaving the psychic crazies building.

Twenty minutes later, Tony brought Sid a soda and a slice. "Closing up soon, trying to get rid of the leftovers. Please don't feel obligated to eat it. How'd you make out with Dan?"

Sid only briefly looked away from his surveillance to acknowledge Tony. "He starts Monday."

"Something wrong, Sid? You look preoccupied." He didn't respond. "Hey, Sid. Did you hear me?"

He looked at Tony. "I'm fine, just thinking."

"I must start cleaning up. If you want to talk after I'm done, hang out... free refills on the soda."

Sid nodded with a smile. "Thanks, but I'll be leaving soon."

Sid watched the psychic crazy club as he ate. He hoped Vito was inside. He wanted to end this tonight.

Did this moron think I wouldn't know it was him? He's the only person who knows I have the gun, and he'll tell me how he got my identity, or I'll make sure he dies in excruciating pain. You screwed with the wrong guy, Vito Rosa!

Sid stayed by the window for a half hour until nightfall, wanting to be discreet entering the club.

If something goes down with Vito, Tony is the only person who has seen me tonight, and I need to keep it that way.

Sid locked the entrance doors behind him, pulled the draperies shut, and then opened the side entrance that shared the alley with the psychic shop. It was dark. Sid took a moment for his eyes to adjust, then walked across the alleyway and used the butt end of his pistol to knock. He waited a minute, and when there was no answer, he hit the door again. The man who finally answered was the same guy Sid had knocked out yesterday. Sid smirked when he saw the bandage on his chin and head.

"Where's Vito?" Sid didn't wait for a response. Instead, he pushed himself inside, pressing the pistol to the man's cheek. "I'm counting to three. Take me to Vito or die."

"He's not here."

"One…, two…,"

"All right, all right! I'll take you to him."

A female voice interrupted. "That won't be necessary, Tod. Drop the gun, Mr. Love!"

Sid looked at the pistol Madame Beth was holding and laughed. "Shoot me, and you all go down. Didn't Vito tell you about my insurance policy?"

"Vito told me about the photos. You're a foolish man. Soon you'll be begging for my help, and it will cost you the life of someone you love."

"You're an idiot if you think I'd ask for your help. Sorry to disappoint you, but I don't love anyone. Your threat is meaningless."

She gave him a sinister smile. "If you don't love anyone but yourself, you'll be begging me for your own life."

"Don't hold your breath. You know you're not going to shoot me because I have the evidence to lock you all up and throw away the key, so put the gun down and let this clown take me to Vito."

She kept the pistol aimed at him. "What exactly do you want with him?"

"I want to know where he got my information and who he's shared it with."

Madame Beth gazed at Sid with empty black eyes. "I don't know what information you're referring to."

Sid backhanded Tod. "I'm done playing. We can all just wait for Vito right here. Let's lock your front door and make ourselves comfortable."

She offered little resistance when Sid took the gun from her hand and had them walk to the front entrance. He heard a sound from behind; then a hard object hit him before he could turn. He groaned, grasping his head.

"What the…?"

He felt a second blow to the base of his skull. He tried to stand and see his assailant, but everything went from gray to total darkness.

Evan watched Sid enter the club. He got out of the car when he saw Sid exit the alley door and knock on the door of the neighboring business. He stood at the edge of the building and peered around the corner. It was hard to see until the door to the psychic shop opened. Sid was standing with a gun pointed at whoever had answered. Evan heard him ask, "Where's Vito?" before pushing the person inside. He tip-toed to the door and heard Sid say, "Shoot me, and you all go down. Didn't Vito tell you about my insurance policy?" Evan snickered.

He thinks these people sent my note and photo.

Evan thought Sid had the upper hand for a moment, but then everything suddenly got quiet. The next thing Evan heard was a woman's voice. "We can't do it here. Take him to his place. It needs to look like an accident."

Evan ran out of the alley when he heard them walk toward the door. He leaned around the corner and watched them carry an unconscious Sid into the club. Evan couldn't determine what was being said inside, but he noticed they'd left the entrance to the neighboring building ajar, so he opened it and stepped inside. He stayed silent for a few moments. Not hearing anything, Evan was confident the place was vacant. He pushed through some curtains and entered a room with chains, leather, and other bondage paraphernalia. *These people are sadistic, masochistic perverts.*

I can understand bondage, but have a hard time understanding how pain and sex go together. To each his own.

He heard someone enter and footsteps heading his way. Evan took cover behind an oversized wooden chair. He listened to the sounds of metal clanging and drawers opening and closing. It occurred to him that they must be gathering some tools to use on Sid. Evan wasn't about to let Sid be killed, especially because things were getting so interesting. When the people left, Evan came out of hiding and entered another room with a pentagram in the middle of the floor and three-foot-tall candles all around. He laughed. Evan could only hope Sid would appreciate what he was about to do. He took a nearby lighter and lit the wick, illuminating the room. He took the candle to the black curtains that covered the store's large glass windows, put the flame to the cloth, and watched the fire climb up the fabric. As the smoke began to fill the building, he ran to the alley, banged on the club door, yelling, "Fire!" and then ran around the back of a dumpster to avoid being seen.

Peering from the shadows, he watched a man come out then yell for the others to come quickly. Two men and a woman entered the smoke-filled building.

Evan ran inside the club, where Sid was tied to a chair. He quickly cut the straps with his pocketknife and slapped Sid in the face. "Wake up, come on. You need to get out of here."

Sid opened his eyes, squinting to bring Evan into focus, but couldn't. "Who are you?" He cringed while Evan helped get him to his feet.

Evan didn't answer the question, saying only, "I'm leaving. You need to get out of here, too. Those people want to hurt you." Evan ran to his car and watched a crowd gather outside as fire engines pulled up beside the psychic shop. He got in his car when he saw Sid stagger into the street. Evan smiled.

No 'Thank you' is required. Let my game continue!

CHAPTER 17

Sid woke to a slap in the face and a voice saying, "Hurry, you need to get out of here."

Sid couldn't focus with the back of his head pounding, but he managed to croak, "Who are you?" The person didn't answer. He just lifted Sid to his feet and ran out. Sid staggered into the alley and saw smoke coming from his neighbor's door. He remembered the psychic crazies had knocked him out and felt a pang of shame that he never saw it coming.

How could I have let this happen, and how'd the fire start? I don't remember anything after getting hit, and who was it that helped me?

He heard sirens out front and reached for his gun, only to find it missing. "Dammit," he muttered. "They took it."

He made his way down the dark alley to the street, where people were lining up to watch the firefighters put out the blaze. Sid leaned against a telephone pole, trying to get his eyes to focus. Someone grabbed his arm, and Sid swung a clenched fist toward the culprit but missed.

"Sid, it's me, Tony. Take it easy. You, okay?"

"Sorry. I was attacked. Somebody whacked me in the head. I need a place to sit."

Tony guided him through the crowd and into the pizzeria. He eased Sid onto a chair and hurried off to bring him a cup of water. "You want me to take you to the hospital?"

Sid took a deep breath and blew it out. "No, I'll be okay. I just need a few minutes."

Tony scrutinized the back of Sid's head. "You've got a lump the size of a softball, and there's blood dripping from your ear. You might have a concussion. I think you need a doctor. Let me take you."

"No, I'm fine, but it would be great if you could get me a bag of ice."

While Tony went to get an icepack, Sid watched the activity across the street through the window. The firemen had the flames under control and were wrapping up their gear. And there, staring at Sid from the sidewalk, were the psychic crazies: Madame Nutjob, the guy he had hit, and another man he didn't recognize.

Sid snarled back.

I'll never underestimate you assholes again!

Tony returned with the icepack and a bottle of brandy. "Here, take a shot. It'll help with the pain and to relax."

As the crowd broke up, customers started streaming back into the pizzeria. "I've gotta get back to work, okay? Let me know if you need anything else."

Sid watched two of the psychic crazies get into a black Jeep. He wasn't sure, but he thought the driver looked like Vito Rosa. The third person he didn't recognize stayed behind in front of the shop, talking to the firemen. Sid held the icepack on his head and sipped the brandy while trying to recall anything about the person who had saved him.

Tony came back to his table. "Feeling any better?"

"Yes, thanks. Hey, was it you who untied me?"

Tony looked surprised. "Untie you? What're you talking about? When were you tied up.?"

Sid wished he hadn't asked. He shook his head. "Forget it. Maybe I was hallucinating."

"I'm worried about you. I'm closing in half an hour. Let me take you to the emergency room."

Sid shook his head again. "I'm fine. I'm gonna head home." He used the table to push himself up, but his knees buckled, and he fell back into the seat. "Or maybe I need a little more time."

Tony threw his hands up. "Why are you being so stubborn? It won't take long to have a doctor check you out."

"I'm sure I'm fine. I just need to rest a while longer."

Tony shook his head and said, "I hope so," as he walked away.

Sid turned to the window to continue watching the man who hadn't left with the others in the car.

I can't believe I let them get my gun, he thought, *I need to track this guy when he leaves, and I can't let this bump on my head stop me.*

Sid used the table to push himself up, and this time, he was able to maintain his stability. He used the wall as a support as his rubbery legs carried him to the door. He left without saying anything to Tony and got into his car, keeping his eyes on the man in front of the shop.

Take me to your friends, and then you're a dead man.

The fire engines left the scene, and a glass company arrived to board up the windows. The black jeep returned to pick up the guy who had stayed behind. The previous passengers were gone, and Sid was positive the driver was Vito. Sid followed a few car lengths back as it drove away, but his blurry vision and pulsating head made it hard to maintain a distance. They didn't seem to notice and stopped at an apartment complex not far from Sid's condo. Sid watched as they got out of the vehicle and saw a couple walking in front of them.

So be it, he thought. He wasn't going to lose this opportunity, even if it meant hurting innocent bystanders.

Sid pressed the accelerator hard. Vito and the other man heard the loud motor and turned but didn't have enough time to move out of the way. Sid's car sent them ten feet into the air, landing a few feet from the couple, who screamed and ran off. Sid was slow getting out of the car but hustled as best he could. The man he didn't recognize was still alive, moaning, but Sid assumed Vito was dead; his brain matter was splattered across the pavement. Sid knelt beside Vito's body and took his gun and wallet, then did the same to the other man. It took Sid a moment to stand, but when he did, he pointed the gun at the groaning man and shot him. "That's for the lump on my head, asshole!"

Sid looked around. Some people were standing in the distance, but he was confident there wasn't enough light to identify him. He took his wallet off the console of his car, left his keys in the ignition, and walked away.

When I get home, I'll report it stolen.

The half-mile walk felt longer with his throbbing head. He disposed of his victim's wallets in a storm drain along the way. The wooziness made him stop to rest twice before he made it to the condo. Sid wanted nothing more than to lie down with a bag of ice. He checked his pockets for a key but recalled they were still in the car, so he could only hope Diane wasn't asleep and would come let him inside. He knocked.

"Who's there?"

"It's me, Sid," he said. "Let me in."

She flung the door open. "Where's your key… Oh my God! What happened to you?"

He staggered inside and fell on the sofa. "Can you get me a bag of ice?"

"Your ear is bleeding. And what happened to your clothes?"

"Not now. Please, just get the ice, would you?"

She hurried to the kitchen and returned with the icepack, a towel, and a first aid kit. "Here. What do you need it for?"

He turned his head to show her his injury. "For this grapefruit."

She grimaced at the sight of it. "You could have a concussion. I'll get dressed and take you to the hospital."

Sid placed the pack on the lump and laid back. "I'm okay. Listen, you need to call the police and report my car stolen."

"You're scaring me. What's going on?"

He moaned. "Make the call, and then I'll tell you."

Diane used the phone by the bar, never taking her eyes off him. "They asked a lot of questions I couldn't answer and said they'll be here soon." She took the towel and sat beside him to clean the blood off his face. "I knew something was going to happen to you. I felt it."

He pulled both guns from his waistband. "Take these and put them in the bedroom before the cops come."

She took them and shook her head. "How'd you get the other gun?"

"Give me a second. My head's pounding. Are there any painkillers in the kit?"

Diane took them out. "Yes, here. Take three; I'll get you a glass of water."

"Forget the water. Get me a bourbon."

Sid thought about the note and newspaper clipping as she went off to fix his drink. It could be a problem if Vito had a copy on him. The police would have questions and a possible motive.

Damn, I wish I did a better job of checking Vito's pockets. I can't worry about it now; what's done is done.

Sid wished there had been more of the crazy cultists there when he took Vito and the other guy out. Having the rest of them still around — including Madame Nutjob — will remain a problem.

All this might not be over, but at least now I have the guns to protect us.

Diane returned with Sid's drink, and then helped him sit up. "Now tell me what's going on," she said.

He took the pills and a long gulp. "I went after the only other person who knew I had the gun, the guy I took it from. It had to be him who sent the note. I was gonna make him tell me who else he told. He wasn't there, so I held his friends until he showed up. But somebody snuck up and hit me. I don't know how I let it happen. I must be slipping. Next thing I know, some guy was untying me in my club and told me to hurry up and leave."

"What happened to the people who tied you up?"

Sid's chuckle was followed by a moan. "Their building was burning. I guess they left to put it out."

She made the sign of the cross. "Amazing coincidence. God must have been watching over you."

He nodded. "Or just lucky."

She picked up the ice pack. "You need to keep this on. So how did you get the other gun?"

"I watched the spectators from the pizzeria window and saw the guy I got the revolver from with some another guy I hadn't seen before. I couldn't confront them, so I followed them."

Diane scowled. "How'd you drive in your condition?"

"I ran them down with my car and took their guns. That's why we had to report the car stolen."

Diane's eyes widened. "Are you crazy? You have the police coming here, and you just killed two people?"

Sid rested his head on the back of the sofa. "Diane, I thought I put my previous life behind me. Do you think I want to be doing this shit again? But this asshole wanted the gun and was blackmailing me. There can be no negotiation! They had to die! It was the only way to be rid of the problem. You do see that don't you?"

Diane dropped her head. "Why couldn't we have told the police?"

Sid laughed. "The police, are you crazy? As soon as the blackmailer suspected the police were involved, he'd contact Big Zac. What are the police going to do to protect us? Nothing. Trust me, it was the only way, Diane."

The doorbell rang. "That'll be the police now," Diane said. "Are you ready?"

"I'm fine. Go let them in."

Diane opened the door to two civilian-clothed men who introduced themselves as Detectives Stacy and Greer. "You called about a stolen car?" Stacy asked.

She stepped to the side to let them in.

Sid didn't like Detective Stacy even at first glance. He'd met dicks like him before, with a permanent smirk to make people think they're smarter than anyone else. Somehow making them feel superior. "It was my car that was stolen. Actually, it's a rental. I was turning it in next week."

"Would it be a 1991 blue Cadillac Brougham?" Stacy asked.

Sid slid back in his seat and groaned. "Where'd you find it?"

Detective Greer walked around, peering into rooms. Sid didn't like the police in general, especially when they were being nosy.

Why in the hell is he looking around the apartment when they're here for my car?

"Can I get you something?" Sid asked.

Greer smiled. "Just admiring your place."

Diane looked at Sid, biting her lower lip. Then she looked up and smiled.

"Can I offer you coffee, water, anything?"

"We're good, thanks," said Stacy, taking out a pad and pen. "When did you realize your car was missing?"

Sid picked up the icepack and put it on his head. "When I woke up with this lump on my head."

He studied Sid for a moment. "You're saying you were attacked, and then the car was stolen?"

Sid nodded. "At my club. Never saw it coming."

"Were there any witnesses"

"How would I know if I was attacked from behind?"

Greer said, "Your car was found half a mile from here. It was involved in a hit-and-run. Two men were killed, and there was a gunshot to the head of one of the victims."

"That's terrible. I'm sorry to hear that. Do you know who they were?"

Stacy looked up from his pad with his embedded grin. "No. Their wallets were taken, but we'll identify them soon. Is there any way to substantiate your story, Mr. Love?"

Sid frowned and turned his head. "Look at this lump. Do you think I did that?"

"We're not accusing you. This is a homicide investigation. We need to ask these questions. What time were you attacked?"

Sid shrugged. "I don't remember. Maybe eight or eight-thirty."

"Is that the time you usually leave?"

He shook his head. "No, I stayed to watch the fire."

"Fire?"

"Yeah, my neighbors. Their building caught fire."

"You were watching the fire while getting into your car?"

"No, the fire was put out first."

"Where were your keys when you got hit?"

Sid tossed the ice pack on the coffee table. "What the hell difference does that make? They took my keys and then my car."

Stacy stopped writing and used his pen to point to Sid's hand. "How much is that Rolex and gold diamond pinky ring worth? It's odd that an attacker would ignore that kind of jewelry. If the motive was robbery, that is."

"Maybe they just wanted the car. You know, so they could mow down people."

Greer blurted. "How'd you get home?"

Sid sighed. "The last thing I remember is walking up the path to this building. I can't remember anything before that or after I got hit."

"Is it possible someone saw you get attacked?"

"I didn't see anyone. Are you almost finished? I really need to lie down."

Greer pointed to the paper and brought it closer for Sid to see. "Is this the best number to reach you at? We may have more questions."

"That's right. So, when can I get a copy of the police report? I'll need it for the rental company."

Stacy looked at his partner and shrugged. "You can pick it up at the precinct tomorrow."

"And where do I pick up the car?"

Greer handed Sid a business card. "The car was impounded as part of the homicide investigation. You can have the rental company call us."

Sid took the card, dropped it on the table, and looked at Diane. "Show them out, babe. We're all done here."

Diane hurried to the door closing it behind the detectives. When they were gone, she turned to Sid. "I think they suspect you. Why'd you do it?"

"They've got nothing. Let me worry about the police."

As she walked to the bedroom, she muttered, "Like you told me not to worry before you left tonight?"

Sid put the ice pack back on his head. He didn't like the questions.

They're just fishing. But I don't like them, especially Detective Stacy's perpetual smirk. I doubt this will be the last I see of them. Right now, they're unimportant. What is important is knowing who else in Vito's clan knows my identity.

Evan did some house chores while keeping an eye on the monitors in Command Central. At nine-fifteen P.M., he began to wonder why Sid wasn't home after leaving him over an hour ago.

What happened to him? Maybe I should have waited to make sure his assailants didn't finish the job. I thought he was a tougher dude.

He looked at Diane sleeping on his screen.

I guess I won't have to share. He must've gotten bagged again, the idiot. I was so hoping to have some fun.

He turned off the monitors and mumbled. "See you tomorrow, Ms. Diane Rivers. Maybe I'll bring you my catch of the day and make you the best fish dinner you ever had."

CHAPTER 18

Diane woke at seven A.M. and hurried to the bathroom, gagging, which soon became stomach convulsions. She knelt, staring into the bowl, hoping it would stop. After a couple of minutes, Diane stood and splashed her face with cold water. She could only hope having a baby would be easier than her pregnancy had been so far.

The morning sun was peeking through the blinds in the bedroom, and Diane adjusted them to darken the room and let Sid sleep, while she went to make herself some tea and toast. She found the remote and switched on the small counter television to see the news.

A reporter was saying, "Two men were run down last night in an apparently deliberate hit-and-run. Eyewitness reports confirm that a 1991 Cadillac intentionally hit the two men. An unidentified man then got out of the car and shot them. Police are looking for the driver, described only as a tall man with a muscular build. Anyone with any information is advised to contact local law enforcement."

Diane ran to the bedroom. "Sid, wake up! Your... car incident was on the news!"

Sid didn't move. She shook him. "Sid, wake up. Did you hear me?" He lay lifeless. Diane rolled him onto his back. "Sid! Answer me." She put her fingers on his neck and was relieved to feel a pulse. "Sid, can you hear me?"

She ran to the phone in the kitchen and called 911.

The ambulance arrived fifteen minutes later. Diane flung the door open and pointed to the bedroom. "He's on the bed. Hurry."

After taking his vital signs, the EMTs were less gentle than Diane in trying to wake Sid. One of them gave him two soft slaps to the face. "Wake up!"

Sid groaned and reached up to grasp his head. "Get out of here, you bastards," he said. "You're not going to get me." He opened his eyes. "Who the hell are you?"

The EMT ignored the question and said to Diane, "We'll take him to the emergency room. You can meet us there."

Diane took Sid's hand as they lifted him from the bed. "I love you."

Sid looked at Diane. "Why? Do I know you?"

Diane's eyes widened at his response. After they rolled him out, Diane turned to the medic. "Why doesn't he know me?"

"I don't know. That's a nasty bump on his head. It may be temporary. Talk to the doctors. They can tell you more about his amnesia."

Diane closed her eyes, took in a long breath, and let it out slowly.

He shouldn't have gone last night. Why didn't I stop him?

After the paramedic left, Diane took a large tote bag from the closet and packed some underwear with a change of clothes for herself and Sid. She packed some toiletries and her medication. Diane checked the drawers and saw the pistols. She pushed one to the back of the drawer and covered it. The other she wrapped in a towel and put it in her bag with Sid's cell phone.

Diane parked the Jeep in the Bay Ridge Hospital Parking lot and hurried to the emergency room.

What if his memory loss is not temporary? What am I going to do?

She went to the nurse's desk and spoke with a pleasant young nurse. "Can you tell me where they took my boyfriend, Sid Love?"

"I'll see what I can find out, but please sit, miss, you look pale. I'll be back soon. Can I get you a cup of water?"

Diane smiled. "That's very nice of you. Thanks."

Diane watched the white coats and green surgical outfits hustle around her, paying her little attention. She sat there for nearly ten minutes before the nurse returned with the water.

She smiled and took the cup. "Thank you. Were you able to find out anything about my boyfriend, Sid?"

The nurse nodded. "He's been taken to surgery."

Diane gasped. "Oh, my God! Why? Is he going to be, okay?"

"I'm not allowed to give out personal medical information unless you're family, but Dr. Jacobs, who's working on him, is one of the top neurosurgeons in the state."

"Neurosurgeon... brain surgery? I need to see him!"

She tried to stand, but the nurse put her hand out. "Please, you should sit. It may be your pregnancy, but you don't look well. Would you like to see a doctor?"

Her insides tightened, and the baby kicked hard. "No. I want to see Sid. Please take me to him."

"It will be a while before he's out of surgery and post-op. Please go home and rest. You can call later to find out his status."

Diane folded her arms. "I'll stay here until I can see Sid."

The nurse nodded. "Okay, suit yourself, but it could be a while."

Sid woke and tried to focus his eyes. Eventually, he was able to make out a picture of fruit on the wall and became aware of machines beeping and hissing around him. He could hear voices, but his view was obstructed by a curtain.

Am I in the hospital?

"Hello?" he said. "Who's out there?"

He wanted to sit up, but one of his arms was restrained. His right hand, though, was free to reach up and feel some kind of contraption on his head.

"What happened? Wait… how did I get here, and who the hell am I?"

He grabbed the bed rail with his free hand and squeezed. He could feel his heart pounding harder in his chest, and the beeping noise of a machine accelerated with it. "Someone talk to me!" he shouted.

A young woman in scrubs pushed aside the curtain and turned down the noise on the beeping machine. "Why are you yelling?"

"Where am I? Who am I? Why is my arm tied down, and what the hell is this thing on my head? Let me up."

She checked his tubes. "The straps are so you lie still, Mr. Love. You've had a bad head trauma."

Sid grabbed for her wrist. "What did you call me?"

She patted his hand. "Your name is Sid Love. You were brought here by ambulance this morning with a head injury. Dr. Jacobs drained fluid from your cranium to relieve the pressure. It seems that you have amnesia. We don't know yet how long it'll last. That's all I can tell you. Dr. Jacobs will be able to answer any questions. I'll let him know you're awake."

He grasped her hand. "Where is he?"

"I don't know, I'll page him."

Sid squeezed his grip. "Stay with me. What's your name?"

She gritted her teeth. "Judy, and you're hurting me. I can't stay. I have other patients."

Sid took a breath and blew it out slowly. "I didn't mean to upset you, Judy. It's intimidating not knowing who I am."

She handed him two pills and filled a cup from the water pitcher beside the bed. "Take this. It'll help with the pain so you can sleep."

He resisted taking them at first because he didn't want to sleep, but he needed something for his throbbing head and took them, "Please, tell the doctor it's important I see him as soon as possible."

"I will. You get some rest Sid and I'll check in on you later."

Diane waited for information and fell asleep. The waiting room was quiet, with fewer people when she woke. She looked at the clock on the wall. I've been sleeping for over three hours. She slowly got to her feet, holding her back. The nurse at the desk was different than before. "I'm trying to find out about my boyfriend, Sid Love. Can you tell me if he's out of surgery and if I can see him?"

The nurse looked at the monitor and punched some keys. "Mr. Love is on the third floor recovering."

"Thank God. Does he still have amnesia?"

She shrugged. "I don't know."

Diane smiled. "I'd like to see him, can I?"

"Let me check his status. I don't know if they're allowing visitors yet."

As soon as the nurse hung up, Diane blurted out. "Can I go see Sid now?"

She shook her head. "He was just given a sedative. He could be sleeping for a couple of hours. The nurse on the third floor told me what your boyfriend needs now more than anything is rest. Maybe you should come back tomorrow and let him sleep."

Diane sighed. "I'll wait. Can you please let me know when he's up?"

"Come see me later, and I'll check for you."

CHAPTER 19

Sid woke and lay in bed alone for hours. There was a disturbing but familiar feeling of loneliness from a time long ago. He could almost recall it, but it frightened him when he tried.

I need to get out of here; how do I get this damn restraint off?

Sid pulled out the tubes and wires and attempted to remove the straps holding down his head.

Nurse Judy rushed into the room. "What are you doing? You need to lie still."

Sid banged the bed rail. "Where the hell is the doctor? You said he'd be here soon, hours ago. I'm lying here, seeing bits and pieces of life like they're parts of a jigsaw puzzle. Nothing makes sense. I can't lie here alone like this, Judy; I'll go out of my mind. There must be something the doctor can do?"

"I'm sorry, but he's gone for the evening. He had a family event."

"Screw him and his family event. Is he the only quack in the building? Get me another doctor."

"I'll get you another sedative to help you sleep. The only other neurosurgeon in the hospital is working in the emergency room. I'll ask him to stop in when he has time. That's the best I can do."

"Your name is Judy. See? I remembered that. I'm not taking any sleeping pills or waiting for a doctor that doesn't show. I'll go out of my skull. Take this thing off my head so I can get up. You can't keep me here against my will."

Nurse Judy took a step back. "We can if we think you'll hurt yourself. We can't let you leave if you don't know who you are or where you're going."

Her face softened, she smiled gently at him, and then reached down to straighten his bed sheets. "Listen," she said, "I have a dinner engagement later and need to kill some time. I'll come back after I clock out, and we can chat for a while. Would that make things any easier?"

Sid let himself relax and sank back against his pillow. "Yes, that's nice of you, and I'll be good, I swear. I just need someone to talk to."

As promised, Nurse Judy returned a little while later, dressed in civilian clothes and hair down. She looked younger and prettier than she had in her scrubs. "I'm back."

Sid looked for the bed remote to raise himself up. "Where's that damn thing?"

She pulled the wire connected to the controller under the covers. "I can help, but let's not raise it too much. If you feel any pain, let me know."

"I wanted you to come back as a friendly face to talk to. Not to be my nurse."

She grinned. "That's what I do, I can't change. If we're going to be friends, you'll have to accept that. Now, what do you want to talk about?"

He looked at the bedside table. "Is there a pen and paper? I'd like to jot things down that I recall."

Judy found a pencil and a small pad in her purse. "I'll do the writing," she said. "That way, you can just tell me what you remember, and I'll write it down."

She sat in the chair beside the bed and flipped the pad to a clean sheet of paper. "I'm guessing you want to try to figure out who you are, right? Your admittance information is here on your chart. You live in apartment 6C at the Shore Road Condominiums on Ninety-fourth Street and Shore Road, Brooklyn."

He stared at the ceiling. "That address doesn't mean anything to me. How long have I lived there?"

"It doesn't say."

"What else is in the chart?"

Judy gave him all the pertinent information available. "You have no relatives and no medical records before this incident. A woman named Diane Rivers gave us your information and your medical insurance card."

Sid's eyes widened. "I don't recognize the name. Where is she? Can we contact her?"

She looked through the chart. "I don't see anything. I can check with the person who admitted you and see if there's more information on Diane Rivers, but Ada is gone for the day. We'll have to wait for her to come in tomorrow."

Sid closed his eyes tightly three times in unison with flashes of light only he could see. Each followed by an image. "Judy, this is crazy. I see snapshots of faces and places, none of which are in any order. There's this knight on a stallion that keeps popping up. How does that play into my memory? We're not living in the Middle Ages, so why would I see a knight? The funny thing is, I feel like once I make a connection to Sir Lancelot, I'll remember everything else."

She nodded. "Sometimes, that's all it takes to trigger your memory. I'm not a doctor, but I think your amnesia is temporary. Be patient, Sid."

He chuckled and winced at the pain. "I've gotta remember not to laugh. I hope you're right. You have no idea what it feels like to try and hold onto a thought that's not there long enough to grasp. It's like trying to grab water."

Judy slid back in her seat. "Do you remember any of your childhood?"

He was surprised at the question and paused to recall something. "Yeah. My parents died in a car crash."

"How old were you?"

Sid closed his eyes. "Dunno. Maybe nine or ten, I think."

Nurse Judy stood and smiled. "That's a start."

Her comment puzzled him. "What do you mean?"

"If you remember your childhood, you can start there and work your way up to now. I've got to be going now, but look at it this way: Now you have something more than water to grab at."

Sid reached for her hand. "Stay a little longer. I hate being alone."

She shook her head. "I'm sorry I can't, and anyway, you've got some piecing together to do now that you have a starting point to work with. Who knows? When I come back tomorrow, maybe your amnesia will be cured. Besides, I don't want to be late for my dinner date. He'll be wondering what happened to me."

"You have kids?"

"No. Haven't met the right guy."

Sid's stomach fluttered. "Children. That means something to me. Is it possible I have a family?"

"As I said, your chart doesn't have any specifics, but sure, of course, there's a chance you could be a father."

"Somehow, I don't see myself as a dad. But thank you. You've given me a lot to think about. Will I see you tomorrow?"

"Yes, I'm working. I'll drop in during my rounds. Good night, Sid."

Evan didn't see Sid come home last night and didn't see him getting dressed this morning as he usually did. Evan concluded Sid's assailants from last night had finished the job and Sid was dead.

I didn't think I'd have to protect him all night.

"Stupid ass deserved to die."

He decided to go fishing and catch a terrific dinner he'd make for himself and Diane tonight.

She'll need some consolation to overcome her grief, and good food always helps. She may not know Sid is dead yet, so I'll break it to her as gently as possible. Diane belongs to me now. I'll take care of her, but I wish I could've had some fun with Sid before his killers took the vengeance away from the mob boss. It would've been fun to watch Sid squirm as they cornered him.

Evan caught a large flounder that he considered worthy of a great meal. Upon returning to his apartment, he dropped his fishing gear and took his chair at Command Central. The monitors came to life, but Diane wasn't there.

"Where are you?" He frowned. "Maybe the coroner called, and she left to identify the body. That would be a bummer. I so wanted to see her reaction when she heard Sid was dead."

Evan recalled overhearing tenants in the vestibule discussing an ambulance outside this morning.

I bet she was the reason for the EMT. They would have taken her to the closest hospital. He grabbed the telephone directory, flipped to medical listings, and ran his finger down the page. "Bay Ridge Hospital."

Evan dialed the phone number. "Hi, I'm looking for a Miss Diane Rivers. Can you tell me if she was treated or admitted?"

A woman abruptly disconnected. "Please hold."

She came back a minute later. "There's no record of a Ms. Rivers."

Evan said nothing and hung up.

Then why isn't she home? There're no friends that I've seen. Other than maybe that pizzeria where Sid hung out. Perhaps she's making funeral arrangements. I'm missing all her emotions and reactions. That sucks.

It was seven P.M. when Evan finished dinner and went to Command Central to confirm that Diane was still not home.

Where is she? I waited for her all day and had to eat by myself. This is no way to start a relationship.

Evan stopped.

Shit, maybe the same people who killed Sid did Diane in also. Oh, man, that would really suck. Time to see what I can find out.

Evan took off his shoes, snapped on a pair of latex gloves, and surveyed the hallway. All clear.

Upon entering Sid and Diane's apartment, he pulled down the blinds and shut the drapes. Diane's scent lingered, and he paused to take it in. Then he went to the bedroom dresser, opened the top drawer, and found the hidden gun. He would have expected Sid to take it with him before confronting his assailants.

He's even stupider than I thought.

Evan extracted the bullets and put them in his pocket. Then placed the gun back where he found it. The second drawer contained Sid's undergarments and socks. He held up one of the T-shirts. "Too big for me," Evan muttered. "I'll throw all his stuff in a trash bag. If Diane's not dead, she'll appreciate not being reminded of that loser."

The third drawer contained Diane's lingerie. The fragrance aroused him more than he could stand. He was just lying down on the bed, about to unbuckle his pants, when there was a knock on the door. He jumped up and hurried to the peephole. Ian, the maintenance man, stood waiting next to a man wearing a cap that said, "Rosa's Plumbing."

Evan disguised his voice. "Who is it?"

"Building maintenance. You called about a broken faucet?"

"We're busy. Come back tomorrow."

A voice bellowed. "Hi. I'm with Rosa Plumbing. If I can just take a quick look at the faucet, I'll return with the correct part to fix it."

Evan shouted. "It'll have to wait. Good night."

After they left, Evan went to the kitchen sink and turned on the water. It worked. So did the one in the bathroom. He shrugged. "Maybe they had the wrong apartment."

He stopped to look at himself in the bathroom mirror. He picked up his chin and ran his fingers along the stubble on his neck.

Diane wouldn't appreciate me looking like this.

He found a razor in a tray on the vanity, and put in a new blade he found in the medicine cabinet. He was happy with the beard grooming when he was done. It looked clean and sharp at the edges. He studied the newfangled shaving instrument.

This is one of those duel track razors I've seen advertised. Sid won't need it anymore. It will be mine when I'm here. I can use it on the nights I stay over. Considering, of course, Diane's alive. I sure do hope she is. I had grand plans for us.

The walk-in closet had Sid's clothes on one side, and Diane's on the other. Evan went through her dresses and took out the ones he liked best.

If she comes home, she can wear these for me.

He laid everything on the bed and took his time arranging each garment. His selection for shoes was a black strappy spike heel. Happy with his choices, he stepped back and admired his work.

She'll want me to choose her outfit every day.

Evan left the apartment, hoping to be with Diane the next time he was there and enjoying a dinner together with his next great catch.

CHAPTER 20

Evan got out of bed but didn't make his coffee as usual. Instead, he went to Command Central to check on Diane and scoffed when he didn't see her.

Maybe she really is dead. Where else could she be unless the information I got from the nurse was wrong and she was at the hospital. Even if Diane's dead, there'll be a record of when she was admitted. I should have protected her after the attack on Sid. After all, she was part of the witness protection program. But there was nothing about her or any woman in the article I found. I assume she was only here because Sid wanted her to be. It would be a shame if she had to die for that jerk.

Evan shut the monitors, made coffee, and took a shower. Then got dressed and wrote down the address of the hospital. He had to be sure Diane was alive, but if she wasn't, he'd need new performers. Life was boring without them.

Sid watched televised news and remembered that George H. W. Bush was the president of the United States.

How can I remember the president, down to his middle initials, and not my own name?

He tried to recollect what happened after his parents died, but only remembered being at the wake and seeing his mom and dad in coffins. The pain of that day tightened Sid's neck and shoulders and made his head pound more than it already was, so he stopped trying to recall anything more of his childhood.

His stomach grumbling was loud enough to be heard across the room.

"I need food." He mumbled.

Sid found the call button and pressed it several times.

When a nurse stepped into the room, he blurted, "I'm starved. Can I get something to eat?"

"Your breakfast should be here soon; I saw the dietitian with food trays in the hallway."

"Great, thanks. Hey, can you tell me where Nurse Judy is?"

"I haven't seen her this morning."

Sid sighed. "Do you know when she'll be in?"

The nurse shrugged. "I have no idea."

He shut his eyes and inhaled. "What's your name?"

"Diane."

Sid grasped her arm. "Do I know you?"

She pulled away. "You're hurting me."

"Nurse Judy told me someone named Diane admitted me yesterday. Was it you?"

She shook her head. "I've never seen you before."

Sid examined her face. "I was hoping there was a connection."

She quickly turned to the door. "Maybe you know someone else named Diane. I'll see if I can find out when Judy's shift is for you."

Sid was alone again, and the head restraint had him feeling trapped. The familiarity of this feeling made him tremble. Sid used the bed control to sit up, and the pressure weighed on his head like a sandbag. He tried to ignore the pain, but after rising to a fully erect seated position, his eyesight went blurry, and his head felt like it might explode. Sid hit the button to recline again and took a deep breath as the pressure subsided. "Where the hell's the...?"

Before he could finish the sentence, Dr. Jacobs walked in. "Sid, how're you feeling? Can you tell me your name?"

Sid wished he could punch him but instead hit the bed rail. "I've been lying here for hours, not knowing who the hell I am. And you want to know my name? You already told me it's Sid. Rather than ask silly questions, take this contraption off and give me something for the pain."

"Don't worry, Sid, your amnesia is temporary. It could be days, weeks, and in rare cases, months, but you *will* regain your memory. I realize it's frustrating, but your brain needs time to reset after the trauma."

"Easy for you to say. I'd think better with this thing off my head. It's driving me crazy."

Dr. Jacobs made some notes and returned the chart to its place at the foot of Sid's bed. "You still have some swelling. Rest today. Maybe we can remove the restraint tomorrow."

"Bullshit! Take it off now."

The doctor sighed and gave Sid a gentle smile. "If you want to get well, I advise you to rest and keep your head as still as possible. However, if you want to go against my recommendations, you can sign a waiver, and I'll have the restraint taken off."

"I'm not a child. I can be still without this on. Give me the waiver."

Dr. Jacobs shrugged. "Don't rush it. Besides, even if you're physically okay, we can't release you until your memory returns or a relative can take care of you."

Sid closed his eyes to recall the information Judy had given him. "My name is Sid Love, and I live in apartment 6C at Shore Road Condominiums. What else do you need to know?"

"You were given that information. You didn't recall it."

Sid laughed. "Does it make a difference? I know who I am and where I live. I'll be ready to leave tomorrow. You just be here to sign the release."

"Let's reassess tomorrow. Meanwhile, I'll allow the nurse to remove your head restraint."

A different but familiar sensation of being released brought more flashbacks — this time of people putting Sid into a car as a child. These recollections didn't upset Sid. There was a feeling of relief being put into the back seat of the vehicle.

Diane stayed the night on the waiting room couch. Each time she inquired about Sid, she was told he was either sleeping or that it was too late for visitors. A nurse was nice enough to give her a blanket and pillow. She was awakened a few times by EMTs rushing through with emergencies that had doctors and nurses rushing around shouting medical terms she didn't understand. Her bladder had her up early, and when she returned from the bathroom, she stopped at the vending machine and purchased a cup of coffee. The waiting room was quiet now, and she felt at peace sipping her java on the couch.

This is relaxing, but I wish I could take a shower. Maybe I should've gone home last night, but I hated the thought of being there alone, feeling helpless and wondering if Sid was okay or if he'll remember me.

Diane folded the blanket and fluffed the pillow to take them back to the nurse's station. There was a new nurse at the desk.

"Good morning. Thank you for these. It helped a lot. Can you find out if I can see Sid Love now?"

The woman looked at the computer and then picked up the phone. Diane's heart beat faster, waiting for a response.

"He's in with the doctor now. You can see him shortly."

Diane sighed. "Okay, how long do you think it will take?"

She shrugged. "Give it an hour. I'm sure he'll be available by then."

After a short while, the waiting room started to fill. Diane took a seat by the window and picked up a magazine. She tried to read, but her thoughts kept going back to Sid and his memory loss.

Diane was startled by Evan standing in front of her.

"Here you are, Diane. I had a feeling I would find you here. You never came home last night. Are you okay?"

"You're the guy who came to our apartment. What're you doing here?"

"I'm sorry for your loss. I'd like to help you through this difficult time however I can."

Diane scowled at him. "What the hell are you talking about?"

"Like I said, to offer my sympathy for the loss of your boyfriend."

"Sid's not dead, you idiot. Now, get out of here."

Evan shook his head. "Nobody's told you yet?"

"Sid's not dead. He's in recovery from surgery. I told you, get out of here. If I see you again, I'll call the police."

Evan studied her face. "He's alive? Are you sure? It doesn't matter. Even if you're right, he won't be around much longer."

"Get out!" Diane shouted

Evan smiled. "You'll need me soon, Diane. I'll be in touch."

Diane waited for Evan to leave before hurrying to the nurse's station. "Some guy just told me my boyfriend's dead. You people have been telling me he's recovering from brain surgery. What the hell is going on? I need to know the truth. Take me to Sid!"

The nurse stood and reached for Diane's hand. "Calm down, honey. I'll see what I can find out, okay? Why don't you have a seat, and I'll be right back?"

Diane took a deep breath and nodded. "Yes, thank you."

The nurse returned with a cup of water and sat down next to Diane, handing her the cup. "Your boyfriend is fine. The doctor was just in to see him. They're going to clean him up and make sure he has his medications. Afterward, a nurse will come down and get you. Another half hour at the most.

Diane studied her face. "So, he's alive, and I'm going to see him, you swear?"

"Yes, but you look pale. Drink the water and rest until they come to get you. Can I get you anything?"

"No. Thank you, you've made me very happy."

Her happiness only lasted a moment.

What if Sid doesn't remember me?

Judy arrived abruptly and startled Sid with her entrance. She handed him the waiver and a pen. "I'm surprised you got Dr. Jacobs to remove the head restraint, even with the release."

Sid signed the paper and handed it back. "I promised to be a good boy."

"Okay, someone will be by in a little while to take it off."

Sid smiled. "Good to see you again, Judy."

"So, have you remembered anything more yet?"

He shrugged. "A nurse named Diane came in earlier, which seemed to trigger something. I must know a Diane. But I don't know more than that. It was like someone dangled the memory in front of me and then pulled it away."

"Actually, that's a good sign." Judy said. "I'm sure it's all going to come back to you soon. What about your childhood recollection we talked about yesterday? Were you able to recall anything more?"

Sid smiled and reached for her hand. "No. And it hurts my brain to try. So, I stopped. It would help if I could talk about it with you. Can't you stay until this thing is off my head? You don't know what it's like lying here alone, looking at nothing but the ceiling. Please stay."

She smiled back at him. "I have other patients to attend to. I'd lose my job. You work on getting your memory back, and I'll return later to see how you're doing with the restraint off."

After Judy left, Sid closed his eyes, trying to piece together the pictures he was seeing in his head. After a few minutes, his eyes became heavy, and just before he fell asleep, another nurse walked in. "Mr. Sid Love, you have a visitor." Then she turned to the woman standing next to her. "I'll let you two talk and I'll be back in about half an hour."

Sid cringed in pain, trying to turn his head toward the door. The woman standing there was wide-eyed and grinning. "Sid! Thank God you're okay. It's me. Diane. Don't you recognize me?"

Sid studied the woman's face. "I'm not sure. You look familiar. Are you the same Diane that admitted me yesterday?"

"Yes, Diane Rivers. We live together, and I'm having your baby. Remember?"

"There is something about you. That scar on your face… why do I feel I had something to do with that?"

She shook her head. "No, you didn't, but it happened because I know you."

Sid's eyes narrowed. "Why would someone do that to you because of me?"

"I'm not sure I should go into details now. There's a lot to tell you."

"You must tell me. I've been lying here since yesterday, not knowing who I am. Do you have any idea how that feels? Start from the beginning. The doctor said my memory could come back if I hear or see something I know."

Diane paused, then nodded. "Okay. Let me close the door. No one can hear what I'm going to tell you."

Sid laughed. "Am I a secret agent or something?"

She smiled. "Or something…."

When the door was shut, she came and sat beside him on the edge of the bed and began: "About a month ago, we lived in Venice Beach, California, and your name was Sal Lovato."

As Sid listened to the details of the trial, the witness protection program, and the deal he had made. There were flashbacks of the court-room and jail cell.

Diane pushed her hair back. "This scar was their message to you."

"And what was that?"

She shrugged. "You can't hide. We'll find you. You pissed off some bad people."

"From what you said, it sounds like they pissed me off first. Why did we choose to move to Brooklyn?"

"I'm not sure, other than that it's on the other side of the country. You wanted to own a nightclub as part of the deal, and I guess this is where they found one for you."

His eyes darted up and down. The mention of the nightclub flooded his head with memories of a judge and his excitement when she agreed to his terms. "Yes…, I do remember wanting the nightclub. What's the name?"

"Camelot Dance Club."

Sid hit the bedrail hard. "Yes, yes, yes! Does the place have a knight on a horse?"

She nodded. "On the roof above the entrance."

A flood of information rushed into Sid's head. "Susie, I remember! Oh my God, it's all coming back to me!"

Diane looked around. "Shh-h-h. Sid, my name is Diane now, remember? You can't call me Susie."

He chuckled from the relief of knowing who he was. "Sorry, you're right, but I'm excited Diane. Thank God you're here! I never felt so alone as I did since being here." He reached for her hand. "I'm so happy you are here, and I don't ever want to forget you again."

Her eyes welled as she leaned over to kiss him. "That's so nice to hear. I was so worried about you." Diane chuckled. "Maybe the hit in the head did something. You've never said anything so sweet to me before."

He closed his eyes and took a breath. "You can't believe the relief I feel right now."

Sid didn't understand his feelings at that moment.

I've never felt this way about Diane before. I realize now I need her as much as she needs me. Although, I think I'll keep that to myself for now.

She squeezed his hand and smiled. "It's okay to say you love me. I know you do."

"What makes you say that?"

"What you just said and your actions before getting hit. I always feel safe when I'm with you, and you've been by my side even when you didn't want to be. You do little things, like cover me when I fall asleep or clean up the dishes after dinner. You love me, Sid. You just can't say it."

Sid pulled his hand away from Diane.

He recalled the anxiety he felt when she previously tried to get him to say, "I love you."

"I care very much for you, Diane, and I am thrilled you're here. Let's leave it at that."

Diane smiled and shook her head. "There's a good man under that hard exterior. You'll let him out one day, and then we'll both be happy."

There was an awkward silence before something occurred to Sid, and he said, "The cops that came to the apartment and were asking questions. Have they been back?"

"I don't know. I've been crashing here at the hospital. But your car was televised on the news the morning you were taken here."

Sid gazed at her. "The guns. Where are the guns?"

She lifted the duffle bag. "One is in here with some clothes I took for you, and the other is where we left it in the apartment."

Sid smiled. "Good girl. Until I'm sure Vito didn't share the information with anyone else, we should both carry a weapon."

"It scares me when you say these things. When won't we have to worry anymore? Is this how we're going to live the rest of our lives?"

Sid sighed. *I wish she would stop saying things like that, what the hell does she expect me to do?*

"I'll take care of everything once I'm out of here. There's nothing to be afraid of. All I'm saying is carry the pistol until I'm sure."

Diane nodded. "Okay, Sid."

Judy and a young man in scrubs came into the room. "We're here to take the restraint off."

Sid grinned. "That's great, and you know what else is great, Judy?"

She clapped her hands. "You got your memory back?"

"Yes! Judy, this is Diane, my girlfriend, and Diane, Judy was my only friend when I couldn't remember anything."

Diane put out her hand. "Thank you for helping, Sid. I was so worried about him."

Judy nodded. "He's going to be okay. What did you say to kick start his memory again?"

She looked at Sid. "I'm not sure."

Sid laughed. "Judy, do you remember when I told you that once I figured out the meaning of a knight on the horse, I would get my memory back?"

She nodded. "Yes."

"When Diane told me about the club — I own named the Camelot and that there was a knight and horse on the roof — it all came back to me. You have no idea what a relief it is."

"I'm very happy for you, Sid. This is Joey. He'll be assisting me with removing the restraint and changing the dressing. We'll have to move your head a bit, so you'll experience some pain. The doctor advised you to take a sedative afterward, and he'll come in and check on you later."

"I don't want to sleep; I just got my memory back. I'll be still and talk to Diane."

"Okay, Sid, but Diane will have to wait outside until we're done here."

Diane took Sid's hand. "You should follow the doctor's orders. I'm going home. I had a terrible night's sleep on the waiting room couch, and my back is killing me. I could really use a shower and bed. Now that I see you're going to be okay, I can sleep. I'll leave the duffle bag here with your things and see you in the morning."

Sid grunted. "Don't go, Diane. I don't want to be alone again in this room."

Judy began removing the EEG wires from his head. "Let her go, Sid. She looks tired; and being pregnant, she needs her rest. How far along are you, Diane?"

"Seven and a half months next week."

"The third trimester is the toughest. Go get some sleep. I'll check in on Sid."

Sid laughed. "Well, I guess I have no say in this. See you tomorrow, Diane, come early… Okay, let's get this contraption off."

CHAPTER 21

Diane parked and took the delivery entrance into her building. It was a shorter walking distance but would need to take the service elevator. Her back and legs ached. The quickest way home was not the most pleasant. The last time she took this route with Sid, they encountered a mouse. Sid laughed when she threw her arms around him, screeching. Diane was ready to face her fears if it meant she could get into bed quicker.

She looked around while waiting for the elevator, and when it arrived, she quickly entered and pushed the button for the sixth floor. She took a breath when the doors closed and grunted when the elevator dinged at the first floor.

A maintenance man got on. "Hi, I'm the building superintendent, Ian. This car is not for tenants. Do you live here?"

"Yes. The sixth floor. It was a shorter walk from the parking lot. I hope it's, okay?"

Ian looked at her belly. "Of course, in your case, I understand. What apartment are you in?"

"6C"

Ian nodded. "Oh yes, you called for a plumber. I let him in your apartment this morning to get a part number for the bathroom faucet."

Diane's eyes widen. "You let someone into my apartment?"

"Well, yes, I came to your apartment last night with Rosa Plumbing. Your husband said to come back tomorrow. I saw the work order. I thought it was strange that he would come on a Sunday but being that he only wanted a part number, I didn't see the harm. We were only inside a minute, and I was with him all the time. He said he'd be back tomorrow to replace the faucet."

"I can't believe this. I didn't call a plumber!"

The elevator dinged on the fourth floor. Ian held the door. "Your husband must have called."

"I don't have a husband. And me and my boyfriend weren't even home last night."

Ian's face tightened, and he released the door. "I'm sorry, he must have had the wrong apartment. I won't let it happen again."

Diane shook her head.

Sid wouldn't be happy with this mishap and would probably call Ian a moron.

She arrived at the apartment and hurried to the bathroom to get the hot water running.

A shower and then bed. It'll feel so good.

She went to the bedroom to undress and get her robe but stopped to look at her clothes laid out on the bed. "Who the hell put these here? The plumber." She went to the phone directory and dialed the number for the building superintendent.

"Hello."

"This is Diane Rivers in apartment 6C. We just met on the elevator."

"Yes, of course. Is something wrong?"

"What the hell went on in my apartment? Someone went through all our belongings."

"It wasn't me, Ms. Rivers. As I told you, I only let the plumber in for a minute to get the part number for the faucet. I was with him the whole time. Neither of us touched any of your things."

"Well, someone did! Who else has a key?"

"I wouldn't know. I don't give out keys."

"This is unacceptable! I want the locks changed today!"

"It's Sunday, Ms. Rivers; I'm off. I'll take care of it for you tomorrow."

"If you weren't working, why'd you let the plumber in?"

"He said he'd be in trouble with his boss if he showed up tomorrow with the wrong faucet. I was trying to be helpful, and it only took a few minutes of my time. I'm sorry. I didn't know he had the wrong apartment. And as I said, I won't let it happen again."

"How am I going to sleep knowing someone can just walk into my home? I can't believe this."

"There's a security chain on the door. Keep it on today, and I'll be by tomorrow with a new lock."

Diane hung up the phone without saying anything and went to the front door to engage the chain.

What's Sid going to say about this? I'm sure he doesn't want me calling the police, and I don't want to call him now. This would only upset him.

She went to the drawer with the gun and took it out. "Thank God it's still here." Then she took it with her into the bathroom and took a shower.

By chance, Evan powered up Command Central as Diane arrived home.

"Well, she's not with her boyfriend; I'll assume she wasn't lying, and he's alive. Now it's time to end the cat-and-mouse game that never really got started, and send the information I have to the mafia boss. The sooner I get Sid Love out of Diane's life, the better."

He moved closer to the monitor when Diane entered the bedroom, where he laid out her clothes. He was disappointed when her only reaction was anger, followed by her calling the building super. Evan yelled at the monitor. "Come on, Diane. You can't see how perfectly put together the outfit was? You'll learn to appreciate me soon."

Damn. It's Sunday, the post office is closed.

"I'll send the letter to exterminate your boyfriend tomorrow."

Sid was finishing his breakfast when Diane arrived the following day. "Good morning, Sid. How're you feeling?"

He smiled. "Better than yesterday. I can sit up without feeling like my head is going to explode. The doctor should be here soon to release me. I wish I had my phone. The contractor was starting work today. He's probably wondering what happened to me."

"You can use the hospital phone, but I did take your cell; it's in the duffle bag I left with you. I'll get it. I shut it off, so you should still have some battery life."

Sid grinned. "You're the practical one; that's why I like having you around."

Diane sneered at him. "Is that the only reason?"

Sid chuckled.

Gotta love that she's always expecting more from me.

"No, it turns out you're also a pretty good cook … and sexy."

She snickered and powered up the phone.

"I guess I'll accept that for now. What's the number?"

He reached for the phone and cringed. "I have it in my contacts."

Diane frowned. "You're still in pain. Maybe you should stay here for another day."

Sid pressed Dan's number. "No way. They're not doing anything for me here except tell me to rest and sedate me. I can do that at home … Hello Dan, It's Sid."

"Sid. We were just talking about you."

"Who were you talking to about me?"

"Uncle Tony. We were worried something had happened to you."

"I'll tell you about what happened later. Are you working at the club?"

"Yes, we started demolition. When you didn't show, I wasn't sure how I was getting in, but I assumed that's why you left the side door open for us."

"It wasn't on purpose. I guess I never locked it after getting hit on the head. It worked out for the best, though. Well, keep going. I hope to be by soon. Any issues, give me a call."

"Yeah, sure, but there's something else you need to know."

"Okay."

"Uncle Tony was just telling me your neighbors had some kind of a meeting last night. A lot of people entered the burned-out building through the alley door. Then two of them paid me a visit this morning at the club. They asked for you and said things would get extremely painful if you didn't give them the photos."

"How'd you respond, Dan?"

"I told them to get out."

"Good man. Call the police if you must. I'll deal with them in my time."

"Do you know what photos they were talking about and what they meant by painful?"

"I don't know what they meant, but the photos I have are going to take these nutjobs down, not for you to worry about. You have a deadline to meet. Stay clear of them and keep them out of the club. Capiche?"

"Understood. Don't worry. Uncle Tony and I are looking out for you."

"Great to hear…. Listen, I have to go, the doctor just came in. Hopefully, I'm being released. We'll talk again as soon I get out of here."

Evan's alarm beeped loudly at seven A.M. He was anxious to get to the post office with the information that would eliminate Sid Love. When he went to stand, all his joints ached. "Oh, man. What did I do, catch the flu or something?"

Probably at the hospital, those places are filled with germs.

He put on his robe and went to the bathroom for aspirin. The bright light penetrated his eyes like daggers. He shielded them for a moment so his pupils could adjust. Evan was about to open the mirrored door to the medicine cabinet when he caught a glimpse of his disfigured face. He touched one of the pus-filled red blotches on his cheek, and it burst. "What the hell is this?"

I'll need to contact the doctor, but too early yet to call for an appointment. I'll work on putting together my note in the meantime. It'll be short and sweet. Come and get your snitch.

Evan managed to get a late morning appointment. When he opened the door to the doctor's office, the waiting room was full. The people who weren't reading went wide-eyed when they saw him. He walked up to the receptionist behind the glass panel. She looked up at him and grimaced.

"My God!" She stopped and swallowed hard. "Do you have an appointment?"

Evan nodded, trying to ignore the pain. "Yes. Evan Locke."

She sprang from her seat to open the door to the examination area. "Come in."

Dr. Messina put on gloves and a mask before examining the sores on his face. "They're boils. I've never seen a case this bad before. When did they start?"

Evan took a deep breath. "This morning, but they're the least of my problems. I'm in agony. Every bone in my body feels like it's on fire. Can you do something for the pain?"

"I'll prescribe something, but we'll need to run bloodwork to know for sure what you've got. I couldn't begin to imagine what it is, but you should quarantine yourself at home until I get the test results back. I'll give you antibiotics and something for the pain for now."

Evan left the doctor's office and wanted nothing more than to go home to bed, but he had one more stop to make at the post office. He took the envelope and slid it through the slot. "Goodbye, Mr. Love."

CHAPTER 22

Nurse Judy entered Sid's room with a smile and a bag. Diane sat on the bed next to Sid. Judy removed papers from the sack. "I bet you guys are anxious to get out of here. We can't release you without completed paperwork. The administrator will be in to finalize everything. In the meantime, look over these post-trauma instructions. I'll go over them with you again before you leave. Inside this bag, there's a change of dressing, some topical antibiotic ointment, and a prescription for pain and inflammation. I'll be back."

Sid took her hand. "Wait. Don't go. I don't know anything about the person who was my best friend the last two days."

She laughed. "Not much to tell. I work twelve hours a day and share my apartment with another nurse. Most of the men I meet are jerks. Present company excluded."

Sid looked at Diane and grinned. "I've had my moments. At least you're smart enough to see one, Judy, and don't worry about your looks and personality, you're bound to find Mr. Right. I'm the new owner of the Camelot Dance Club on Eighty-second Street and Seventh Avenue. The same place with the knight and horse on the roof that jogged my memory. It's currently under renovation but come see me in six weeks. It'll be the hottest club in the area. I'll set you up with free drinks."

Judy nodded. "I remember the Camelot. There're not many knights around, so I'm surprised the Camelot didn't connect with me when you talked about seeing one on a horse. And… umm… not sure I should tell you this, Sid, but I heard some bad things went down inside, like cutting up people in the kitchen?"

Sid shrugged. "That's okay, Judy. I do know about the history. I found out a little late, but it doesn't matter. Nothing was proven. I hope you won't let some urban myth stop you from coming to see me. Who knows, it may be where you meet the man of your dreams?"

Judy snickered. "I'll come to see you, Sid, but with no expectations. Nightclubs are usually where jerks breed. I must be going. Other patients are waiting. Nice seeing you again, Diane."

Sid and Diane left the hospital and took a cab home. On the way, Sid said, "You want to know something, Diane? When I lost my memory, I wondered what kind of person I was — good or bad. Now that I know, I've gotta wonder why you're with me."

Diane took Sid's hand. "You're a good man. You don't do bad things out of hate or anger. It's always been about business or following orders. What happened with those guys and the car the other night, you did to keep us safe."

"I think conducting business justifies only some things I've done. I was hoping I could put that life behind me when we came here, but now I'm not sure I'll be able to."

She sat back against the seat of the cab. "Maybe that guy didn't tell anyone else before you ... you know," she whispered, "killed him."

Sid grunted. "I hope you're right. If he did share what he knew, we'll know soon enough. Keep your eyes open, look over your shoulder and let me know if you see anything suspicious."

The car stopped at the front entrance to the building. Diane paid the driver and helped Sid out of the car and into the lobby. Diane pushed the elevator button. "Sid, did you call for a plumber before you were hurt?"

He squinted. "No. Why're you asking?"

"Something strange happened. Some of my clothes were laid out on the bed when I arrived home yesterday, and I didn't take them out.

The building super said he let a plumber in the apartment, yesterday morning before I got home to get a part number for a broken faucet."

Sid shrugged. "Maybe you forgot you took out the clothes and the plumber had the wrong apartment."

"The building super said the plumber was here Saturday night and that you wouldn't let them in and told him to come back tomorrow."

Sid's eyes widened. "Did you tell him I wasn't home?"

"Yes. All he said was that he saw the work order and a man inside the apartment said to come back tomorrow morning. That's why he let him in the next day when no one was home. He said they were only in the apartment a couple of minutes."

The elevator door opened, and Sid followed Diane into the cab. "Did you check to see if anything was taken?"

"Yes, but it doesn't look like anything is missing. The building super is supposed to be by today with a new door lock."

When Sid entered the apartment, he looked around. "Where's the revolver, Diane?"

She pulled it from her purse. "It's here. I got spooked last night after learning someone was in the apartment and slept with it under my pillow."

Sid took the pistol. "There're no bullets in it."

"Oh my God, Sid! You mean I've been protecting myself with an empty gun."

He nodded. "Looks that way... I'm fairly certain there was ammo in it, but everything is a little fuzzy from that night."

First, the photo and now an intruder that possibly stole the bullets from the gun. Could this possibly be connected? I don't want to get Diane paranoid, but this is not good.

"Should I call the police?"

Sid sneered. "For what? Nothing was taken, except maybe the bullets, and we can't show them the gun. Especially the one I took off the dead guy. I have more ammo."

He went to the bar and poured a bourbon. "I'm going to get cleaned up and shave, feeling grungy. Then I'll take some pain meds and get some sleep. My head is starting to throb again."

Diane sighed. "With everything going on, I don't think I'll be able to sleep. I'm calling the building super and find out when he is changing the lock."

Sid took his drink and headed to the bathroom. "That's a good idea. Wake me when he gets here; I want to talk to him."

Sid looked at his bandaged head and two-day-old beard in the mirror. "You're a sight."

He couldn't stop wondering if the intruder was somehow connected to Vito Rosa. If he wasn't, why was nothing taken? I'm not one hundred percent sure the bullets were ever in the gun. Although I find it hard to believe the creep I took it from was carrying an unloaded pistol.

Sid reached for his razor and yelled to Diane when he couldn't find it. "Have you seen my razor, Diane?"

She walked into the bathroom. "It was right by the sink on the tray where you always leave it."

"Well, it's not here now."

She looked through the drawers and medicine cabinet. "It's gone … I don't recall if I saw it when I took a shower. Could this have something to do with the intruder?"

Sid laughed. "Why in the hell would anyone want my razor?"

Diane fell back, leaning against the vanity. "None of this makes any sense. The plumber no one called for, and an intruder, but nothing was missing except bullets and a razor. There's something weird going on here, Sid."

He nodded. "It does seem odd, but you need not worry about it." He rubbed his whiskers. "I guess I'll have to live with this rat's nest on my face another day. I'm gonna to lie down before my head explodes." Sid entered the bedroom and sat on the end of the bed.

Diane's right. There's something not right about all this. We can't trust anyone, but for now, I need to rest my head and get some sleep. I can't think straight with my head pounding.

Sid woke in darkness to the sound of the doorbell chiming. He turned the night table lamp on and grunted when he tried to stand. "Hey, Diane. Who's at the door?" He stumbled into the living room, where Diane was asleep on the couch with the television on. The clock said it was 7:30 P.M. "Who the hell is it at this time of night?"

He looked through the peephole and sighed. Detectives Stacy and Greer stood at the threshold when Sid opened the door. "You boys again. Forget something?"

Greer said, "Do you know a Vito Rosa or a Jake Hart? The two men that were run down by your car."

"No." *Shit! They made the connection back to me?*

"Well, they seem to have known you. Vito Rosa is a known gun runner wanted by the police, and he had your name and address on him. It also turns out Vito Rosa worked for his family business next door to your club at the psychic readings shop."

"Those people are a bunch of weirdos. They're using that business for more than just voodoo mumbo-jumbo."

Stacy said. "What do you mean?"

Sid chuckled. "You just told me he was a gun runner working for his family business. What do you think they're doing? I'm sure I don't have to spell it out for you."

Greer grunted. "No, you don't need to spell it out. Why do you say they are weirdos? Have you met them?"

"I never said I met them. You see this bandage on my head? I spent the last two days in the hospital. Why don't you find out who bashed my head in instead of asking me questions about murders I had nothing to do with?"

Detective Stacy said, "Vito Rosa obviously knew you, and it was your car that ran him down. You're not under arrest, for now, but you *are* a person of interest. Normally, we'd bring you downtown to answer questions, but considering your injury, why don't we come back tomorrow?"

Sid shook his head and cringed. "No way, I don't want to see you again. Just ask your questions now, and let's get it over with."

"How long have you owned the Camelot Club?" Stacy asked.

"Four or five weeks."

"Have you ever had business dealings with the psychic shop next door to your club?"

"No."

"Do you know Madame Beth?"

"No. Never heard of her."

"Have you ever met Vito Rosa?"

"No."

"Well, that's interesting. Madame Beth told us you went to their shop last week, asking where you could get a gun."

"I don't recall that. Did she say I got one?"

"No, but she said Vito paid you a visit the next day."

Sid shrugged. "I don't recall that, either."

"The night of the fire. Why were you at the Camelot?"

"It's my club. I was taking care of business."

"Do you know how the fire started?"

"How the hell would I know that?"

"You previously said you didn't see who hit you. Did you hear anything?"

"No."

"You also previously said you don't know how you got home. Do you remember waking up after getting knocked out?"

"No."

"Is there anyone who can corroborate that you were at the club the night you were attacked?"

Sid was about to mention Tony but changed his mind.

I'd have to be sure about what Tony saw and heard first.

"No."

"Do you know of any reason why Vito Rosa would have your name and address in his pocket?"

"No."

Damn it, why didn't I check his pockets?

"Okay," Stacy said. "We're done for now. You have my card. Call me if you plan on taking any long trips."

After the detectives left, Sid closed the door and locked it.

Vito, having my information in his pocket, proves nothing. I just need to stick to the story.

He tried to watch television with Diane but couldn't take his mind off Madame Beth and the possible connection to the intruder.

If there is a connection, I can let them think they got the best of me or have the upper hand. I'm going down there tomorrow and make it clear to Madame Sicko that she's telling me what she knows.

"I'm going to the club tomorrow morning" Sid said.

"No, you're not," replied Diane. "The doctor said you need to rest for a couple of days."

"I only need to check on the contractor. Shouldn't take more than an hour."

She dropped her head and sighed. "Why do I need to worry about everything you do? Why can't you follow the doctor's orders and stay home? You shouldn't be driving with the medication you're taking. Don't you understand if something were to happen to you, the baby and I would be alone? Please don't go, Sid."

I understand she's afraid, but she can't be throwing this guilt at me. After my amnesia, I realize I need her, but why does she have to make me angry.

Sid walked around the table and sat next to Diane. "I promise to be home before noon. I've just got to check on things so I can make sure the club opens on time. It's our future. You can understand that, right?"

Diane nodded without looking at him. "I guess I have to."

Sid saw a tear roll down her face.

Damn, now she's crying.

"I promise, I'll only be out for a little while. And when I get home, we can discuss finishing the baby's room. Does that sound good?"

Her eyes widened, and a grin spread across her face. She threw her arms around him. "You don't know how long I've waited for you to show you care about the baby. Thank you, Sid."

Sid chuckled.

I guess I hit the right button. I don't really care about the baby, but I want Diane to be happy.

"We're in this together. That's why I must take care of business and make sure no one else knows about the photo and note."

Diane's eyes narrowed. "You said you were going to the club, not investigating the source of the note!"

He grasped her shoulders and looked her in the eye. "I have to do both, and you need not worry. I will do what I must to protect our lives and future. So can you please try understanding when I need to do things?"

Her head dropped. "Do I have a choice?"

Sid lifted her chin. "So, did you get the carpet you called me about?"

Diane smiled. "I do understand your life, Sid. Although I wish I didn't… I haven't made a decision on the rug. I've been collecting color samples and swatches. Do you want to see them? I can get them. They're in the baby's room."

Sid liked seeing Diane happy. "Sure, go ahead and get them."

CHAPTER 23

The next morning, Sid pulled up outside the club. He glanced up at a picture Diane had hung from the car's rearview mirror. It was of Diane and him at the Memorial Day party where they met. "Fun times. Boy, have things changed," he muttered. He got out of the car and walked down the alley beside the club's side entrance, pausing to look at the door of the psychic shop.

I need the element of surprise. Let's see; maybe I'll get lucky.

He pulled the doorknob. It was locked.

This won't be easy, but I won't underestimate them again. Anyone who knows my identity must be disposed of even if they agree to the photo swap deal I offer. There is no other way to be sure.

The alley door to his club was held open by a rope tied to the railing. The sound of hammers, screw guns, and voices echoed in the room. Sid asked a worker where Dan was, and he pointed to the kitchen.

Dan was standing at a plywood table, shuffling through some papers. "How's it going, Dan?"

Dan swung around, looking surprised. "I wasn't expecting to see you today, Sid. Your head's bandaged up pretty good. How are you feeling?"

"Not too bad as long as I take the pain meds. How's it going here?"

"Good, good. I've only got a small crew working for now. Once the demolition is done, I'll bring in the carpenters, plumbers, and electricians."

"Have you seen my neighbors again?"

Dan laughed. "No, I haven't seen those creeps today."

"If they come by, kick them out, and then make sure you let me know immediately, got it?"

Dan shrugged. "Don't worry, I'll take care of it…. but something's disturbing about these people. Maybe you should give them what they're looking for, and they'll go away."

"This is not your concern. I'll handle this. You just keep them out of here. Capiche?"

Dan nodded. "Sure."

Sid pointed to the front doors. "Let's look at the entrance. I have an idea to put torches on each side of the door to look more like a castle."

When they went outside, Dan stopped Sid and pointed to the two people getting out of a car. "The man with the lady was one of the two that were here yesterday."

Sid gazed at them and took a step back behind the door. "Dan, I don't want them to see me. Let's talk inside."

"Okay."

Inside the club, Sid watched Madame Beth and her male partner open the entrance door to the psychic shop, which was still covered in plywood. "Hey, Dan. Do me a favor, would you? I'm going to talk to them, but I want my visit to be a surprise. When I leave, wait till you see me in front of their building, then go bang on their alley door four or five times."

Dan shrugged. "Okay. What're you going to do?"

"I'm going to talk with them and hopefully make a deal, but I don't trust them and want to be sure how many are inside when I enter through the front entrance. Your distraction should help."

He nodded. "From what Uncle Tony told me, and what I've seen, you're right. They shouldn't be trusted. Be careful."

"One other thing, Dan, and this is very important. What you see and hear regarding my visit with these crazies stays between us. Can I count on you for that?"

Dan didn't hesitate "Of course. Nothing to worry about."

Sid liked that

Sid couldn't see inside with the boarded-up windows and waited to hear Dan's knock. When he did, he slowly opened the entrance door and peeked inside before walking in. The vacant room still smelled of smoke. Sid heard voices coming from the hall leading to the alley and took out his gun. He listened carefully to make sure it was only the two people and stood behind the wall at the corner of the corridor.

Madame Beth was speaking to the man. Sid waited for them to enter the room before he revealed himself. "Ladies and gentlemen, it's time to play, 'Let's make a deal!'"

Sid thought Madame Beth went white when she saw him. "You? How could you be here?"

"That's not a very nice welcome. I've come to settle our differences."

She looked at her partner. "How can this be, Jay? Is Satan protecting this man? There is no way the curse didn't work. It always works."

Jay shrugged. "I don't know. Maybe Gary took someone else's razor."

Sid tried to decipher what they meant.

Did these sickos take my missing razor? Do they actually believe in curses? They seem genuinely surprised to see me unscathed by their efforts. They're about to find out a gun works better than their voodoo crap.

"I'm here to make a deal, but first, give me the keys to the door!" When no one moved, Sid lifted the revolver. "This can be easy, or this can be hard. Give me the keys!"

Jay took them from his pocket and handed them over.

Sid went to the front door and locked it. "Good, you're catching on. Now let's make a deal. Are you in or out? I don't have time for your games."

Madame Beth squinted at him. "What's the deal?"

"It's easy. You give me the names of anybody who knows about my past and the photo you sent me, and I'll only kill them. You get to live, and I'll give you the original pictures and the letter the last club owner left behind — all the evidence that could put you in prison."

The man she had called Jay said, "What're you talking about?"

Madame Beth shot him a piercing stare. "I know what you're talking about," she said to Sid. "Bring me the originals, and then we can talk."

Sid shook his head. "This is a one-time offer. Tell me who else knows about me, and I'll give you the evidence."

"I don't know how you escaped the curse, and you need to pay for my son's death, but we have no idea what you are talking about."

Sid pressed the gun to Jay's temple. "Gimme an answer by the count of three, or he dies."

Madame Beth held up her hand. "Hold on, don't shoot. No one else knows about you. Only me," Madame Beth said.

"One..., Two...."

"Stop! Wait! He knows nothing. Don't kill him. The truth is, I don't know what you're talking about, either."

Sid cocked the revolver. "Why should I believe you? You just admitted you tried to kill me."

She shook her head. "No, we weren't going to kill you until we had the original photos. If the curse worked, you would be in agony now and would have gladly turned them over to us to stop the pain."

"Do you have dementia or something? You just said a few seconds ago that I should be dead."

"I never said you should be dead. What I said was you shouldn't be here. I had no intention of killing you right away. I wanted you to suffer first for running down my son."

Sid pointed to Jay. "Where is the other guy who was with you yesterday at my club?"

"I don't know who you're talking about."

Sid hit him on the head with the butt of the gun and, causing a stream of blood to run down his face. "Let's try it again. Where's the other guy that was with you?"

Madame Beth answered; "That's my other son Gary, and he's not here."

"Where is he?"

"I don't know?"

Sid pointed the gun again at Jay's head. "Are you sure you don't know?"

"He works as a plumber. I don't keep track of where he goes."

"Does he have a cell phone or a pager?"

Madame Beth grunted. "A pager."

Sid took out his cell and handed it to her. "Page him now."

She dialed the number and then handed the phone back to Sid.

"How long does he take to call back?" Sid asked.

She shrugged. "Not long during business hours if he can find a pay phone."

Sid's cell rang minutes later. "Is this Gary?"

"Yes, who's this?"

"That's not important. Come to your family psychic business right away; your mom and Jay are waiting."

Sid flipped the phone closed and looked into a dark room with a table, chairs, and a candle at the center of a pentagram. He pointed with the gun. "We'll wait for your son here. Go sit down." He looked for the light switch but couldn't find one. "Where're the lights?"

Madame Beth sneered. "There is no electricity in that room. The energy inside comes from those able to connect with the spiritual world."

Sid laughed. "Hilarious. Well, I don't want to sit in the dark. Let's find another room." Sid pointed the gun to the adjacent door. "Let's see what dark magic is in here."

He flipped the light switch and illuminated an office with two chairs — one behind the desk and one in front. Sid waved the gun for them to enter and took the chair behind the desk. "You can decide who sits where."

Jay sat on the floor, letting Madame Beth sit opposite Sid. "We don't have any photos of you," she said. "Why do you think we do? There's no reason to hold us here."

Sid leaned back in the chair. "Elementary deduction. Your son Vito was the only one that knew I had the revolver. So, when I received a photo and note to blackmail me and give up my gun, it didn't take long to figure out who sent it. Your son Vito wasn't very smart. My reason for holding you is to find out who else Vito told. Once I know, I'll get the information you have on me and trade it for the information I have on you. Then we can all leave and move on with our lives."

Except. I'll be moving on; you'll all be dead.

Madame Beth said nothing but continued to stare at him. Sid tried to ignore it and went through the desk drawers.

What the hell is with her? Her eyes are black like Vito's, but her stare is so intense it makes me uncomfortable.

The ledger books showed the business making tens of thousands a month. "You make this kind of money telling fortunes? I don't believe it."

There was no response, just a continued cold, dark gaze from Madame Beth that was now irking Sid.

"Listen, Madame Nutjob, find something else to look at, or Jay is going to have more than a gash on his head."

Where's her son? I need to end this. She's starting to creep me out.

Sid heard a noise coming from the front entrance. Then a man's voice, shouting, "Mama, why's the door locked?"

"Cone in," Sid said. "We've been waiting for you."

Sid nudged Gary into the room with Madame Beth and Jay, then locked the front door again.

Gary sat on the floor next to Jay. "Sorry, Mom, but why didn't the curse work? Do you think I took the wrong razor?"

Sid gazed at Gary with the hat that said "Rosa Plumbing."

"Were you the intruder in my apartment who took my razor? You people are sicker than I could ever have imagined."

Gary replied, "All I know is you killed my brother, and you should suffer and die."

Sid took Gary by the arm. "Come on, let's go confirm all the doors are locked. You two don't try anything, or Gary here will suffer the consequences." They checked the alley door first, and Sid could hear the loud construction noise.

The work next door will muffle the shots.

They checked the front entrance and returned to the office, closing the door behind them. Sid looked around and was pleased there were no windows.

This room is perfect. It should shield the noise of the gun well. Let's get this over with.

He pointed the gun at Jay's head and looked at Gary.

"Do you know him?"

"He's, my dad."

Sid fired the gun, and Jay fell back, his chair hitting the floor with a thud.

"He's dead," Sid said, looking at Gary, "and the next person to die is your mom. Who else knows about my past?"

"Please, don't kill her. I swear, we don't know what you're talking about."

Sid pointed the gun at Madame Beth. "I'll give you to the count of three to tell me who else knows about me."

Gary jumped out of his seat. "We don't know what you're talking about! I swear. All I know is you killed my brother, so we put a curse on you. You should be begging for relief right now. That's all I know."

Sid squeezed off the next round, and Madame Beth fell next to her husband. He turned the gun on Gary.

"Do you want to die, too? Tell me, who else knows?"

Gary grimaced. The color had drained from his face, and it looked to Sid like he was wearing a white plastic Halloween mask. "Why did you do that?" Gary whispered, tears glistening in his eyes. "They didn't know anything. In the name of Satan, don't kill me. I don't know anything."

"I don't believe you," Sid said. "Now go see Satan and your family in hell."

He squeezed the trigger.

Why would he not tell me unless he really didn't know? Is it possible Vito didn't tell any of them? I guess it is, but it had to be Vito that sent the note. No one else could have known about the gun. I assume Vito would have shared the information with his family but died before he had a chance. Whether they knew or not, the secret dies here with them.

Sid went through all the drawers and files in the office, checked all their pockets, and found nothing that could incriminate him.

Where would they have put a copy of the photo?

He took Gary's pager since Sid's phone number would appear on it. Then he wiped down anything he'd touched before leaving and locking the office door. He retraced his steps since entering the building and cleaned anything else he may have left a fingerprint on before leaving through the alley and locking the door on the way out.

In the alley, Sid went to Gary's plumbing van and flipped through a clipboard of papers. Most of which were work orders. He found the one for his apartment and took it. After finding nothing else connecting him to the Rosas, he started the van and drove it six blocks to the address of the last work order. It was a factory building on a dead-end street.

It could be a while before anyone realizes the van's abandoned.

Sid wiped down whatever he touched. Then he made sure he wasn't seen before locking it and walked back to get Madame Beth's car.

Getting rid of her car won't be as simple. It's on the street, and it will be hard not to be seen getting into it. Whatever it takes. Maybe the note and photo are in their car. Then I can feel better about killing them and knowing the information is destroyed.

Sid stood at the edge of the alley, hoping Dan or any workers wouldn't unexpectedly come outside. He waited for two people walking by to pass and then quickly entered the car. He started it and drove away without being noticed. He went to the waterfront parking area about a mile from Shore Road Condominiums to go through the car. Besides car info, the glove box contained a claw that looked to be from a chicken's foot, a horn that could be from a goat, and a small book with a pentagram on the cover. He went to the trunk and was unsuccessful in finding the photo. He picked up one of the black robes.

Sick people, but what did they do with the picture. The last place to search would be their home. I can't chance getting seen there. I'm going to have to wait. If I don't hear from anyone else, that should be the end of it.

Sid thought about leaving the car in the parking area but realized it was too close to his apartment.

I'll have to find a better spot where it won't be found for a long while.

He drove around for twenty minutes before spotting a street off Fort Hamilton Parkway that ran below the bridge ramp. There were several abandoned, stripped cars there.

"Bingo." Sid smiled.

After wiping down the car interior and handles, he took the keys from the ignition along with Gary's pager. He walked along the waterfront and stopped to throw in the keys and pager.

Now the only thing I need to get rid of is the gun. Seems a shame to give it up after everything I went through to get it. If I get rid of it, we'll only have the one gun. I can't take the chance of it being found.

Sid looked around before pulling it out from his shirt and tossing it in the water. Then he walked a few blocks before getting on a bus back to the club.

Sid arrived and found Dan.

"I'm leaving Dan. I'll see you tomorrow."

He gazed at Sid. "You were gone for a while. Is everything okay? Did you surprise them?"

Sid nodded. "Yeah, they were surprised, but we couldn't come to a deal. If you see them again, let me know. Okay? I'm going home. I need my pain pills my head's pounding."

CHAPTER 24

Sid arrived home to find Diane vacuuming. He tapped her shoulder, making her jump.

"Sorry. Didn't mean to startle you. Why're you cleaning when the doctor told you to rest?"

Diane hit the 'Off' button and scowled. "You were supposed to be here two hours ago. What do you think is going through my head when you don't even call? Then I try to call your cell, and it goes to voice mail. What's the sense of having one if it's not on? And don't lecture me on doctor's orders if you can't follow them yourself."

Sid grasped his head and groaned. "Please, Diane. My head's pounding. I'll explain after I get some pain meds."

Diane snarled as he walked away. "Your head wouldn't be pounding if you stayed home and rested, as the doctor said."

Sid returned with a cold bottle of water and plopped on the couch. "Give me a few minutes for the meds to kick in, Diane, before you start yelling at me again."

Diane sighed and then smiled. "I won't, and you rest. I'm going to sit on the terrace for a while and read. Let me know when you're feeling better."

Sid leaned back and closed his eyes. "Thanks, Diane. Sorry I was late."

Diane was watching television on the other end of the couch when Sid woke. He thought he had only closed his eyes for a moment, but there was a noticeable time lapse. "Hey." He said to her in a froggy voice.

She looked at him. "You're finally up? You've been sleeping for almost two hours."

He was surprised to hear how long it was. "I thought I just closed my eyes." Sid moaned as he pushed himself erect in his seat. "I'm hungry. What do you say we go to Denali's for an early dinner?"

"We can't. That guy is coming to do the fire-alarm test. He was supposed to be here earlier, but the company called and said they were running late."

He shrugged. "I forgot. So, what have we got around here to eat?"

"I can make a grilled cheese sandwich. Or maybe scrambled eggs and toast?"

"Grilled cheese sounds great."

At least she doesn't sound mad.

"I'll make one for myself, too." She paused and clutched her stomach. "Oh my God, Sid, the baby just kicked. There it is again. Put your hand here." She placed his hand on her belly, and they both waited.

Sid was about to pull away when he felt her stomach bulge. "That was the baby?"

She grinned. "Yes."

"Does that happen often?"

"Yes, lately, but it was the first time you were here to feel it. Isn't it wonderful? I can't wait until we can hold it in my arms."

Sid felt his stomach flip. Feeling the kick made it surreal.

This baby's going to complicate our lives. I don't want it but saying that will only cause a fight.

"He's kicking because he's hungry like me. All that talk of grilled cheese got him riled up."

Diane laughed. "He? What makes you think it's a he?"

"I don't know. Can't doctors tell the sex nowadays?"

She nodded. "Yes, I originally wanted to know so I could decorate the room in the right color, but I thought more about it and, I don't want to know. I'd rather be surprised. Wouldn't you?"

He shrugged.

"Doesn't matter."

I wish I could tell her I'd rather there's no baby..., I can never love it like she will.

While Diane went to the kitchen, Sid headed to the bedroom to get the revolver from the dresser drawer, and confirmed it was loaded. He slid the gun inside his belt and covered it with his shirt when the doorbell rang.

At the door stood Ian, the maintenance man, and an official-looking guy with a badge and clipboard. Ian smiled.

"We're here to do the fire alarm inspection. Is it a good time?"

"Not especially, but come on in, and let's get this over with."

They dragged in a ladder and some other equipment. "We'll start in the kitchen if that's okay," Ian said.

Diane was finishing up the sandwiches when they entered. She nodded to Ian and the other man and said, "Lunch is ready, Sid. Should we wait for them to finish?"7

The man with the badge looked at the smoke detector on the ceiling. "We shouldn't be long."

Sid took his plate from Diane and sat. "I don't want a cold grilled cheese sandwich."

The fire official took his ladder to a duct register on the wall and removed the vent cover. He looked at Ian and then at Sid before conducting his smoke detector test and reinstalling the vent cover. "I'm finished here," he said. "I'll move to the bedroom."

Sid took the last bite of his sandwich and followed. "Good grilled cheese, Diane. I'm going to stay with them until they're finished."

The inspector continued the same procedure. After removing the vent cover in the bedroom, he grinned at Sid.

"Something amusing to you?" Sid asked.

The man shrugged. "No. Sorry. It's none of my business."

"*What's* none of your business?"

"The cameras."

Sid paused to comprehend what the man said. "What the hell are you talking about? What cameras?"

The inspector pointed. "Inside the ducts. There's one in the kitchen and one here. I assumed you knew about them."

"I don't know about shit! Finish your inspection. I want to know how many cameras there are."

Ian looked nervous. "Maybe we should call the police?"

"I'm here to do a fire alarm test," the inspector said, "not investigate hidden cameras. If you didn't put them there, then yeah, you should call the authorities."

Sid closed the bedroom door. "Keep your voices down. I don't want my girlfriend to hear this until I know what's happening. Do your inspection but leave the vent covers off."

I've got to figure out who put these there. The psychics couldn't have done this and if Big Zac knew where I was, he'd just kill me, not install cameras. This isn't making sense. Holy shit… ! Did I kill the wrong people?

Sid's heart pounded, his face tightened, and his insides turned over as each of the five cameras was revealed. He grabbed Ian's arm as the inspector tested the last location. "I need to know where the wires are coming from that control the cameras. If you can confirm the location and help me get to the bottom of this — there's five hundred dollars in it for you."

Ian's eyes widened. "Really?"

"Yes. But get it done immediately. I want to know today."

Whoever put these cameras here will pay dearly. I'll keep this from Diane for now. She'll just freak out.

As promised, Sid sat with Diane to go through color swatches for the baby's room, but he had a hard time concentrating waiting for Ian to get back to him. *Where's Ian? He must have found something by now.*

Sid heard Diane raise her voice. "Sid, where are you? You're not hearing a word I say."

"Yeah, sorry. I have something on my mind."

Diane sat back. "Should I be worried?"

Sid shook his head. "Something to do with the construction at the club…, so, what were you showing me again?"

The doorbell rang as Diane handed him the sample. Sid jumped up. "I'll get it."

Ian nodded when Sid opened the door. "I know where the wires go."

Sid turned. "Diane, I'm going with Ian, the building super. I'll be back in a few minutes."

Sid stepped into the corridor and crossed his arms. "Where do they go?"

"Apartment 6A. Evan Locke's apartment. He sublets your apartment. I guess that's how he had access."

Sid stomped up the hallway to Evan's door. "Open it up."

Ian shook his head. "I can't do that. I could lose my job. Evan Locke has been a long-time resident. I can't just enter his apartment without his consent unless it's an emergency."

"Tell whoever you answer to it was urgent! I'll back up your story."

Sid pounded on the door. "Your Peeping Tom days are over, Evan. Come out here, you son of a bitch."

When no one answered, Sid put out his hand. "Give me the keys."

Ian sighed. "Please, I can't."

"Listen, Ian, I already told you I'm giving you five C-notes. I'm not playing games here. Give me the key, or you get crap, and I take it anyway."

"I can't do that…."

"You'll do it now. Don't let me have to ask again." Sid said.

Sighing, Ian unlocked the door, peeked inside, and called out, "Evan?"

Sid pushed him aside and marched into the apartment, quickly examining the rooms. A foul odor was coming from the bedroom. The smell of human excretion was an unpleasant but familiar odor for Sid. He flashed back to the room where his bathroom was a bucket.

When Sid pulled the covers back on the bed, Ian jumped. "Oh my God! What happened to him? He looks like a monster or something."

Sid gazed at Ian. "Are you sure it's Evan?"

"He had white hair and a white beard. It must be him, but his face is unrecognizable. Should we check his pulse to see if he's dead?"

Sid scowled. "You can. I'm not touching him. He may be contagious, but it's a safe bet to say he's dead. He pissed and shitted himself on the way out. Let's get away from the stench."

Ian nodded. "I guess I should call the police?"

Sid opened the door to a room full of monitors and computers, but everything was turned off. He punched buttons, bringing the equipment to life. The first screen showed Diane sitting in the living room. The other monitors showed the rest of Sid's apartment. He stood there shaking his head in disbelief.

If Evan weren't dead, I'd be killing him right now.

Ian went to the phone on the desk and picked up the receiver. "I'm calling the police."

Sid took the phone from his hand and hung it up.

"Not yet. I want to know what pictures he has of us."

"What if the cops find out I let you go through his stuff? We shouldn't be here in the first place."

"You can call the police when I'm done. Tell them you went inside when no one answered the door for the fire inspection."

Ian sighed. "Okay. That's believable, I guess."

Sid watched Diane on the screen, flipping through a magazine.

I've got to get rid of anything he found in my past and be sure no one knows about or uses this equipment again.

"Ian, I need you to cut all the camera wires going to the computer and remove all the cameras in my apartment while I search this place."

"Aren't you going to want the cops to see them?"

He shook his head. "No, and I don't want you telling them about them, either."

Ian cocked his head. "That doesn't make any sense. Wouldn't you want them to know?"

"I have my reasons. Tell them you went into the apartment for the fire inspection and found him dead. There is nothing else you need to say. Capiche? When I'm done here, I'll close the door on my way out, and then you can call the authorities."

Ian paused, gazing at the floor, and then looked at Sid. "When do I get the money?"

Sid reached into his pocket and took out a billfold. He counted out two hundred and fifty dollars. "Half now and half after the cops leave."

Ian took the money. "Why can't I have the rest when I take out the cameras?"

"Because I want to make sure you don't say anything about what we found."

Ian folded his ladder. "I don't know anything about finding anything."

Sid smiled. "Good man. Tell Diane I'll be back soon."

When Sid was alone, he went through the cabinets and drawers in the computer room. He found a notebook of dates and times he and Diane had come in and out of the apartment, and in the bedroom dresser, he found a pair of panties that looked like Diane's. He put them in his pocket. The closet held fishing gear and a blow-up sex doll. He shook his head and looked at the body on the bed. "You were a sick pervert."

Sid walked through the apartment, looking for places Evan might have hidden photographs. The desk by the front door caught his eye.

He opened the top drawer, and there it was: the photo Sid had received with the blackmail letter. He also found a scrapbook of photos. All the pictures were of women naked in the apartment. One looked familiar, whom he had met on the elevator. "That degenerate must have been doing this for years." Inside the tray of the top drawer, there were .38 caliber bullets.

These must be from the revolver.

Also in the drawer was Diane's jewelry. He put them in his pocket and muttered. "Can't believe he came into the apartment multiple times and went through our stuff. I'd crack him in the head with a bat if I thought it would do any good." He looked through a phone book and wondered if Evan had friends and family with whom he could've collaborated. He walked around the apartment, examining the framed photos. There weren't many. Except for an old couple he assumed was his mom and dad, all the pictures were of him holding a fish. *The pervert must have been a loner.* Sid took everything, including the scrapbook, and left.

Ian was finishing up when Sid got back to his own apartment. "I'm done. You can make the call. Remember, you know nothing."

He nodded. "I got it. I don't understand it, but I got it."

"Good. If I don't get any visits from the police, you can stop by tomorrow and pick up the rest of your money."

After Ian left, Sid went to the kitchen, where Diane was sitting with a mug in her hand. "Where'd you go?" she asked. "Ian wouldn't tell me. You can't keep me in the dark, Sid. I can tell something's wrong."

The tension building inside Sid exploded. "Can't you sing a different song? I'm tired of hearing it. I took care of the problem, and it has nothing to do with you or the baby. So, leave it alone."

Diane got up and left the room. "I thought I was starting to see a change in you, Sid, but now I'm not so sure."

Sid sat down and went through the papers and scrapbook.

If Diane knew about this, she'd completely lose her mind. I'm doing her a favor by not saying anything, and what does she mean when she says I changed. I'm the same person. I don't understand her at all.

Sid put the papers in a pile and buried them in a dresser drawer. "I'll find a place to burn these at the club tomorrow, and that should be the end of it. Then I can get back to business."

Just hope I did a good job cleaning up after the psychos. It's a shame they died for the wrong reason, but the world is a better place without them, so I don't feel too bad.

PART THREE

THE
RECKONING

CHAPTER 25

Terminal Island Penitentiary, May 4, 1992: Big Zac and Anthony Rinaldi met in the prison courtyard to play chess. Before setting up the board, Big Zac passed Anthony the letter he had received that morning.

Anthony read it and smiled. "Is this a joke?"

"Don't know, it came anonymously. If it's true, we have all of Sal's information here, including his new name Sid Love. Put Nicky Bones on it. He's good at seeing through bullshit."

Anthony gave the letter back to him and continued setting up his chess pieces. "This is great. I feel like we just hit the lottery."

"We'll know when Nicky gets back to us. Until then, I'm not getting my hopes up."

Anthony nodded. "I'll make the call and tell him to make this investigation priority. He hasn't had much luck finding Sal. He said it's like finding a needle in a haystack. I'm sure he'll be happy to hear we may know his location."

Big Zac made the first chess move. "Just make sure Sal's taken alive so he can be questioned. Is that understood?"

Anthony nodded. "Sure." He stared at the game board, but his thoughts were not on the move.

I can't allow Sal to be questioned.

Sid was at his desk in the Camelot when Detectives Greer and Stacy walked in. He glanced up at them, then went right back to his paperwork. "Something I can help you with?"

"We hope so," Stacy said. "Your neighbors, the Rosas, have been reported missing. They're not at home, and the building next door is locked up. Have you seen them?"

Sid didn't bother to look up. "No. That all?"

At least they hadn't found them yet.

"Funny. I was just talking to your contractor. He said the last time he saw the Rosas, they were here looking for you. He also said you were trying to set up a meeting with them. Did you meet?"

Sid sat back and stared at them. "Briefly."

I'll tell them it was business, but I told Dan to keep his mouth shut.

Greer crossed his arms. "What was the meeting about?"

"Not that it's any of your business, but I wanted to make them an offer to buy the burned-out building so I could tear it down and turn it into a parking lot."

"Were they receptive to the offer?" Greer asked.

Sid shrugged. "Like I said, we only talked for a bit. They were in a rush to leave."

Detective Stacy asked, "Is that the last time you saw them?"

"Yes. Now can I get back to my work?"

Greer nodded. "Yes. You have my card. Call if you see them."

Sid laughed. "Sure thing. And if *you* find them, tell them to come see me. I still want to buy that property."

Sid watched them leave.

It's just a matter of time now that they're looking for the Rosas. I wish I had known about the hidden cameras in the apartment before whacking them. Now I have to deal with the police when I didn't have to. Still, I feel safer without those nutjobs around.

Diane was hanging curtains in the baby's room when the phone rang. She slowly stepped off the stool but lost her balance and fell against the crib. It took her a moment to stand and examine herself to make sure she wasn't injured. She grasped her stomach. "You, okay?" she asked the baby. The phone continued to ring as she slowly walked to the living room and picked up. "Hello?"

"Good afternoon. This is Inspector Roland with the New York City Health Department. Is this the residence of Mr. Love?"

"Yes. I'm his girlfriend. Is something wrong?"

"That's what I'm trying to find out. I am calling about a Mr. Evan Locke. Do you know him?"

Diane's mouth dropped. "Yes, I do know him. What's this about?"

"Evan Locke died from a rare strain of the Ebola virus that isn't usually seen in the United States. We're trying to track down anyone who may have come into contact with him."

"Have you or Mr. Love been around him?"

"I was around him less than two weeks ago in the Bay Ridge Hospital waiting room, and he was in our apartment a while before that. What does that mean?"

"I'm going to need both of you to come to our Brooklyn health office tomorrow to be tested and vaccinated."

Diane took a pen and jotted down the address as he gave it to her. "How dangerous is this?" she asked.

"It can be fatal, but the only way to contract the virus is through bodily fluids, so the odds are good that you're not infected."

"I'm pregnant. Will the baby be okay?"

"If you're clear, the baby will be, too. This is just a precaution. See you tomorrow. Good-bye."

Diane dropped to the couch and held her head in her hands. "What next?"

Sid arrived home at four P.M. with flowers and found Diane in the baby's room, fussing with the curtains. "You're supposed to be resting."

"I know, but it keeps my mind off everything else going on. You bought me flowers?"

He handed them to her. "I'm sorry if you think I'm uncaring; I'm not. I just want to keep us safe and shield you from things that will make you worry unnecessarily. Trust me, things will be better soon."

Diane took the bouquet and kissed Sid. "This is so unexpected. Thank you. I'll get a vase and put them in water." When Diane returned, she placed flowers in the center of the coffee table. "They're beautiful..., I hate changing this happy moment to something serious, but I received a call today from an Inspector Roland of the New York City Health Department. Turns out our creepy landlord Evan died of a deadly virus. I knew he had died, and thought it was odd when the coroner's office had the corridor closed off. I had to walk to the other end of the building for the elevator."

"I remember. But what did this Roland guy say?"

Diane shrugged. "Inspector Roland wants us at his clinic tomorrow to be tested."

"He was contagious?"

She nodded. "Yes, but only through bodily fluids. He said they're testing everyone that could have been in contact."

Sid remembered his encounter.

Good thing I didn't touch him.

"Did he tell you the name of this virus?"

"He said it was a rare strain of Ebola that's extremely rare for this country.

Sid stood. "Okay, I guess we better make sure."

Diane smelled the flowers and smiled. "What do we do with the rent if the landlord is dead? Do we keep mailing it to the same PO box?"

"No, we'll put it on the side until someone contacts us. That guy had no friends or family, so it may take a while."

Diane stared at Sid for a moment. "How do you know he had no friends or family?"

Sid stuttered. "Um... Ian told me a while ago that the guy subletting us the apartment was a loner."

"Doesn't it seem odd? If he lived on our floor, why didn't he come here to collect the rent?"

Sid shrugged. "I don't know. Maybe he wanted to be anonymous."

I went into that freaking creep's apartment. The test better come back negative. Damn it, what else can happen?

CHAPTER 26

Diane looked at the clock on the dashboard and scowled when Sid parked in the lot across from the health department. "We're late," she said. "The appointment was for nine. I hope we won't have to come back."

"I'm sure they'll wait. I just hope they're ready for us. I know how these places are, and I'm not spending the whole day here."

Sid took Diane's arm to help her up the steps and held the door. Glancing inside, security caught his eye. "Dammit," he said. "We have to go through a metal detector. What the hell? It's the health department, not the FBI. Wait here. I've gotta go back to the car."

Diane grumbled. "You brought the gun?"

Sid pulled her aside and whispered, "Keep it down. I'll put it in the car and be right back. Just stay here."

When he returned, Diane said with a huff, "Can we go in now?"

"Yes. Let's get this over with."

After giving their names, they were ushered to a room where they waited thirty minutes, frustrating Sid. "We were a few minutes late, not a half hour. When the hell are they giving us the test?"

Diane sighed. "Please be patient, Sid."

Before Sid could respond, a man and a woman in white coats entered the examination room. "I'm Inspector Roland," the man said, "and this is Nurse Sara. She'll be taking your blood samples." The inspector read through the questionnaire and looked at Diane. "How far along are you?"

"Seven and a half months next week."

He pulled a pen from his jacket and jotted down some notes. "Are either of you experiencing any of the following: headaches, joint pain, fever, rashes, vomiting, diarrhea?"

Sid shook his head, but Diane nodded. "I have headaches, vomiting, and occasional diarrhea."

The inspector smiled. "That could be common with pregnancy. Let me clarify. Have you had any of the symptoms consistently over the past three days?"

As the nurse swabbed Diane's arm and inserted the needle, she replied, "No."

He pointed his pen toward Diane. "Other than what you told me over the phone, can you recall any recent encounters you might have had with Evan Locke?"

"No," Diane said again.

Then Roland pointed to Sid. "How about you? Any contact with Evan Locke?"

Sid rolled up his sleeve for the nurse. "No."

Roland jotted down something and looked back at his notes. "Miss Rivers, you told me on the phone that Evan Locke came to see you in the hospital?"

Sid looked at Diane. "I don't know anything about that."

She nodded. "When you were in the hospital with amnesia, that creep visited me with flowers to offer condolences. He thought you were dead. After you regained your memory, I forgot to tell you."

Roland jotted down something. "Do you know the date and time he went to the hospital?"

"I don't remember exactly it was the day after Sid was admitted for a concussion."

"I'll look into it." He tucked his pen away in his pocket. "Unless you've had more recent contact, it's unlikely either of you will have contracted the virus. If you don't hear from me in twenty-four hours, you're both clear. Thanks for coming in."

Diane had Sid drop her off at home after returning from the health department. A half-hour later, she heard a noise at the door and went to look through the peephole. She recognized the face but couldn't remember where she'd seen him before. The vague recollection made her nervous, but she didn't know why. The door handle moved, and she heard a scraping noise. Diane looked through the peephole again and saw the man doing something to the lock. She turned the deadbolt and put on the security chain. "Who's out there?" she shouted.

"I'm with the maintenance company. Is this the residence of Sid Love?"

She took a step back and crossed her arms. "Why you trying to get in this apartment?"

"I'm not. I was just checking to see what type lock the building uses."

She looked through the peephole again.

Something is very wrong.

"There's no Sid Love here. Go away."

He stared at the lens in the door and smiled. "I was told he lives here; I'll try again later."

What the hell does that mean? He doesn't believe me. I should call Sid.

Diane dialed Sid's number, and he answered quickly.

"Hello."

"Sid. A man was here. I think he was trying to break into the apartment. He said he was with a maintenance company, but I didn't believe him."

"Did you open the door?"

"No. I heard something and looked through the peephole. He was doing something with the lock. He looked familiar, Sid. I don't know from where, but I could swear I'd seen him before. Then he asked for you."

Sid raised his voice. "He asked for me?! What did you tell him? Did he give a name?"

"He said he had information you were here and that he'd be back later."

"Shit. Do not open the door for anyone, even if you think you know them. Keep the doors locked. Tell him I'll be home at four-thirty if he comes by again, and then call me so I can come in the back way. Don't worry, I'll find out who it is. Have the police been there?"

"No. Why would they be?"

"My neighbors at the club are reported missing. The police came by asking a lot of questions. I thought maybe they would go by the apartment also."

"What's going on, Sid? I'm scared."

"Don't worry about the police. I'll find out who this guy is. Keep the doors locked and call me immediately when he returns."

"I will…. I love you, Sid. Please be careful."

"Okay, I'll see you later."

Diane hung up.

Why is it so difficult for him to say I love you?

Anthony met Big Zac in the prison courtyard, as usual, to play chess. Anthony wished he'd find someone else to play with.

Doesn't he get tired of beating me all the time?

Big Zac moved a pawn forward. "Has Nicky found any information on Sal?"

"I don't know. We don't go into detail over the phone, but from what I gather, he hasn't confirmed Sal's location yet."

Big Zac looked at Anthony. "You told Nicky I want Sal alive, right?"

Anthony nodded. "Yes, sir."

Wish he'd stop asking me that.

Big Zac stared at the chessboard. "I know we talked about this, but tell me again why Sal killed that cop."

Anthony moved his bishop to attack. "Come on, boss. How many times are we gonna go through this? Sal played the guy for the money, and he got in over his head and killed the pig. Then, the scum saved his ass by pointing the finger at me."

"Your moves are so predictable," Zac said, studying Anthony's face. "Sal was your soldier and testified that you gave him the rogue order for the hit."

Anthony shook his head. "I'm not even gonna dignify that with an answer. How many times you gonna ask me? If you think I'm lying, just say so."

"You know, Anthony, with all the time I have to lay in my bunk and think, I keep wondering why Carmine Simone let the deal go down if it didn't come from me? At the trial, Sal said he gave you a briefcase with fifty thousand. You said you never saw any money, but whether you saw it or not, the money wouldn't have been there if Carmine didn't think there'd be an exchange. How did Sal get Carmine to think it was me setting up a deal? Carmine hasn't been taking my calls. I figure he's distancing himself as far as he can from the dead cop."

Anthony took a deep breath and blew it out. "I told you Sal never gave me any money, and I don't know how he could have set up a meeting with Carmine; maybe he didn't. Nothing at the trial confirmed that there was a transfer of money other than Sal's statement."

"But Carmine confirmed he gave the dead undercover cop the money in his testimony. So, what happened to it? There's a lot of unanswered questions, Anthony, and that bothers me."

"Sal must've hidden the money. You think I would take the money and cut you out?"

Big Zac scowled. "If you were the one who gave Sal the order, yeah. I read through the transcript a bunch of times, and you know what bothers me? The amount of detail Sal gave in his testimony."

Anthony moved his knight. "I'm sure he put a lot of thought into that fairytale he told in court. Come on. Let's just play the game. Your head's working overtime on conspiracy theories. You know I wouldn't have screwed you. I've been your captain for what now? Over twelve years? Not to mention I'm your nephew. Doesn't that count for anything?"

Big Zac took the knight with his pawn. "Your head's not in the game. Is this conversation distracting you?"

Anthony sighed. "You're trying to make it sound like I was conspiring with Sal or something. I don't appreciate it."

"The way I see it, there's two different stories about why I'm here: yours and Sal's. Only one can be the truth. The unanswered questions are keeping me up nights. So, until I'm happy with the answers, I'm gonna keep asking. You read the Bible, Anthony?"

"It's been a while. Not since going to Sunday school as a kid."

Big Zac grinned. "Since being here, it's hard not to see that book everywhere I go. For God's sake, there's even a copy in the bathroom. Then there're all those born-again inmates spouting Bible quotes. I was bored a few weeks ago and started reading the Gospels. I grew up Catholic, so I kind of already knew the stories. The Bible's full of wisdom. Know what I've learned?"

Anthony shrugged and didn't look up from the chessboard.

"Truth and light are the same," Big Zac said. "Each is absent of darkness. You can take a lamp and hide it to keep others from seeing it, but the light is still there. It's just hidden. The same goes for truth. You can hide it, but it's still there, waiting to be revealed. I'll find the truth. It's just a matter of time."

Anthony made a move, and Big Zac quickly attacked. "Check."

"You're right, Zac. I don't have my mind on the game. I'm going to put another call into Nicky to see if there are any new developments."

I'm tired of you questioning me.

"Remember. I want him alive."

"I know, boss."

Sid was directing two of Dan's workers with a large safe into his soon-to-be office by the kitchen. It took some work getting it inside, making it harder to get out, Sid thought. There was only one way in and one way out with no windows. Sid took extra precautions in making his office secure, including a steel door with two deadbolt locks. After the safe was in place, Sid worked on setting up the desk. He went to see Dan about the lighting and found Detective Greer and Stacy talking with him. "What's going on here?"

Dan shrugged. "They want to borrow some tools to get into the building next door."

Detective Greer's mouth curled down. "Hi, Mr. Love. We have a warrant to search the building next door and were asking your contractor for some tools to get inside."

Sid laughed. "You two are like the Keystone cops. Would you like some cake and coffee too? Get the hell out and buy your own tools."

Detective Stacy turned away. "Let's go. We're not getting any help here."

Sid waited for them to leave and turned to Dan. "Don't help them or tell them anything. Don't talk to them at all. Refer them to me, and if I'm not around, tell them to come back when I am. Do I make myself clear?"

"I'm sorry I told them about your meeting with Madame Beth. They caught me off guard. I won't let it happen again. But why are they asking questions? What do they say you did?"

"They think I hit myself on the head, knocked myself unconscious, and ran down a couple of guys with the car I reported stolen. They've got nothing. They're looking for a scapegoat. Don't talk to them. Capiche?"

Dan nodded. "Understood."

Sid walked out the front door and watched the detectives work to get inside the psychic shop building. They were amusing to watch, and eventually entered. Twenty minutes later police vehicles arrived. A half-hour after that, a van from the coroner's office arrived. Neighbors began to crowd the street. Sid joined them, standing by his front door as the Rosa family was wheeled out in bags. Greer and Stacy followed behind the gurneys but stopped to look at Sid after the bodies were placed in the vehicle.

When Sid saw them heading his way, he went back inside and sat at his desk.

I'll soon know if I did a good job cleaning up.

They walked in and stood in front of Sid. "Your neighbors were murdered. Do you know anything about that?" Stacy asked.

"Why would I?"

Stacy looked around. "We'll need to speak with the workers."

"You can do that later, on their own time. They're on my time now."

Detective Greer crossed his arms and stared at Sid. "This is a homicide investigation, and if you do anything to obstruct it, I will lock your ass up. Are we clear?"

Sid sat back and maintained eye contact with Greer. "You go ahead and do that, but I'll be putting in a complaint to your superiors for harassment and disruption to my business."

Greer laughed. "I guess I should be worried." He turned to Stacy. "Tell all the laborers to form a line outside this room for questioning. You can leave us, Mr. Love. I want to talk to each man alone. They can return to work when I'm done with them."

Sid stood. "This is my office. You guys are a real piece of work."

If they found anything, I'd be under arrest already. Let them talk to the workers. They're just fishing.

Greer and Stacy questioned each person, needing Dan's assistance for a few who didn't speak English well. When they were done,

Detective Stacy walked up to Sid. "I know you did this, you son of a bitch, just like you killed those two guys with your car. You're not getting away with it."

"If you have something, arrest me, asshole. If not, get out." Sid grinned, watching Stacy stomp away with a red face.

He's going to be a thorn in my side for a while, but I have to keep my cool and stick to the story.

Dan walked up to Sid when they left. "Everything okay, boss?"

"Yes, what did they ask you?"

Dan shrugged. "Have I ever seen those people from next door, and did I ever see them with you? I told them the same as I did last time they asked."

"Good. They have nothing on me."

"They seem to be going through a lot of trouble if they have nothing."

"This is none of your concern, Dan. It's my business, not yours."

"Sorry. Didn't mean to pry."

Sid smiled and slapped Dan's back. "No problem. But let's not worry about the damn police and stay focused on getting this club finished."

I know I can trust Dan, but sometimes he's too inquisitive.

CHAPTER 27

Sid tried to take his mind off the police investigation and worked with Dan on stage lighting. When they were done, he looked at his watch. "It's eleven-thirty. I'm going to the bank to take care of some business, then I'm going to see Tony and get some lunch. I'll bring back a few pies for you and your men."

Dan smiled. "That'll be great. They'd love a free lunch."

When Sid entered, the pizzeria staff was hard at work, getting ready for the lunch crowd. "Hey, Tony. How are you doing today?"

Tony looked up while pounding dough. "I'm great. Especially after seeing those murdering bastards get taken away. They must have finally screwed with the wrong person. I wish I knew who did it so I could give them free pizza for life."

Sid nodded. "I wish I could tell you, but the cops don't seem to have any leads."

Sid laid a hundred-dollar bill on the counter. "I know you're busy, Tony. When you get a chance, make five pies for the crew and a few bottles of soda. I'll be back. I'm going to go to the bank."

Tony came around the counter with a concerned look on his face. "Wait a minute, we need to talk," he said, pulling Sid to a quiet table. "What do you think happened over there? I mean … I'm happy they're gone, but what happened? A police officer came here to ask questions. He was one of the detectives who investigated Darlene's case if you can call it an investigation. He told me it was Madame Beth, her husband, and their son who they found dead and that their bodies have been there almost two weeks."

"Yeah," Sid said, careful not to say too much. "Yes, that's what I heard also."

Tony continued, "Then he asked me a bunch of questions. He wanted to know if I saw you with them."

"What did you say?"

"Nothing. But the police seem very interested in finding out who killed those creeps. They barely investigated finding my missing wife two years ago, so why would I help them now. Even if I knew something, I wouldn't tell them shit."

Sid nodded.

I won't have to worry about Tony. Maybe someday I can share what I know and give him closure.

"Maybe one day you'll find answers to what happened to your wife."

Tony sighed and slid out of his seat, "I hope you're right. I pray about that all the time." Tony went back behind the counter. "I'll have the pies ready when you get back."

Sid was at the bar at Denali's restaurant, waiting for his takeout order for dinner when something on the local news being broadcast on the TV above the bar caught his ear. He leaned back to watch. The image was of the psychic shop next to the club, and the newscaster was saying:

"The Rosa family - including Beth and Jay Rosa and their son, Gary, longtime owners of the Psychic and Spiritual Readings shop here on Seventh Avenue - were found dead this morning in their recently fire-damaged building. The police said it was a homicide investigation but have not yet released any details."

Sid's stomach tightened as he watched the broadcast of the burned-out building and the bodies being taken away. He could see the Camelot club next door.

Shit, I can't believe this is being televised next to the club. If anyone con-nects them to the Camelot, the news will read that the whole block is cursed.

Paul came out with the food in a bag. "How's Diane doing? Haven't seen her in a while."

Sid put money down on the counter. "She has her good days and bad. I hope things can return to normal after the baby comes."

Paul gave a deep laugh. "Boy, are you naïve! Your life will never be the same after the baby arrives."

Sid shrugged. "But I won't be the one feeding it or changing the diapers."

Paul shook his head with a grin and handed Sid the food. "You keep believing that, but you're in for a rude awakening. Give Diane my best."

Sid turned to leave and was startled to see Nicky Bones entering the restaurant. Sid turned his back to him and sat down at the bar again so he could watch Nicky from the mirror behind the bar. Sid took a breath and felt a wave of relief when Nicky went to the bathroom after ordering.

This is my chance to get out without being seen.

He hurried to his car and waited for Nicky to leave.

Why is he here? That pervert Evan must have contacted Big Zac. This is not good, but at least I have the element of surprise…. Damn!

Sid followed Nicky, careful to stay a few cars back.

Where you going, Nicky? His destination will confirm his reason for being here. Although not likely, I'm hoping this is a coincidence. I always liked Nicky; it would suck to kill him.

Sid was Nicky's mentor and the son of Big Zac's cousin. He had taught Nicky to always look behind when on assignment and leaving a place. Sid would tell him,

If someone were following, that's when they'd be most visible.

He was happy Nicky seemed to have forgotten that lesson.

After a few turns, Sid suspected Nicky's destination and sighed when he turned onto Shore Road.

It had to be Nicky who scared Diane at the apartment earlier.

"Damn, Nicky. You're not giving me much choice."

He put his pistol on the console and drove around the back of the building when he saw Nicky's car pull into the condominium parking lot. Sid parked in the shadows and called Diane.

"Hello."

"Diane, it's Sid. The guy outside the apartment today was Nicky Bones, Big Zac's man. He's coming up to see you now."

"Oh my God, where are you?"

"I'm downstairs. Keep the door locked and stay quiet until you hear from me again."

"I'm scared, Sid. What are you going to do?"

Before Sid could answer, the fire alarm in the building went off.

"Sid, the alarm… I need to leave."

"No! Stay put. It's Nicky's distraction to get you out of the apartment."

"But what if it's a real fire?"

"It's not. I'm outside now, and there is no fire. Don't move, Diane. I'll be back for you."

"Please hurry, I'm so afraid."

Sid started towards the front entrance hugging the building. He looked around the corner and saw groups of people exiting.

What's Nicky doing? Waiting for us to come out, or is he going in. He couldn't do much with the crowd around. He must be heading to the apartment.

Sid returned to the rear of the building and entered a stairwell while people exited. Fewer people descended as Sid climbed the stairs until he was alone on the fifth-floor landing. He took out his gun and was cautious, continuing up to his floor. It was possible for Nicky to be hiding even though it was unlikely he'd be waiting for him in the stairwell.

He doesn't know I followed him, so he wouldn't expect me, but I can't underestimate him. Luckily, I still have the element of surprise, but what's his game plan?

When Sid arrived at the sixth-floor landing, he heard banging and someone shouting fire. He opened the door just enough to see down the hallway.

Nicky was at the apartment door, hitting it with the butt of his gun and yelling, "Fire Department, you need to evacuate the building."

Sid took out his phone and called Diane. She answered, but it was hard to hear her above the alarm.

"Sid, is that you?"

"Yes. Don't open the door."

"I'm not, but the fire department is yelling for me to get out, and I can't see them through the peephole. I'm so frightened. I don't know what to do."

"Diane, I told you there's no fire. I'm on the floor and can see Nicky. He's trying to lure you out. Listen carefully. Without going near the door, shout for him to stand where you can see him. Don't actually look. Wait five seconds and yell that you called the police. Do it now, and don't hang up."

Nicky stopped banging when he heard Diane yell out. He stepped in front of the door. Put the gun to the peephole and fired.

Sid listened for Diane. "He tried to kill me, Sid."

"I know I'll take care of it from here. Stay low and away from the door."

Sid saw him working on the lock and yelled, "Hey, what are you doing?" and slammed the stairwell door hard, so Nicky would know where the shout came from. Then Sid went one flight up to the roof landing, scooched down, and waited. When Nicky entered the stairwell, Sid aimed the gun at him from above and called his name.

Nicky turned and raised his pistol, but Sid fired first, hitting him in the chest. Nicky fell backward down the stairs and lay at the bottom, blood puddling around his head and seeping down his chest. Sid checked to make sure he was dead. "Sorry, it had to be you, Nicky. I always liked you."

Sid used his keys to enter the apartment and found Diane doubled over. "Hey, are you okay? Relax. It's over. Nicky's dead."

Diane's face grimaced as she let out a moan. "Something's wrong, Sid. I think the baby's coming. But it can't be now. It's too soon. Oh my God, Sid, take me to the hospital."

Sid took two deep breaths.

This is when she decides to have the baby.

"I don't think the elevator is back in operation yet. Do you think you can do the stairs?"

Diane moaned, "I don't think I can."

Sid sat down and put his arm around her. "I'll call for an ambulance."

"Please hurry."

Sid made the call and tried to make Diane comfortable, but her groans got louder. He looked down and saw a lot of blood. His memory of sitting in a puddle of blood after he was raped hit him like a lightning bolt. He recalled thinking he was going to die and wished he would have at the time. Sid's insides tightened as Diane seemed to be losing consciousness. He yelled, "Try to stay awake, Diane. Help is coming soon."

Sid stared at the stain of blood growing around her. "Where the hell is the ambulance?" He dropped his face into his hands. "What am I supposed to do?"

CHAPTER 28

Sid entered the emergency room, went to the nurse's station, and asked the first nurse he saw about Diane.

Not lifting her head from the keyboard, she asked. "What's her name?"

"Diane Rivers. I'm her boyfriend. Has she delivered the baby? How is she?"

"Take a seat. As soon as I have a moment, I'll see what I can find out."

After twenty minutes, Sid went back to the nurse. "You said you would check on my girlfriend, Diane Rivers. What've you found out?"

"I did. The doctors are with her and prepped her to take the baby. There's not much else to tell you."

"I'm the baby's father. Diane's scared and needs me. Can I be with her?"

The nurse shook her head. "That's not possible."

Sid sighed. "She's worried and frightened that something's wrong with the baby. She lost a lot of blood and was unconscious before coming here. I want to know how she is and let her know I'm here. I won't get in the way.

"No. I'm sorry. Have a seat, and I'll check on her later."

Sid's jaw tightened.

The hell with these people. I have to know she's okay.

"You won't have to," Sid said, dashing past the desk and through the doors marked "HOSPITAL PERSONNEL ONLY."

He heard the nurse yell for security, but he didn't stop until he saw Diane lying on a gurney in one of the emergency bays. She was unconscious and looked pale, almost pure white. Someone cried, "Code Blue!" Sid stared as a cluster of people in scrubs gathered around Diane. A doctor shouted, "Clear!" and applied paddles to Diane's chest. Her body jumped, but she remained unconscious. "Again!" The doctor said, and her body jumped again. This time, she took a breath. Sid saw it and called out, "I'm here, Diane!"

Sid tried to get closer, but two prominent men in security uniforms grabbed him under his armpits and started to drag him away. Sid took hold of a doorjamb and wouldn't let go. "Listen," he said, "I'm the father of her baby. I have every right to be with her." One of them rolled his eyes at the other, but then they shrugged and put him down. Sid stood up straight and smoothed the wrinkles from his clothes.

He tried to see around the hulking guards blocking the door. Then, he tried again to push his way passed them. "You don't understand she needs me. It's my fault she's here. I can't let her die."

A nurse saw Sid's altercation with security and came over. "Mister, you're not helping her or the doctors by causing a commotion. Right now, she needs your prayers, and we need your cooperation. Please calm down. We're doing everything we can to save both her and the baby. Come on. Let the guards take you back to the waiting room. I promise to let you know the moment her status changes."

Sid stared into the nurse's eyes. "You tell those doctors I don't care about the baby. If a decision needs to be made between Diane and the baby, I want Diane alive. Do you understand me?"

"We'll do everything we can."

Sid sat in the waiting room, resting his face in his hands, elbows on his knees, looking at the floor. His mind bounced from Diane to the possible repercussions of Nicky's death when he noticed two legs in front of him. He didn't have to look up; he had seen those shoes before. "I'm really in no mood detective. Come back tomorrow."

"We need to ask you some questions," Detective Stacy said.

Sid lifted his head and slid back into his seat. "How did you know I was here?"

"Neighbors we questioned in your building told us an ambulance took a pregnant woman from the sixth floor. We assumed it was your girlfriend, and you'd be with her."

"Okay. Make it fast."

"A man was found shot and killed in the stairwell of your building. Would you know anything about that?" Stacy said.

Sid grunted. "No. Go harass someone else in the building."

"Can you tell us why Diane was taken to the hospital? Was she giving birth?"

Sid shook his head. "I don't know. She was bleeding, and why should it matter to you?"

Stacy looked up from writing on his pad. "Because we're wondering if there's a connection between her and the guy murdered in your building."

Sid's nose flared. He wanted them gone. "She's here because she was bleeding. Now get lost."

"I guess we're done here for now. But you should understand something," Stacy said. "Six people are dead, and *you* are the common denominator. As they say in the movies, don't leave town."

Sid watched them walk away.

The only way they can connect me to Nicky is with the gun. I have to find another weapon and get rid of the revolver. If they find a reason to get a search warrant, I'd better have gotten rid of the evidence. Now I have to worry about these two clowns on top of Diane.

Not long after the detectives departed, one of the emergency room doctors stepped into the waiting room and stood beside Sid's chair. "We delivered the baby by C-section and — "

Sid interrupted. "I don't care about that. Tell me about Diane."

"I'm sorry," the doctor said, "but Diane is on life support, and I won't lie to you — her condition is dire. She lost a lot of blood and went into shock."

Sid felt his legs go weak. "Are you saying she's gonna die?"

"There's a chance she won't make it through the night. The baby — it's a boy, by the way — is also having issues. His lungs weren't fully developed. He's in the operating room now. We expect him to survive, but he'll need to be in NICU for a few weeks."

"I told you I don't care about the baby. You need to save Diane. She can't die. Do you understand me? I swear to God if she dies...!"

Sid leaped out of his chair, pushed past the doctor, and stomped down the corridor, pausing to kick a "Wet Floor" sign as he passed.

A priest strolling down the hallway dodged the sign, and then turned to Sid. "You're obviously distraught, my son. Can I help?"

He looked at the man with the collar. "Yes. Tell your God to keep my girlfriend alive."

"I'm Father John; the resident Priest. Can we walk and talk a bit?"

Sid shook his head. "There's nothing to say. My girlfriend's dying, and there's nothing you or your God can do to stop it."

"Is your girlfriend Catholic? I can perform last rights."

"How about you pray for her to live instead of giving her some sign-off that doesn't mean shit?"

The priest stopped walking and turned to Sid. "Why don't *you* pray for her?"

"Ha! I was ten when my parents died. God didn't hear me then, and he's not going to hear me now. You're the priest. If God listens to anyone, it'd be you."

Father John pointed to a door. "My office is right here. Would you like to sit for a while? I can offer you a cup of coffee. It's not great, but it's salvageable with plenty of cream and sugar."

Sid turned to walk away. "Maybe some other time."

"Can I share something with you before we part ways?"

Sid stopped, leaned back on the corridor wall, and gave a tense nod. "I'm not sure I want to hear this, but go ahead."

Father John smiled. "Do you know what justice is?"

"A penalty for screwing up."

The priest grinned. "Close enough. Now, can you tell me what mercy is?"

"*Not* getting a penalty for screwing up."

Father John chuckled. "Do you know what grace is?"

"It's like getting special treatment."

The priest nodded. "You're on the right track, but it goes deeper than that. The only true grace comes from God. Our Lord provides blessings to everyone, believers, pagans, and sinners alike. God loves everyone and wants all to experience his grace."

Sid smirked. "You're talking about luck. I've seen real scumbags win big at the casino. Are you saying that's God's grace?"

"Winning money could be a result of grace because our Lord works in mysterious ways, but not likely. It's not the way he usually works. Winning can be a curse from the devil. The way to know it's God's grace is following an event of mercy or blessing you feel in your heart a need to change."

Sid frowned. "So, God has a few choice people he helps, and the rest of us can go to hell?"

The priest put a hand on Sid's shoulder, and Sid considered pushing it away but didn't.

I don't want to be rude, but he's not helping.

"Whether you know it or not, *you* have been the recipient of God's grace. There is no person living on this planet who hadn't experienced God's grace even when they were undeserving."

"Father, I know you're trying to help, but not now."

When mom and dad died, I was cursed, not blessed.

"The only blessing I ever had was Diane; now she may be taken away. I wish I could believe what you're saying, but I don't."

The priest smiled. "Pray for your girlfriend and ask for God's grace. He knows your heart and your sins. I'd like to pray for you both. Can you tell me your name? And your girlfriend's?"

Sid stared at him.

He's strange, but still, there's something comforting about him.

"Sid. And my girlfriend's name is Diane."

Father John walked away. "Well, Sid, if you ever need me," he said, nodding toward the door. "You know where to find me."

Sid nodded and walked a few steps before turning back to ask if he would go to Diane's room with him. He didn't understand how Father John could have walked away so quickly, but he was gone.

CHAPTER 29

Sid went to the nurse's desk. "I want to see Diane Rivers."

The nurse looked at the computer monitor. "She's in intensive care. Are you family?"

"I'm the father of her baby."

The woman gazed at him and pointed. "Go through the double doors and make a left at the end of the corridor. She'd be in room 1100. The third room on the right."

Sid cringed when he saw the tubes and wires connecting Diane to the equipment keeping her alive. He stood at the foot of the bed.

This is happening because she wanted the baby. I told her not to have it. Why didn't she listen to me?

Her foot moved under the sheet, and he grasped her hand.

"I'm here," he said. "Please don't die, Diane. I know I never told you this, but I need you. None of this makes sense anymore if you're not with me. The baby's here… it's a boy." He chortled. "I think you already knew that. He's had a rough time, but they think he's gonna make it. Did you hear me? Your baby's going to be fine, and he's going to need you."

Diane's hand tightened around his.

She heard me!

"Don't worry," he said. "I'm here, and we'll get through this, but you need to fight."

With his free hand, Sid stroked her hair. "I had an interesting conversation with a priest earlier. Yes, a priest. Don't be shocked. We talked about you. He told me that God's grace can heal you and that I should pray." Sid took a breath and blew it out slowly. "They're not giving you much hope. Damn it." Sid kissed her head. "You're the only person in the world who could make me consider asking God for help. But I will, if you just please don't die."

A nurse walked in. "Sid Love, is that you?"

Sid smiled. "Judy. Good to see you. I wish it was under better circumstances."

Judy lifted the clipboard from the end of Diane's bed to read her chart. "She lost a lot of blood during childbirth and went into shock."

He nodded. "The doctor told me there's not much hope. Be honest with me, Judy. What're her chances?"

Judy set the clipboard down and shook her head. "It doesn't look good," she said, "and it doesn't help that she has a rare blood type. We are waiting for more AB-negative blood to come in. She used up what we had during the delivery."

Sid put out his arm. "Take my blood."

"Not possible. When you were here, I remember your blood type was O-positive. It's not a match."

Sid fell into a chair next to the bed. "Are you saying there's no hope?"

"I've worked here too long to say there's no hope at all. It may not look good, but… don't give up. Pray for God's grace."

"What did you say?"

"Pray for God's grace. Why?" she asked.

"You're the second person who mentioned God's grace today."

Judy smiled. "My Nana used to say it all the time."

Sid turned to look at Diane. "Do you think God can heal her?"

"Yes," Judy said, "but that doesn't necessarily mean he will."

"How does he decide who lives and who dies? Why would he take Diane?"

Judy inspected the monitors around Diane's bed. "You're asking me questions I can't answer. I'll pray for her, Sid. I'm sorry I can't be more comforting. Hey, would you like to see the baby?"

"Baby?"

It's the baby's fault Diane is here.

"Yes, your baby is most likely in NICU. I can take you there."

Sid shook his head. "He's Diane's. I never wanted him. If she dies, he might as well die with her."

"I wouldn't have expected that from you. What'll the baby do when she dies?"

"*When* she dies? What happened to God's grace?"

"I'm sorry," Judy said. "I shouldn't have said it that way. But just the same, you can't ignore the baby. He doesn't deserve to be kicked aside on the day of his birth. He's already had a rough enough go of it."

Sid stood and looked at Diane. "I could never be a father to that baby if she dies. Anyone I ever loved was taken from me, and if that's true for Diane, then that baby is better off without me."

Judy came over and squeezed his arm. "I was there for you when you had nobody, remember? You were frustrated, angry, and scared."

He turned to her. "Scared?"

"Yes, tough guy. You were alone and frightened. Where would you have been without my compassion? That baby is like you were with amnesia — alone and afraid. How can you just abandon him?"

Sid got up and kissed Diane's forehead. "Please don't put guilt on me, Judy. There are things you don't understand. Right now, all I want is for Diane to live." *Not long ago, I wasn't sure I wanted her with me. Now I don't know what I'll do if she's not.*

Judy straightened Diane's bed sheets. "Talk to her, Sid. Let her feel your presence. Love is the greatest healer there is."

He took a breath and smiled at Judy. "I hear you, but our relationship… well, it's complicated… I'm going to get a cup of coffee. Would you like one?"

"I have to finish my rounds, but thank you."

Sid followed Judy to the corridor. "Thanks for the talk, Judy. You always give me shit to think about."

Judy nodded. "Please think about the baby also, Sid."

Anthony was in the prison yard with Big Zac and said, "I should've heard back from Nicky by now."

"How late is he?"

"It's been two days."

"Give it another day. If you don't hear from him, send the Crow."

Anthony nodded. "Okay. You sure that's the right choice? He can be a bit messy."

Big Zac laughed. "Messy but efficient. If Nicky's in trouble, there's no one better to help. If he's dead, there's no one better to finish what he started. You know what? Forget what I said about waiting. Get the Crow on this today. Do it now… and make sure the he knows I want Sal alive.

"No problem."

Anthony waited for a pay phone for what felt like forever. He dialed Bobby Crow's number, but the call went to voicemail. "This is Anthony, pick up the phone; I know you're there!"

After a moment, Crow answered, "Yeah, Anthony, what's up?"

"Nicky Bones was sent to check out a lead about Sal, the snitch at Shore Road Condominiums in Brooklyn, New York."

"Really?"

"Yeah, and it's been two days since he's checked in to the hotel. Find him and report back. Leave today. Update as soon as possible, and if you see the snitch, make sure it's the last time anyone sees him alive. You got all that?"

"Yeah, I got it."

Anthony hung up.

I'll tell Zac he was killed in a shoot-out. That's believable. I sure hope this is over soon so Zac will stop questioning me.

CHAPTER 30

Sid sat in the cafeteria, drinking coffee. He felt hopeless and defeated, knowing Diane could die and the club would never open now that Big Zac knew where he was.

I should've never taken Diane with me. We still have enough money to find new lives in a different place, but my hopes of owning a nightclub are over.

"I can accept that. God, if you just let Diane live... Please."

Sid heard himself ask God for help and was surprised at the plea because it came out as if he talked to God on a regular basis. There was only one other time in his life he asked God for help. At age ten, he had promised to listen to his parents and never do anything wrong again if God would just bring them back. God didn't answer that prayer. Instead, he was punished at the hands of the Nortons.

God didn't help me then. Why would he listen now? But I can't help but keep thinking about Father John and how he told me to pray for Diane. There was something comforting about him. He offered hope, and right now, I need something to grasp on to, because I've got nothing. Prayer may be the only hope I have. I'll speak with Diane about this. She may not be able to respond, but it'll feel good to talk with her.

Sid took the last gulp of coffee and strolled back to see Diane, stopping on the way at the gift shop to buy flowers. He hoped her eyes would be opened to see the roses, but instead, he found her room vacant. He went back to the door plaque and checked the room number. "What the hell, where is she?" He hurried to the nurse's desk. "Diane Rivers was in room eleven hundred. Where did you take her?"

The young nurse at the desk typed something and studied the computer monitor. "She was taken to the fifth floor."

"Why wasn't I told? What room is she in?"

"Five-fifty-five."

Sid ran to the elevator and pushed the button. Thirty seconds later, when it still hadn't arrived, he crashed through the stairway door and took the steps two at a time to the fifth floor. He was gasping when he reached the nurse's station. "Where's room five-fifty-five?"

The chubby middle-aged woman's eyes widened. "Are you okay? Maybe you should sit for a minute."

"I don't need to sit. Where's Diane Rivers room?"

The nurse picked up a clipboard. "Are you family?"

"Why does everyone keep asking me that? Yes, I'm her baby's father. Now tell me where her room is."

The nurse glanced at her computer monitor. "She's still on life support, but her doctor will be talking to you about taking her off. I'm sorry to have to tell you that."

Sid caught his breath and pulled his shoulders back. "Tell the doctors if they take Diane off life support, I'll put them on life support. Where's the room?"

The nurse pointed to the corridor. "It's the fifth door on the right."

Sid walked quickly at first, then slowed down as he got closer. He stopped and took a breath before turning the corner into Diane's room. She didn't look very different from when he'd seen her earlier. He kissed her head and held up the flowers. "I was hoping you'd be able to see these…. They're trying to write you off, Diane, and they're wrong. I'm not going to let them disconnect you from these machines, but you've got to fight. Not just for me but for your baby."

He told Diane about his anguish over her possibly dying and how he was sorry for getting her involved. He told her the club would never open, but it didn't matter. Father John had offered hope. "I don't understand everything he said, but I want to because I feel like I'm in a hole

I can't get out of. I'm going to go talk to Farther John again." He kissed Diane. "Don't worry, I'll be back soon."

Sid knocked on Father John's office door. After three tries and no answer, he turned to leave, and then noticed a pair of doors with the word *CHAPEL* written above. He peered through the glass and saw a few people sitting in the pews facing a marble stone alter and behind it was a large mural of a hand reaching out of the clouds. Sid stepped inside and sat in the last pew. Under his breath, Sid whispered, "Father John told me your grace can make Diane well. I know I have no right to ask you for anything, but please heal her if you have the power. She's a good person. Don't blame her for what I've done. She has a baby now that needs her, and I need her. Please tell me what I need to do, and I'll do it. Thanks for listening." Then Sid stood and walked out.

Waiting for the elevator, Sid spotted a sign that said NICU, with an arrow pointing down the hall.

It would make Diane happy if I told her I saw the baby.

Ignoring the 'bing' of the arriving elevator, he turned on his heel and marched down the hallway.

The NICU was filled with incubators and equipment that hissed and beeped. When Sid entered, a nurse looked up and smiled at him. "Can I help you?"

"My girlfriend — Diane Rivers — had a baby boy yesterday. I'm the father. I'd like to see him."

"Okay, you have a seat here, and I'll be back in a minute."

The thought of seeing the baby made his stomach do flip-flops.

I should be waiting to do this with Diane. I'm not sure why I'm here.

Sid was about to leave when the nurse returned and told Sid to follow her. The baby inside the plastic bubble was smaller than Sid had expected. "That's him?"

The nurse smiled. "Yes. Tiny, isn't he? But he's strong. Talk to him. They like to hear people's voices. There's also an opening on the side where you can put your hand into a glove and touch him. Don't worry.

It's safe and stimulates the baby when they feel someone touching them. I'll leave you two alone to get to know each other."

Sid stared at the baby for a long while. It was the tiniest person he'd ever seen. "Hey, little guy. Your mom can't be here now, but she will be. She's a fighter, and she loves you very much." Sid stuck his hand into the hole and stroked the infant's leg. The baby immediately reached down and grasped Sid's finger. A jolt of energy traveled up Sid's spine at the contact. Suddenly, tears were rolling down Sid's face and peacefulness came over him that he'd never experienced before. He swallowed hard.

"Listen, little guy, I'm gonna go and see your mom. I'll tell her all about you." He tried to remove his hand, but the baby's grip on his finger tightened.

It's as if he knows me and doesn't want me to leave.

Sid recalled the love he had for his dad. "Maybe someday we'll play ball together like I did with my dad." Sid pulled his hand from the glove. "Your mom needs me. I'll be back soon … I promise."

When he got to Diane's room, Sid spoke to her about the baby.

"He's so tiny, but he grabbed my finger, and he's strong. He's going to be okay, and you need to be there for him. I never said this before, but … I'm sorry for how I've treated you. You didn't deserve it. I never had a person in my life I cared about before. It's always been about what people can do for me. I never knew love or how to love, but now I think I do. When the baby took my finger, something happened that I can't explain. It was like a cork being pulled out of a bottle. Feelings started flowing, stuff I haven't felt since I had a mom and dad."

He stroked her head and leaned over to kiss her forehead.

A doctor entered the room. "Are you a relative?"

Sid nodded. "Yes, I'm the father of her baby."

"And what's your name?"

"Sid Love. What's this about?"

The doctor checked Diane's eyes with a penlight. "She's non-responsive, Mr. Love, and we're declaring her clinically dead. Do you want to remove life support?"

"Absolutely not."

The doctor wrote something on Diane's chart. "Then you should talk with the finance department and see what your insurance covers. I'm sorry I don't have a more positive diagnosis."

After the doctor left, Sid took Diane's hand. "I know you can hear me, Diane, and we're not giving up… Damn it, fight."

CHAPTER 31

Sid didn't want to leave Diane's side, but he knew he didn't have much time before Big Zac sent another assassin. *I need to be ready.*

Sid went to multiple stores to pick up everything he needed to booby-trap his car.

Sid parked his car on the dead-end street under the bridge ramp, the exact spot where he'd gotten rid of the psychic's vehicle. It was the most remote place he could think of to rig his car for a flash fire. He laughed when he spotted the psychic's car, still there but now stripped of everything but the frame.

Confident there was no one around, he opened all four doors of his car and began removing seats. He used duct tape to conceal the batteries, wires, and toggle switches under the dashboard. As he worked, Sid recalled Eddie Blaze, a deceased soldier of the Barrelli family and his mentor when he started working for Anthony. Eddie had once told him a flash fire was just as efficient as a conventional bomb without all the noise. The first time Sid saw one of Eddie's car flash fires go off, it nearly took a building with it. Sid finished inserting the batteries and connecting the toggle switch. If he did everything right, the steel wool he put over the bare copper wire would create the spark he needed. Smoke rose from each location. He added gunpowder and dry hay, and then reinstalled the seats. Finally, he broke off all the inside door handles except one on the driver's side. It was after three o'clock when he finished. Before he returned to the hospital, he drove to the Camelot and parked.

Sid sat across from the club and looked up at the knight on the horse.

This would have been such an incredible place, but it'll never happen now. It was a nice dream while it lasted.

Sid hoped it would be a few days before Nicky's replacement arrived. *I've got to sell the club fast, but with no time, how do I get a reasonable price for a half-renovated building?*

"What the hell am I going to do? Should I let Dan continue?"

I won't tell Dan anything for now. I need to have a plan first.

Sid hit the steering wheel and mumbled, "Our lives depend on what I do, and right now, maybe for the first time in my life, I haven't got a clue. Come on, Sid, stop thinking about Diane and concentrate. We need a plan fast."

Sid sighed, got out of the car, and walked toward the building. He didn't have a plan yet but was happy he previously withdrew all the cash from the bank, to avoid leaving a paper trail of money transactions.

I'll leave all the money in the safe for now and be ready to make a fast exit out of Brooklyn.

Sid went to his office, took out the deed, and studied it. He knew the building was worth money and that he needed all the cash he could gather before going into hiding with Diane.

I don't have weeks or months to sell the property. I only have days after that; I'd be taking a chance the sale could be traced back to our new location.

Sid questioned if Diane would be with him at a new location and quickly removed the thought.

"Diane will be with me. I have to believe that."

Dan knocked on the door. "Sid? You in there?"

Sid pushed the safe door shut and let the contractor in. "Hi, Dan. I was going to see you before I left. I needed to pick up some papers. How are things going?"

"Really well. I think we're going to finish on time."

Sid smiled. "Of course you are."

A lot of good it does me now.

"How's Diane?"

Sid shook his head. "Not so good. I'm going back to see her after I leave here."

Dan gazed at Sid. "I know you probably don't want to hear this now, but the police were here asking questions again. They showed me a picture of that guy shot in your building. They wanted to know if I'd seen him around here. I told them no."

Sid nodded. "Okay, thanks."

"There was also another guy here looking for you. He said he was an insurance agent and had some important papers for you to sign."

Sid's eyes widened.

Shit, can they really have sent a replacement for Nicky already?

"What'd you tell him?"

"I told him you were at the hospital visiting your girlfriend. I asked him for a business card, but he didn't have one. I thought it was strange, especially for an insurance agent, so I didn't tell him anything else."

Sid's heart was pounding. "He asked for me by name?"

"Yeah."

"Did you tell him what hospital Diane is at?"

Dan shook his head. "He asked, but I didn't tell him."

"How long ago was he here?"

"Maybe two hours. Is everything okay? Did I say too much?"

Sid took the contents and cash from the safe, put everything in a briefcase, then pushed past Dan. "I have to get to the hospital. If he comes back, call me right away."

Sid parked the car on the street just outside the hospital parking lot and looked at the clock on the dash. It was five-forty-five.

Dan said this guy was at the Camelot a couple of hours ago, so whoever he was — Nicky's backup, it had to be — he could have already been to the hospital, and gotten to Diane.

Sid looked around.

He'd be waiting for me at the entrance if he was here. He would wait until I was leaving, but he doesn't suspect I know he's here, so that gives me the upper hand. There must be a service entrance.

Sid started the car and circled the building. The doors behind the trash container on the loading dock looked like a possible entry. He parked in the shadow of the dumpster, checked the safety of the revolver, and took the briefcase. He opened a door that led to a hallway and hurried to the next set of doors, which led him to a room full of bodies covered in sheets. A man sitting at the desk looked up at him. "It's about time. Why do you undertakers take so long to pick up a body? I don't have another available gurney. The next cadaver will have to go on the floor."

Sid laughed. "I'm not here to pick up any bodies. I just took a wrong turn. Can you point me to the stairs that go to the lobby? I can find my way from there."

The man walked Sid outside to the corridor and pointed. "At the end of the hall, make a left."

Sid opened the door and surveyed the crowd in the lobby.

I don't know who else Big Zac sent, but I do know most of his henchmen. Odds are good. I'll know him when I see him.

Not recognizing anyone, he climbed the stairs to the fifth floor, then took a moment to catch his breath.

I need to start exercising again.

The maintenance man mopping the floor was too old to consider an adversary. Sid smiled at him. "Hey there, would you mind checking to see if anyone is in room five-fifty-five? Sorry to bother you, but I want to see my sister and I don't get along with the rest of the family. I'd rather visit when she's alone. You know how it can be with family."

The man chuckled and put his mop in the bucket. "Sure, I know. My wife's sister Helen's someone I try to steer clear of." He leaned the mop handle against the wall and poked his head into Diane's room. He turned back to Sid with a grin. "No visitors."

"Thank you," Sid said.

Sid went into the room and checked Diane for a pulse. Everything seemed as it was before he left.

If Zac's man is here, he'll wait to get me before coming for Diane. Or maybe he hasn't been here yet."

He looked at Diane. "Has anyone been here?"

Something caught the light on Diane's cheek, and he realized it was a tear. "Are you crying?" he asked. A second bead rolled down her face. He took her hand. "Hey, are you hearing me?"

He wasn't sure, but he thought he felt Diane's finger move.

"Can you hear me?", he shouted; then took a deep breath and blew it out.

"I'm sorry, Diane. I didn't mean to yell, but the thought of you waking up excites me. I believe you will recover soon through God's grace. Believe it or not, I went to the chapel today and talked with God. I sure hope he heard me. Right now, he's our only hope. I felt helpless and defeated until Father John told me about grace; I believe we will leave here together.

I'm sorry I got you into this, Diane. I really thought being a nightclub owner was something I could be successful at, but I know now how wrong I was about everything. Anyway, what's done is done. My job now is to keep you and the baby safe."

Sid felt her finger move. This time, he was sure of it. "You can hear me." He chuckled. "Yes, I said the baby, too. He was amazing, Diane. We connected in a way I can't explain, and he's waiting to meet you."

Sid stared at her. "If I tell you something, will you fight harder because I need you to, or will you be devastated? You're a tough woman. Remember the hard ass façade you put on when we first met?

It was part of what first attracted me to you. What I'm about to tell you is bad, and it's the reason you need to use all your tenacity and get well quickly!

Big Zac has sent another henchman for us. We'll have to leave here soon, and I'm not sure how we're doing that while you're connected to these machines. Fight Diane, please fight." Sid kissed her. "I have to leave now to deal with the problem."

He felt her finger move again. "Don't worry," he said. "I'll be back."

Sid left the room and took the stairs back to the service entrance. He was ready to take on his adversary but wanted to make sure it was on his terms.

He drove to the front of the hospital, parked as close as possible to the brightly lit entrance, and stood outside the car.

He should be able to see me from here, but I'm safe. He won't do anything in public. I'm here on a visit, as far as he knows. He'll be waiting for me to come out. I left the car doors unlocked, so that's where he'll wait: in the back seat, where he'll order me to drive to a secluded area. That's when I'll fry his ass. For now, it needs to look like I'm just here to visit Diane.

Sid turned and walked into the building. He stopped twice to see if he was being shadowed.

Good, it doesn't look like he's following. Now I need a place to kill some time. Best if I don't go to Diane's room.

CHAPTER 32

The cafeteria down the first-floor corridor was an excellent place to kill time and busy enough to make it an unlikely place for a confrontation. Sid bought coffee and took it to the only empty table where he could have his back to the wall and watch the entrance. He was sitting back sipping coffee when Father John walked in. Sid waved and got his attention.

The priest smiled. "Sid, right? You're a hard man to forget."

"Yes, Father. I'm happy to see you. I went to your office earlier, but you weren't there."

"Sorry I missed you. What was it you needed?"

"I wanted to ask you for a specific prayer I could say for Diane. I haven't talked to God in a very long time. I thought you might know a good prayer. I wanna make sure he hears me."

Father John smiled. "Yes, there are prayers, but what you need to do, Sid, is actually simple. Earnestly ask for God's forgiveness for your sins, and then thank him for his mercy and healing your girlfriend. God wants you to repent and be thankful. These are two things God responds to."

"How can I just say I'm sorry and be forgiven? It can't be that easy. And how do I say thank you for something that hasn't happened yet?"

He smiled. "What I said was ask earnestly for forgiveness. You can't just say that you're sorry. You must mean it and being thankful for something God hasn't done yet is the greatest form of faith. God's blessings are never far from sincere faith."

Sid sighed. "If I told you some of the things I've done, you'd call me a monster."

The priest took out his wallet and showed Sid a photo. To Sid's surprise, it was a mugshot of Father John... but without the collar.

"Twenty-five years ago, I got involved with the wrong crowd and did drugs. We met two girls one night, and the people I was hanging out with raped them. I passed out and didn't remember being a part of it, but it didn't matter. The women said I did, and I spent six years on Rikers Island. Back then, people called *me* a monster. I learned about God's grace from a prisoner serving a life sentence. What he taught me changed my heart. When I got out, I knew I wanted to do for others what he did for me, so I entered the seminary. You see? Sometimes God uses our circumstances to change us. It's a form of God's grace. We're all sinners and undeserving, but God loves us unconditionally, no matter what we've done. Pray for Diane, Sid. God will hear you."

Sid's eyes connected with the priests. "I did. When I couldn't find you, I went to the chapel and asked God to heal Diane, but she's still not waking up."

Father John patted Sid's arm. "She may not, but that doesn't mean your prayers are not being heard. In the short time, I've known you, it seems to me God is at work changing your heart. Don't be afraid to turn away from your past and repent. Have faith, Sid. God's miracles are never far from faith. Understand?"

Sid looked around to make sure no one else could hear. "I've heard priests can't repeat what people tell them in confidence. Is that true?"

"Yes. Is there something you want to confess?"

Sid nodded. "I'm about to kill a man — or be killed, depending on how things go. This person wants Diane and me dead, and I'm not gonna let him hurt her."

"Listen, Sid, we both know what you're talking about is wrong. Whatever the reason, it's still wrong. Don't you see? God is already changing your heart. Don't go back now."

Sid dropped his head and stared into his cup. "I don't have a choice."

"There's always a choice. I beg you, don't follow through with this. You're asking God to heal Diane, but you're willing to take a life. Don't you see the contradiction? Violence begets violence, and as long as you live like this, God won't be able to help you. There's a better alternative. You need to find it."

Sid lifted his head and squinted. "What happened to God's grace helping everyone?"

Father John chuckled. "You can't intentionally sin and expect a blessing. You do understand that don't you? If you want mercy, you must give mercy."

"I'm trying. Not sure I understand everything, but you're offering me the only hope there is. I'll consider other options, Father, but not sure there are any."

He nodded. "I'll be praying for you, Sid, and your miracle."

Sid smiled. "I went to see my son in NICU after leaving the chapel. That tiny baby was the closest thing to a miracle I've ever seen."

Father John's eyes widened. "You never mentioned a baby before, but yes, they certainly are miracles. Why's he in NICU?"

"Premature. They operated on a hole in his lung."

"I'll add him to my prayers. How's he doing?"

Sid's smile widened. "Amazing. So tiny yet so strong and alert... I think I'd like to go see him again while I have some time." Sid put out his hand to shake Father John's. "Thank you for the conversation and for your prayers. You've given me much to think about."

"God bless you, Sid."

Sid headed to the NICU but decided to go to the chapel when he got to the floor.

I need time to think about a plan. I also want to pray but haven't got a clue as to what to say.

Sid entered the vacant chapel and sat in the back pew. The quiet was deafening at first, but before long, he found it comforting. After a few minutes, a thought struck him; it was a revelation, and the alternative Father John knew there was. "Okay, God," he whispered, "if I can do this without violence, I'll do it. Does that mean you'll let Diane live?"

Sid sat a while longer, partly working out the details of his new plan and partly waiting to see if God would answer his question. Sid looked up and whispered. "You don't have to answer me, but I'm going to follow through on my end and do this without violence. Please heal Diane is all I ask." Finally, he left and stopped at the NICU. The same nurse he'd met last time greeted him. "Here to see the baby again?"

He nodded. "If I can."

"He's doing so well. He might be able to leave the NICU soon. Come with me."

The baby was kicking his feet as they approached. "He's still awake," the nurse said, "and he looks happy to see you. I'll be right over there if you need me."

Sid put his hand into the glove, and the baby immediately grasped his finger. "I don't know for sure what's going to happen, little guy. My plan could backfire, and I may never see you again. If that happens… well, hopefully, your mom will tell you only the good things about me. Your mom's not doing well right now, but I talked with God, and he's looking over her. She's gonna be a great mom." Sid wiped a tear. "If everything goes as planned, I'll see you soon with your mom. If not, I have a plan B. It won't be a foster home, and you'll be safe." Sid removed his hand. "I don't have much time. I've gotta go. I sure do hope I get to see you again."

CHAPTER 33

Sid saw it was nearly seven-thirty P.M. when he left NICU. He muttered, "I'm going to need to work fast." Then took the stairs to the nurse's station on the fourth floor and found Nurse Judy. "I need your help," he told her, "but I don't have time to explain. Please wait for me in Diane's room."

She pouted. "How long do I need to wait? I'm in the middle of my shift."

Sid took her hand. "Just ten or fifteen minutes, okay? Thank you. You have no idea how much this means to me." He quickly turned and left.

He took out his cell phone and paused before dialing.

My calls may be traceable on the cell. Can't take any chances. I'll get rid of it.

Sid found a pay phone by the elevator and called Dan.

"I'm sorry to bother you this late," he told him, "but I need your help."

"What's the matter? Sounds important."

"Life and death, please hurry. Meet me at the hospital, and bring Tony with you."

Sid hung up without waiting for a response and rushed to the gift shop, where he purchased stationery and envelopes.

This is going to work; it has to.

Entering Diane's room, he thanked Judy for waiting.

"Can you tell me what this is all about now?" she asked.

He nodded. "Yes. I need you to change Diane's room tonight and list her in your records as deceased."

"Are you out of your mind? I can't do that. I'd lose my job."

"I realize what I'm asking, and I'll pay for your help."

She stood. "No. Can't do it."

Sid put up his hand to stop her from leaving. "I'll give you ten thousand in cash to get her room changed tonight. That money's so you can bribe the people you need to help. You'll get more. A lot more."

Judy sighed. "I'm not doing anything illegal."

Sid took hold of her shoulders and looked her in the eye to make his point. "Errors are made all the time. That's what this will look like. Just enter Diane as deceased. A mistake."

"Why?"

"I don't have time to explain now. Please, just get it done."

Judy shook her head and moved toward the door. For a moment, Sid worried she was refusing to help, but as she left, she muttered, "I can't believe I'm doing this."

Sid brushed back Diane's hair and kissed her, then pulled up a chair next to the bed and sat down. "I have some work to do, but I'm right here if you need me."

He took the stationery out and chuckled when he realized he had forgotten to buy a pen. "Damn, Diane, I'm sure you wouldn't have forgotten a pen if you were in my shoes. Be right back."

He went to the nurse's station and found Judy talking with a young doctor. "Hey, Judy, sorry to bother you. Can you give me a pen?"

She handed him one and gave him a brusque nod that told him to go away so she could finalize the deal she was in the process of making with the doctor.

Sid nodded back and returned to Diane's room, where he drew up a series of notes. He was just finishing when Tony and Dan walked in. Tony opened his mouth to speak, but Sid raised his hand. "Give me just a sec." He read over each note and then stood with them in hand. "Thanks for coming."

"Dan said this was life and death. What's going on?" Tony asked.

Sid patted Tony's shoulder. "Please be patient. I'll explain everything."

Sid took out the briefcase and opened it. He counted out ten thousand dollars and put it in an envelope.

Dan and Tony stared at the case full of cash. "That's a lot of dough to be carrying around," Tony said.

Judy came in and paused for a moment when she saw Tony and Dan. Then she turned to Sid and said, "It's all set."

He handed her the envelope with the money.

"Don't worry," he said to Judy, tilting his head toward Tony and Dan. "They're friends. Deliver this and return as soon as possible." He handed her the papers he held. "Please also make copies of these documents on your way back."

She glanced at Tony and Dan again. As she left, she muttered, "I wish I knew what was going on."

Tony crossed his arms. "That makes two of us."

Sid smiled at Tony. "I'm sorry I made you close up the pizzeria early, but it'll be worth your while, I promise."

Tony walked over to Diane's bed. "How's she doing?"

"I wish I knew. The doctors want to pull the plug. But I saw a tear run down her face today, and I felt her finger move. So, I haven't given up on her."

"That seems like a good sign," Tony said. "How's the baby?"

Sid grinned. "So tiny but strong. He's gonna be okay."

They stood in silence for a moment until Judy came in and handed Sid the papers. "Enough of the mystery. Tell me what this is about," she said. "Now."

"Okay," Sid said while sorting through the papers. "Here goes. All three of you helped me when I really needed you. None of you knew me, but you helped me anyway. You've made me understand the meaning of friendship."

"You never had a friend?" Dan blurted out.

Sid shook his head. "Not really. I've had plenty of business associates and people who did things for me because I could do things for them. But they weren't friends. Now let me finish. We don't have much time."

He paused and took a deep breath.

This won't be easy, he thought. *I need to be as honest with them as possible, and honesty had never been my strong suit.*

"Diane and I are in the witness protection program. My testimony put some powerful people in jail, and now they know where we are. The only way to stop them in their pursuit to kill us is for them to think we're both dead."

Judy's eyes widened. "That's why you wanted Diane listed as deceased."

"Yes, and thank you for getting that done."

Sid looked at Tony and Dan. "Any questions?"

Tony nodded. "Why are you telling us this now?"

"Because I need to make sure the people sent to kill us think I'm also dead. Which means I won't be back." He held up the papers in his hand. "I wrote up these agreements." He stopped and handed each of them a paper. "I need the three of you to care for Diane and the baby after I'm gone. As compensation for your help, I'm turning over the Camelot to the three of you."

Sid opened the briefcase. "There's two hundred and seventy thousand in cash here. Use it to keep Diane alive. You can take her off life support when the money runs out — if she hasn't woken up on her own yet. But she will. And when she wakes up, whatever money is left belongs to her."

Sid took an envelope from the briefcase. "There's a hundred grand here. If something happens to Diane, you are to use every penny of this money to help the baby find a good home. Under no circumstances do you put him in a foster home. Is that understood?"

Judy said. "No. You can't put this on the three of us and disappear. What the hell are you talking about?"

Sid took a breath and blew it out slowly. "Judy. Listen to me. I'm talking about Diane's life and the baby's life. I'm offering you three a chance to make some money and help me. I need… No, *we* need you! Please!"

Judy looked at Tony and Dan. Both shrugged. "Okay, Sid. What's the deal?" Judy said.

Sid removed papers from the briefcase and signed them. "This is the deed for the Camelot property."

Tony took the paper. "Is this a joke? I don't think it's funny."

"It's not a joke. Read the agreements. If you have no objections, sign them and the deed."

Sid had two separate envelopes and handed them to Dan and Tony.

Tony opened the envelope, and a key fell out. "What's this?"

Sid took a breath.

I hope he doesn't hate me when he finds out everything I've been hiding.

"It's to a safety deposit box at Bay Ridge Savings. The contents of the box should give you what you need to bring closure to Darlene's death. I'm sorry, Tony. I should have told you sooner."

Then Sid looked at Dan. "There's twenty thousand in your envelope for the work you've completed. If it's more than that, I hope your part ownership of the Camelot squares us."

Dan looked at Judy and Tony. "None of us know anything about running a nightclub, Sid. We'd have to sell it."

Sid nodded. "I understand. The building belongs to you three now, so you're free to do what you want with it. I estimate you can get a hundred and fifty, maybe two hundred grand, for the building as is. More if you finish the renovations."

Tony said. "This might be a stupid question, but why isn't the witness protection program protecting you?"

"Because I was a greedy, arrogant jerk. The judge knew what I was demanding in exchange for my testimony would come back to bite me in the ass one day and had me sign an agreement. They're not going to lift a finger to help us, and I have nothing to offer them now that would make them change their minds."

Tony squinted. "How will you make it look like you're dead?"

"I can't tell you that, but you won't see me again. That's all I can say."

Sid handed Judy another envelope. "Please give this to Diane after she wakes up and after she's seen the baby. Not before, okay?"

Judy nodded. "Of course. Whatever you want."

Sid smiled. "Thank you, all of you, for everything. Now, I'd like to spend a little time with Diane before they move her. Have a good life, all of you. Just make sure Diane and the baby are a part of it."

Tony wiped his eyes. "No worries, Sid. We'll look after them."

Sid smiled and handed Judy a key. "This is the key to my apartment. Diane can never go back there. Please go and remove all her things. Don't go alone. Take Tony and Dan with you. I don't know if the people after us will continue watching the apartment after they think I'm dead, but don't take any chances. Go together."

Judy hugged him, and the others followed suit as they left the room.

Sid took Diane's hand and squeezed it. "Please don't hate me. What I'm doing is for you and the baby. I wish things could be different, but I don't have another solution. The baby's amazing. He held my finger again today."

Sid saw a tear. "Hey, you're crying again. You can hear me, can't you?"

He wiped her face. "You wanted that baby more than anything, and now all you have to do is get well so you can be with him. You'll never have to worry about Big Zac again, and you'll have some terrific friends to help you raise our son. I wrote you something — you'll see it later... We never talked about a name for the baby. I wish we had. How would you feel about Salvatore? He kinda looks like a Sal. Strong and handsome." Sid chuckled. "Just a thought. I'm sure whatever name you give him will be the right one." Sid used his thumb to wipe the stream of tears rolling down her face and felt her hand tighten in his. "I never said I love you, but I do. I even love the baby. Bet you'd never thought you'd hear me say that. Get well soon. He needs you."

With that, Sid kissed her once more, and then took the stairs to the service entrance, where he intercepted two young maintenance workers. His plan depended on the greed of these two strangers. It didn't take long to get them on board with his proposal.

"Now it was time for Sid Love to die."

CHAPTER 34

Sid stood in the shadows, watching his car. He expected the assassin to be cowering in the back seat, waiting for him. Sid looked for some movement to confirm that someone was there. Soon enough, passing headlights revealed the top of a man's head peering over the door.

From behind Sid walked quickly toward the car, gun in his hand. He threw open the car door and pointed the gun at the person in the back seat. It was Big Zac's longtime henchman, Bobby Crow. Sid laughed. "I should've known it would be you, Bobby. Give me your gun."

Bobby handed it to him. "How did you know I was here?"

Sid chuckled. "You didn't make a very believable insurance agent. Now give me the piece you've got strapped to your ankle."

Bobby obeyed. "What are you gonna do? You can't shoot me here."

Sid looked around and saw an elderly couple who stopped to watch.

Witnesses doesn't matter; if all goes as planned, I'll be assumed dead soon.

Sid yelled at them.

"Keep moving."

He turned back to Bobby.

"Get out of the car. Unlike our pal Nicky, I'm gonna let you live, so you can send a message back to Big Zac. Take me to where you're parked. You know better than to try anything, Bobby, since we both know I have nothing to lose by putting a bullet in your head."

They walked across the lot to Bobby's car. Sid told him to get in the back seat and then followed, pulling the door closed behind them.

He cut the seat belts off and sliced a hole in the upholstery to reveal the steel frame below. "Turn around and put your hands behind your back."

Bobby complied. "Why are you tying me up? I'm unarmed, and you're holding the gun."

"Because I need time to drive away while you work on releasing yourself."

Sid finished tying Bobby's hands, and then said, "Okay, listen up now. Diane... I mean, Susie... is dead. She died during childbirth. You can check the hospital records if you want. You tell Big Zac he'll never find me where I'm going, so best not to try. I'm getting in my car now and then I'm leaving."

Bobby chuckled. "You think Big Zac is going to stop looking for you? He found you once. He'll find you again."

"Maybe, maybe not. I don't have many options, do I?" Sid opened the car door. "If I see you again, Bobby, I won't be so nice."

Sid slammed the door shut, walked back to his car, and waved to the maintenance men waiting inside a laundry truck. They pulled up behind Sid's car as they were told. Sid made sure he shielded his car from Bobby's view and walked up to the truck window. Sid took out the wad of money and showed it to them. "You already received the down payment; you get the balance after it's done. When I give you the signal, move fast, and wait for me to get in the truck."

The driver nodded. "Okay."

Sid opened the driver's-side door of his car and motioned for them to hurry. They carried a cadaver into the driver's seat and returned to the truck. Sid flipped the toggle switch, slammed the door, and left with the maintenance men. He peered through the back window and watched as his car burst into flames, quickly turning into an inferno of smoke and flames.

The burnt corpse would be unrecognizable, and there'd be no reason for Bobby not to believe the body's not mine.

Sid was a couple of blocks away when an explosion shook the ground.

They'll never identify the body now.

The maintenance guys dropped Sid off at Shore Road Condominiums. Sid paid them and then showed them his gun. "Don't talk to anyone about our business arrangement. You don't know my name, and I don't know yours, but I know where to find you. Understand what I'm saying?"

They both nodded. After watching them drive away, Sid went to the apartment and packed a bag. When he was done, he stopped in the baby's room. Diane had done such a great job decorating. He couldn't help but think it was a shame they couldn't stay.

Before leaving, he went to the bar, poured himself a bourbon, raised the glass, and looked up. "Here's to God's grace." He gulped the drink and left.

Diane woke to the sound of a piercing fire alarm and three people in her room. She recognized the woman as the nurse who had taken care of Sid — maybe Judy was her name? But Diane didn't know the two men with her. She couldn't speak with the tube down her throat, and she didn't have enough strength to move her arms. She moaned, but no one heard her over the piercing alarm.

Before trying again to get their attention, an explosion shook the building. People began yelling and running through the hall with the fire alarm wailing.

Judy leaped up. "I'm going to find out what's going on."

The taller of the two men turned to the white-haired man and shouted over the sound of the alarm, "You think this has something to do with Sid?"

"I don't know. Maybe."

Judy returned soon after the fire alarm stopped. "Car fire in the parking lot. The gas tank exploded." She looked at the two men, "What kind of car does Sid have?"

"Jeep Wrangler," the taller man said.

"I can't be sure," Judy said, "but it sure looked like a Jeep. The fire department is trying to put out the fire. People outside were saying there was a body inside. I couldn't tell with all the smoke. Do you think it was..."

Diane moaned loudly, and this time, they heard her. Judy was the first at her side.

"Oh my God, you're awake." She took Diane's hand. "Do you know where you are?"

Diane gave a slight nod and grunted.

"I'm going to get the doctor," Judy said. She turned to the men. "Talk to her."

Diane thought the white-haired man looked familiar, but didn't recognize the taller one. The elder leaned down and gave her a smile. "Hi, I'm Tony," he pointed, "and this is Dan. We were good friends of...,"

Diane tried to say, "Were?" but instead just let out another moan.

Dan leaned over to Tony and whispered something.

Tony sighed. "I'm sorry. Let's wait for Judy to get back. All this will be easier to explain when we're all together."

Diane tried to say, "Sid?" but again, it came out as nothing more than a groan.

Judy entered with a doctor who checked Diane's pupils, heart, and lungs. "This is most encouraging. She's breathing on her own. When I saw her earlier, she was unresponsive." He picked up Diane's chart from the end of the bed and laughed. "This says she's deceased. Obviously, that's a mistake. Ms. Rivers, you would appear to be very much alive."

The doctor had Judy assist him in removing the respirator. Before the doctor left, he said, "This is quite amazing."

Diane was relieved to have the respirator removed. She said, "thank you," in a low, raspy voice.

Judy, Tony, and Dan huddled around Diane's bed. "Hey, we have a lot to tell you when you're feeling up to it," Judy said.

Diane shook her head and in a soft raspy whisper she said, "Sid? And the baby?"

Judy nodded. "Your baby is in the NICU unit. They had to operate on his lungs, but he's doing well now."

Diane looked at the two men and then back at Judy. "And Sid?"

Judy looked at Tony and Dan. Diane saw Judy's eyes well up.

"Somethings happened to Sid?"

She nodded. "Before I tell you, I want to tell you why we are here."

Diane looked at them. "Why are you here?"

Tony smiled. "Sid brought us together to help you." Judy nodded. "Yes, he said the people he put in prison know where you guys are and that the only way to keep you and the baby safe was for him to fake your death. And his."

"So, where is he?" Diane said.

Tears were running down Judy's face. "We're not sure. There's a chance his plan backfired. His car exploded in the parking lot with someone inside."

Diane's eyes widened. "Was it Sid?"

"We don't know. But I don't know who else it could be. Unless maybe it was the person coming after you two. There's no way to know right now. Maybe ever. I would think the body would be burned beyond recognition."

Diane began to sob. "If it was the killer who died, Sid would be here."

"Not necessarily," Dan said. "The guy he put in prison still knows where he is. Sid said he wouldn't be coming back until he was sure they stopped looking. If he did fake his death, he did a damn good job."

Diane wiped her tears. "Why are you three helping me?"

Tony took out the agreement and deed and held them up. "Sid gave the three of us the Camelot building as compensation. He wanted us to look after you and the baby."

Judy took Diane's hand. "We're your family now. Sid wanted to be sure you were safe and cared for."

Diane nodded. "Sid knew how afraid I was to be alone if something happened to him. I can't believe he might be dead. I don't know whose body was in the car, but I don't believe it's Sid." Diane recalled Sid talking to her when she was still in the coma, in a place somewhere between waking and sleep. "Maybe I dreamt it, but did Sid see the baby?"

Judy smiled. "Yes, and after he did, I could sense a change in him. He told us to make sure the baby got a good home if you didn't survive. But I guess we don't have to worry about that now."

Diane's eyes welled. "Can I see him?"

"He can't leave NICU quite yet," Judy said. "The nurses tell me he's doing well, but he's still underweight. I'll ask about bringing you to see him."

Diane smiled. "Please do it soon."

Judy turned to leave. "I'm going to NICU now." She smiled at Tony and Dan. "They'll keep you company."

Diane tried to raise her voice, and it crackled. "That would make me so happy."

When Judy left, Diane said, "Sid didn't talk to me about either of you, which is not unlike him. He didn't tell me much about his life outside of the two of us. I'm glad he had friends he could trust. I didn't think he really trusted anyone."

"I don't think he had many options," said Tony. "Sid was smart. He couldn't put all his trust in one person. There would be no one to answer to if that person ran off with the money. But having all three of us makes it hard for one to screw over the other two."

Diane could tell by Judy's smile when she entered the room with a wheelchair she had good news. "Are you ready to see your baby?"

Diane tried to sit up and fell back. "Oh my God, yes. Please help me up."

Big Zac sat with Anthony in the courtyard for their usual chess game. "You hear from the Crow?"

"Yeah. Sal and that girlfriend of his are dead."

"You were supposed to get Sal alive."

Anthony shrugged. "I only know what the Crow said in a message — that Sal's dead. No details yet. I don't know what happened. Maybe there was a shootout or something."

"You sure you didn't tell the Crow to kill Sal?"

"Of course not."

"Well, I had Mikey call the Crow. You sure you don't want to change your story?"

Anthony frowned. "Listen, what did you think you were going to get out of Sal? He'd do anything to save his skin, including throwing me under the bus. Come on, man. I'm your nephew. Let's not let this come between us."

"It's your disobedience that's coming between us." Big Zac stood and walked away. He stopped and turned back to say, "At the very least, you're a liar, and you're the reason I'm in this hellhole."

When Anthony felt the blade enter his back, he tried to run but fell. He heard someone yell for a doctor just before everything went black.

Diane was beaming after she visited with the baby as Judy wheeled her back to her room. "He's so small, and he seems so alert. They said I should try and pump milk to give him now and that maybe I could put him to my breast in a day or two. Isn't that exciting?"

Tony and Dan were waiting in Diane's hospital room. Helping Diane back into bed, Judy said, "It's all very exciting, but you've got to get your strength up so you can be healthy for that baby of yours."

Diane felt her smile disappear when she looked over and saw Tony, Dan, and Judy giving one another an odd look. "Is something wrong?" she asked.

Judy held out the envelope. "Sid wanted you to read this after you saw the baby. It's sealed for your eyes only."

Diane took it and stared at it. Her stomach flipped, and her hands began to shake. "I'm not sure I want to read this. What if it's bad?"

"You'll never know until you open it," Tony said.

She used her finger to release the flap, took out the paper, and read.

Susie,

If you're reading this, you're alive. I knew you would wake up, even when the doctors thought you were going to die. I love you, and I love the baby. Bet you never thought you'd hear me say that. I'm so sorry for the way I treated you. I didn't realize how much you meant to me until you weren't there. I couldn't let anything happen to you.

Isn't the baby amazing? He's small but strong. When I saw him, I knew it was my job now to keep you both safe. With Big Zac knowing where we are, I had come up with a plan to kill the new guy he sent, but (believe it or not) a priest named Father John, there in the hospital, talked me out of it. I prayed, and God gave me a new plan. (Yes, I prayed.)

I knew Big Zac would never stop looking for us unless he thought we were dead, so I had to make it look like we were. If everything works as I planned, I'll get to see you again someday. I hope so. But if things go wrong, please know I did it for you and the baby. Either way, you don't have to worry about Big Zac.

Judy, Tony, and Dan are good people. They'll help you and the baby get back on your feet. Understand this: Whether my plan worked or not it would be best if they all believed I'm dead. Do NOT tell them, or anyone, there's a chance you'll see me again. When the time is right, and if I can make it happen, I'll contact you. It may be a while, but don't give up hope. I'm not.

We never talked about a name for our son. I wish we had. Maybe you'd consider naming him Salvatore. Just a thought.

Stay well and safe. I believe, through God's grace, we'll see each other again.

With love,

Sal

Diane folded the letter and looked at the people surrounding her bed. Tears rolled down her face.

"Through God's grace?" That doesn't sound like Sal. What did that priest say to him? I believe Sal's alive, but no one else can.

"It <u>was</u> Sid's body in the car. He only told you he was attempting to fake his death because he didn't want you to try and stop him."

They all reached over to touch her shoulders. "We're so sorry," they all said.

Diane nodded. "I'm grateful for you all coming, but I think I need to be alone for a while."

"Sure, we understand," Judy said. "It's getting late anyway. We'll see you tomorrow."

As they filed toward the door, Diane called out, "Wait… Judy. Do you know where I can find a priest named Father John here in the hospital?"

"Father John? Why do you ask?"

"Sid said in the letter that he talked to him."

Judy looked puzzled. "That's impossible. Father John died in a convenience-store robbery two months ago. We don't have a new chaplain yet."

Diane looked over the note. "But Father John talked with Sid right before the car fire. How can that be?"

CHAPTER 35

Sid bought an atlas and sat in the bus station, deciding where to go. He didn't want to be too far from Diane, but he didn't want to be too close, either. He planned to check up on her in a couple of weeks after he had time to grow a beard and shave his head to disguise his appearance. It might take months before he would feel safe enough to approach her and the baby. For now, the question still remained: Where was he heading, and how was he going to earn money since the ten thousand in cash he took for himself wouldn't last long? The only other job he'd ever had was at the Venice Beach marina. It was where he worked, taking care of Anthony's boat and where they first met. He ran his finger around the northeast shoreline on the map and stopped at Rhode Island.

A small, out-of-the-way state no one ever talks about, maybe three or four hours away from Diane. Since most of it is surrounded by water, with my background I should be able to find work on the docks. Okay, Rhode Island it is.

Sid watched the changing landscape as the bus traveled through the most beautiful country he'd ever seen. The bus was filled with people, but Sid felt alone. He missed Diane, and he longed to touch the baby again. Having them missing from his life now brought a feeling of emptiness he had only known once before when his parents died. The loneliness of being in solitary confinement didn't compare to what he felt now because this hurt inside and made his heart ache.

Sid wasn't paying much attention to the other people on the bus, but a little girl of maybe eight or nine caught his eye as she was boarding. A man around fifty-five or sixty was holding her hand. The girl's eyes met Sid's, and he saw something there that unsettled him as they took their seats across the aisle from him. Sid was by the window, and the girl was in the aisle seat. As the bus moved, she continually gazed over at Sid.

Something wasn't right. Sid was sure the girl was scared; somehow, she knew he could see it. Setting aside his worries, he realized he needed to find out if she was in trouble. As the bus's wheels hummed beneath him, Sid planned to confront the man she was with. If Sid was wrong…, well, he might end up having to walk the rest of the way to Rhode Island. But he had to know the girl was alright. He decided he would try to talk to the girl at the next rest stop.

Half an hour later, the bus pulled off I-95 to a service area. Most people got off to get something to eat or use the bathroom. Sid watched the girl, but the man with her wasn't getting up, and he still held tight to her tiny hand. Sid knew he was going to have to force the issue. Taking a bottle of juice from his bag, Sid moved to the seat behind the man and poured the liquid over him.

The man jumped up. "Hey, what the hell are you doing?"

Sid threw up his hands. "I'm sorry, it was an accident." He opened his wallet and took out five dollars. "Why don't you get cleaned up and buy yourself and your kid here something to eat? Call it a token of my apology."

The man pushed the girl into the aisle and dragged her toward the exit.

Sid grabbed his shoulder. "Leave the girl here. I'll watch her."

The man stomped away faster, dragging the child behind him. This time, Sid stopped him. "Leave the girl. I want to talk with her."

The man squinted at Sid. "You're either a weirdo or a cop. Which is it?"

"Neither, But I think you're the weirdo and a pervert. Maybe I'm wrong, and that's why I want to talk with the girl."

"Go to hell. She's coming with me." The man said.

Sid looked around. The driver was just outside the door of the bus, and there were still two sleeping passengers, but that didn't matter. He grabbed the man by the shirt collar. "You can stay here or get cleaned up, whatever you like, but the girl stays with me until you come back. If she gives me the right answers, you can go on your merry way."

The man threw a punch… it must have been the slowest punch anyone had ever thrown at Sid. Failing to connect, the man fell over into the adjacent seats and, in doing so, dropped the girl's hand.

Sid slid off his belt and used it to strap the man to the armrest. "Now you have to stay while me and the girl have a little chat. Don't do anything stupid. I'm watching you."

"You can't do this! Let me up! I'm going to sue your ass."

"You best be quiet, or I'll gag you, too."

Sid put out his hand to the girl, and she willingly grasped it. Sid took her to a seat near the front of the bus, and they sat. Looking nervous, she kept glancing back at the man she boarded with.

Sid gave the girl a gentle smile. "Do you know that man?"

She shook her head.

"Why are you with him?"

She shrugged. "He said he had toys for me."

"Did he hurt you?"

She spoke softly, not meeting Sid's eyes. "Yes."

"Where?"

She looked down and pointed at her crotch.

Sid's remembrance of the pain and shame of his own rape made his blood boil and rush to his head.

The Nortons got away with what they did to me, but this asshole is going to pay. "What's your name?"

"Molly"

"Well, Molly, you don't have to worry about him hurting you anymore. Do you want to see your mom and dad again?"

She began to sob. Unable to answer, she just nodded and covered her face with her hands.

Sid's own emotions bubbled up from within. He knew what she was feeling all too well. Shame, mixed with rage. He looked back at the man.

He doesn't deserve to live.

"I'll make sure you see your mom and dad again. Stay here. I'll be right back, okay?"

Sid crouched down in front of her when she grabbed his hand. "It's okay, Molly. I'm just going to get someone who can help."

Sid backhanded the restrained man in the face as he exited to get the bus driver. "You have a radio on the bus?"

"Yes, but it's only for emergencies."

Sid didn't want to leave Molly alone, or the man for that matter. "Come with me. You need to call the police."

Sid went over to Molly, put his hand on her shoulder, and pointed to the man. "She's been abducted and raped by that pervert."

The driver got into his seat and made the call.

When it was done, Sid sat next to the girl. "The police will take you home as soon as they get here. I have to go."

Molly reached for Sid. "Can't you stay until they come?"

He shook his head. "No, I'm sorry. I have something I need to do."

The bus driver said. "They're on the way. About fifteen or twenty minutes."

Sid went to the man and released the restraint. "Come on, you're coming with me."

"Where're you taking me? I'll stay here until the police come."

"Sorry, but that's too easy."

"Where're you taking him?" the bus driver asked.

Sid held the man by the shirt collar. "To the bathroom. I may rough him up a bit. You got a problem with that?"

244

The driver looked at the girl and then at the man. "No, but what do I tell the police?"

"You don't have to tell them anything," Sid said, pushing the man out the door.

The man struggled, shouting, "No! Don't let him! He's going to kill me!"

Sid smacked the back of his head. "Get moving. I'm not going to kill you and you can thank a friend of mine for that."

Sid pushed him to the side of the building where the bathrooms were and used a credit card to open the locked door. Once inside, he told the man to take off all his clothes.

The man's face went white. "What are you going to do to me? I'm sorry. I'll never do it again! Please!"

Sid removed a lace from the man's shoe and handed it to him. "I don't know how many times you did this to little kids, but this time you picked the wrong girl and the wrong bus. Tie this tight around the base of your penis and under your testicles."

"Oh my God, you're going to castrate me." He began yelling. "Help! Help, please, someone help me!"

Sid took one of his socks and stuffed it in his mouth. "This is going to be painful, but how painful is up to you. Tie the string tight. I don't want you bleeding out. I want you to live and remember this. The police will find you and call an ambulance. You won't die. Now hurry."

The man followed his instructions, bawling the whole time. When he was done, Sid said, "Sit on the floor."

The man shook his head and moaned.

"Fine, but if you move, you may lose more than your balls."

The sobbing man fell to his knees and sat against the wall.

It was then that Sid saw Father John. "How are you here?" Sid said.

Father John's presence was momentary. He said the word *Mercy* and was gone.

Sid looked at the man. "You deserve more than just being arrested, but my friend doesn't want me to hurt you. Through God's grace your justice is not in my hands. So, what the hell do I do with you?"

"Let me go. I'll never do it again," the man said.

Sid chuckled. "Yes, you will." He took the wallet from the man's pants and flipped through the contents. "Russel Booker, I have all your information and your little phone book. I'll be keeping track of your case. If you are acquitted, I'll be coming after you."

Russel grinned. "Can we leave now?"

"I can, you can't. Stand up."

Russel followed the instruction. "What're going to do?"

Sid scowled. "I'm not going to kill you or castrate you, but I am going to embarrass you." Sid used Russel's belt to tie him to the overhead pipe. "The first thing the police will see is your naked body. How does it feel to be humiliated?"

"You can't leave me like this," Russel said.

Sid laughed. "Okay, we'll go back to plan A. Sit down."

Russel pleaded. "No, no, no, I'll stay like this."

Sid held up Russel's wallet. "Remember, I have all your information. You'd best confess if you know what's good for you."

Sid returned to the bus but knew he didn't have much time before the police arrived. He went up to Molly. "Everything is going to be okay now."

She threw her arms around his neck, and his eyes welled, "I have to go. It was nice meeting you, Molly."

He looked at the bus driver. "The guy is in the bathroom, don't forget to tell the cops."

"Hey, wait, where are you going?" The bus driver yelled.

Sid hurried through the parking lot to the on-ramp of I-95 and stuck out his thumb. He could only hope someone would give him a lift before the police showed up and started asking questions about the pervert he tied up in the restroom.

I can't let the police question me and take the chance of revealing my identity or to have my picture in the news.

Sid was in luck. Two cars passed before a pickup truck driven by a middle-aged couple with a large dog between them stopped.

Sid smiled. "I missed my bus and don't have time to wait. I'm heading to Rhode Island. Can you take me a ways before you turn off I-95? I'd really appreciate it."

The man looked at his woman, and she shrugged. "You seem all right." She nodded toward the dog. "Dagger here doesn't seem to think you're a murderer or anything. Hop in the back. We can take you as far as New Haven."

Sid got into the back of the pickup and stayed low. Peering over the truck bed, he saw two police vehicles pulling into the rest stop. *The cops will deal with the man who hurt Molly.* Sid doubted they'd put too much effort into looking for the man who tied up the naked pervert.

It was night when Sid finally arrived in Rhode Island. He hitched two other rides after the first couple dropped him off in New Haven. The last ride dropped him off at a motel, where he paid cash for a room. Once inside, he turned on the television. A story on the local news caught his attention:

The Connecticut state police have arrested a man at a rest stop on I-95. According to a police statement, a man was found tied up and naked in the bathroom. The man is alive and is being treated at the local hospital. Testimony from an unidentified witness said the man police found had abused and raped a nine-year-old child he was traveling with. A nine-year-old girl at the scene confirmed the allegations, and the suspect confessed, according to a police statement. The child's parents have been contacted, and police believe she will be returned to their custody this evening.

Reporters at the scene say some people call the person who tied up the alleged child molester a hero.

Sid stood up and flipped off the television. He was relieved, knowing Molly was safe, and headed home to her parents. He reached for his wallet and took out a picture of him and Diane. "So much has changed since we met, Diane… I mean, Susie," he said softly. "You gave my life meaning, and I miss you. I wonder what you would think about what I did today. The news said some people are calling me a hero. I wonder what they would have thought if I killed that monster or castrated him like I wanted to."

Sid took a breath. "If Father John is right about God's grace, I must show mercy to receive mercy. This way God can heal you and bring us together again."

Sid propped the picture up against the bedside lamp. "Good night, Susie," he said as he turned off the light.

CHAPTER 36

Sal found a job at Fairview Marina in Warwick, Rhode Island, and an apartment nearby. He got up each day at five A.M. and worked till five P.M. It was hard work and long days. Sal didn't mind because when he was done, he was too tired to do anything but cook dinner and go to bed. His thoughts before nodding off were always of Susie and the baby.

Sal took the name Jack Long for his new job and made a deal to work for less money if he was paid cash. Randy, the owner of the Marina, liked Sal and sometimes allowed him to take his forty-foot schooner out on his only day off, Sunday. It was relaxing, and a time he could clear his head and contemplate when he would make an attempt at seeing Di… Susie. He still didn't know if she was alive but prayed to God each day that she and the baby were safe.

After a month, Sal saved enough money to buy a used Lincoln Town Car. It was eight years old, and the paint job had seen better days, but it ran well and was bigger than the midsize and compact cars they were pushing at the dealer. Sal had shaved his head soon after arriving in Rhode Island and grew a beard that was now fully grown in. The gray in it made him look older, but he didn't care because the less he looked like Sal Lovato or Sid Love, the better.

Once the car was registered, and on the road, Sal arranged with his boss to take an entire weekend off. He didn't tell him or any of his co-workers where he was going. Sal was excited. Right after receiving his pay Friday, he packed his bag and a cooler with some water and sandwiches. Too anxious to sleep, he was driving to Brooklyn at four A.M. He estimated it would take three hours.

Sal murmured about what he'd do if Susie was dead. "I can't think negatively. She's alive. I refuse to believe she is not. I did what Father John said. I let Bobby Crow live, and that Booker pervert keep his balls. I showed mercy and prayed every day for God's grace on Susie and the baby. I don't know what I'd do if… No! Susie's alive. I refuse to believe God wouldn't heal her."

He arrived in Bay Ridge, Brooklyn at seven-fifteen in the morning and exited the Belt Parkway a mile from the Shore Road Condominiums. Sal recalled the Locke pervert guy who informed Big Zac, destroying the dream of the nightclub.

I must accept that, but I refuse to accept life without Susie. I wonder what would have happened if Locke didn't give up our location. Who knows, maybe Susie would have died from hemorrhaging because I wasn't there to call the ambulance. But I was there, and I believe that was God's grace, and that's why Susie must be alive.

Sal stopped for a coffee and roll, before driving to the Camelot. To his surprise, it looked like it was still under renovation, and there was no "For Sale" sign. It was Saturday, and he wasn't sure Dan would have men working, but Sal imagined how wonderful it would be if the club opened, even without him. It was a quiet morning. The block was scarce of people, with barely any traffic. The psychic business still had yellow tape around saying it was a crime scene.

Sal chuckled, thinking how disappointed Detective Stacy was when they found the fried corpse.

He may be the only one who believes the body wasn't mine. But without proof, he'll have to accept it.

Sal took out the information he had gathered on Judy, Tony, and Dan, in Rhode Island. He originally never asked them for their addresses, which he laughed about afterward, thinking he put all his trust in these people and didn't have their home addresses. He read through the Brooklyn phone listings he obtained from the phone company. Tony and Dan were easy because he had their phone numbers, but Judy took a while longer. He assumed his first stop would be Judy because it would likely be where Susie and the baby would go. He took the last bite of his roll and put the car in gear. "The moment of truth."

Judy Stiles lived in an apartment complex on Sixty-fifth Street and Tenth Avenue. Sal walked inside and checked the mailboxes to make sure he had the correct address. After confirming Judy lived in apartment 2B, he left and sat in the car. He had to wait now and hoped he'd see Susie. After an hour, he saw Judy leave and get in her car. He wanted to run after her and find out if Susie was there and alive, but he couldn't take the chance. The only person Sal would reveal himself to would be Susie. He sat for another hour and feared she wasn't there or worse.

There's no way she's living with Dan or Tony. Susie must be here.

Sal stepped out of the car and went into the building. He stood inside the vestibule, staring at the intercom button to apartment 2B. Sal remembered Judy saying she lived with another woman. Without knowing for sure who was there, he had to be discreet. He pushed the buzzer, and a woman answered who didn't sound like Susie. "Hi, I have a delivery for a Miss Diane Rivers."

The response came back quick. "There is no one by that name here."

Sid went back to his car. He didn't think Susie was here because there was no hesitation in the response of the woman who answered.

I'll try Tony's house next.

Sal went to Tony's home on Seventy-eighth Street and Twelfth Avenue. The area known as Dyker Heights was a high-end neighborhood with large Victorian houses. Tony had a wrap-around porch, driveway, and garage. Sal thought it was odd to have such a large home for one person.

Sal knew Tony was at work but decided to at least try the doorbell and see if anyone answered.

With all the space in this house, it's possible Susie and the baby came here.

He pushed the button and heard the chime, but no one answered. A voice came from across the driveway. "Who are you looking for?"

Sal smiled at a gray-haired woman in a sweat suit. "I'm looking for the owner."

"Tony's not here; he's working. What did you want him for?"

He stumbled on his words, trying to respond. "Um-mm... I was told he has an apartment for rent."

"Tony didn't tell me he listed the apartment. I guess his niece and her baby are moving out."

Sal's voice rose. "What did you say?"

She seemed startled by his response. "His niece and baby are currently in the apartment. I'm surprised she's leaving. Diane seemed to like it here."

A chill ran up Sal's spine. "Where's the entrance to the apartment?"

"Around back. If you want to see it, you should call Tony. He works late. Do you have his number?"

Sal walked to the car. "Yes, thanks for your help."

The woman watered plants, picked weeds, and gathered her mail. Sid waited for her to go inside her home. She was the nosey neighbor type, and it was best if she didn't see him go to the apartment door.

Sal's stomach fluttered at the thought of seeing Susie. After the woman left, Sal waited and watched for any activity that looked suspicious. When everything looked clear, he went to the apartment door and knocked.

A voice from the other side shouted. "Who is it?"

He put his mouth close to the door so as to not yell. "It's me, Susie."

The curtain on the window pushed back, and the door flung open a moment later. "Oh my God, it's you, Sid. Oh my God."

He put his finger to his lips. "Shh-h-h. Keep it down," he said. Then walked inside and shut the door.

Sal smiled and wrapped his arms around her. "Thank God you're alive. I knew He wouldn't let you die."

Susie's eyes welled with tears. "Who wouldn't let me die, Sid?" she asked.

"I'll tell you about it some other time. Please call me Sal. No reason to use the aliases anymore. You look great, Susie, and your hair looks fantastic short."

She rubbed her hand on Sal's bald head. "Look at you, with the beard and bald head. I almost didn't recognize you."

A cry came from another room. Sal turned quickly. "Is that the baby?"

She smiled and took Sal's hand. "Yes, do you want to see him?"

"More than anything."

Sal was surprised at how much the baby grew in a month. "Wow, look how big he is. What are you feeding him?"

"Salvatore likes to eat."

"You gave him my name?"

Susie picked up the baby. "You asked me too, remember? Would you like to hold him?"

Sal tensed up. "I don't know how."

Susie positioned Salvatore in his arms. "Don't worry, he won't break."

They spent the afternoon talking and playing with the baby. Sal told her how he carried out his plan at the hospital and how worried he was about her. "They wanted to pull the plug on you, but I wouldn't let them. I prayed for God's grace to save you. I knew he would."

Susie looked at him with a tilted head. "You told me you talked to Father John in your letter and how he gave you hope, but I don't understand something."

Sal picked up a toy and waved it in front of baby. "What do you mean?"

"Judy told me Father John died in a convenience store robbery two months before you met him."

He looked at Susie and chuckled. "He was as real as you and me, but I guess that would explain seeing him in the rest stop bathroom."

"The rest stop bathroom?"

Sal nodded. "It's a long story. I don't know if Father John was an angel, but if he was, it was through God's grace he came to me and saved both our lives."

"What do we do now, Sal. Are we done running and hiding?"

Sal went back to playing with Salvatore. "We'll have to keep our eyes open for a while and avoid paper transactions, but I'm not leaving you again. How much money is left?"

She went to a window seat, lifted the cushion, and removed a briefcase. "After paying the hospital bills, there's a hundred and eighty thousand. Tony asked if I wanted him to deposit the money in his account for safekeeping until I could open my own account, but I told him no. I had a feeling you'd be coming back soon and wanted to make sure we had cash."

Sid opened the case. "Good girl. Then you and Salvatore can come back with me today to Rhode Island."

"Today? How can I just up and leave without telling Judy, Tony, and Dan? They have been so good to the baby and me."

"You'll leave a note. I'm sure they'll understand. You can't say it in the note, but we will visit them one day. Come on, I'll help you pack."

Sal drove on I-95 with his new family, happier than he ever remembered and grateful for his new life with Susie and Salvatore.

Thank you, God, for everything!

FROM THE AUTHOR

Thank you for reading the book! I hope you enjoyed the story.

Killing Love is my third Inspirational Thriller novel. I endeavor to write suspenseful plots with protagonists who live broken and sinful lives. My stories include strong language, drinking, and otherworldly vices to make the character seem real in today's society. The protagonist will ultimately be transformed when God and family become important in their life.

I purposely don't invoke or promote any religion with the message of God because many people today won't give God a chance if they think religion is connected to him. I want to spark an interest in God's love and the importance of family. I don't want the message to be blaring, but instead, I make it a subtle catalyst that inspires the protagonist to change.

Because of the secular content in trying to make characters real, I don't use the Christian or spiritual genre to identify my books, but rather call them an *Inspirational Thriller*.

So why do I use the message of God and family in my novels?

Because when you look back on the history of the world and America, God and family are the foundation, the roots, and the fabric that has kept our society thriving. However, our world and nation have drastically turned away from God and family. All you need to do is look at the news daily to see the effect it has had on people. Never in my life have I seen more people depressed, angry, and suicidal.

Unless God and family are reinstated in our culture as necessary and needed for our society to prosper, the deterioration will continue, and our future will look bleak.

www.ingramcontent.com/pod-product-compliance
Lightning Source LLC
Chambersburg PA
CBHW030246200626
46816CB00002BA/526